D0190048

THE
CHEERLEADERS

9 40582718

THE
CHEERLEADERS

KARA THOMAS

MACMILLAN

Published in the US in 2018 by Delacourte Press,
an imprint of Random House Children's Books, a division of Penguin Random
House LLC, New York.

This UK edition first published in 2020 by Macmillan Children's Books
an imprint of Pan Macmillan
The Smithson, 6 Briset Street, London EC1M 5NR
Associated companies throughout the world
www.panmacmillan.com

ISBN 978-1-5290-5352-4

Copyright © Kara Thomas 2018

The right of Kara Thomas to be identified as the
author of this work has been asserted by her
in accordance with the Copyright, Designs and Patents Act 1988.

All rights reserved. No part of this publication may be reproduced,
stored in a retrieval system, or transmitted, in any form or by any means
(electronic, mechanical, photocopying, recording or otherwise),
without the prior written permission of the publisher.

Pan Macmillan does not have any control over, or any responsibility for,
any author or third-party websites referred to in or on this book.

1 3 5 7 9 8 6 4 2

A CIP catalogue record for this book is available from the British Library.

Typeset by Jaclyn Whalen
Printed and bound by CPI Group (UK) Ltd, Croydon CR0 4YY

This book is sold subject to the condition that it shall not,
by way of trade or otherwise, be lent, resold, hired out,
or otherwise circulated without the publisher's prior consent
in any form of binding or cover other than that in which
it is published and without a similar condition including this
condition being imposed on the subsequent purchaser.

In loving memory
of Kezban Mustafa

the depth of my interactions with my half brother.

Mom's eyes are on me. I keep my own eyes on a carton of white rice. I grab a plate and spoon some onto it.

"What's wrong?" Petey asks. It takes a second for it to sink in that he's speaking to me. Tom is watching me now too. My mother makes a face as if she just swallowed down vomit.

"Can I go lie down?" I ask.

"Go ahead," she says.

When I get to the hall, I hear Petey whine, "How come she gets to do what she wants?"

I practically have to crawl up the stairs to my room. The over-the-counter painkillers my mom picked up for me are seriously garbage. I would call Matt, my ex-boyfriend, because even though he denies it, he's friends with people who can get the strong stuff. But Matt graduated and he's not in Sunnybrook anymore and we haven't spoken since July.

My heating pad is still packed in one of the storage tubs Mom and I bought from Bed Bath & Beyond before the move. I dig it out, biting my lip. The nurse at Dr. Bob's office said it would be like bad period cramps. But it hurts so much I want to die.

I break into a sweat from plugging in the heating pad and flop onto my brand-new bed. King-sized, like my mom and Tom's. She insisted—a queen would have looked too small for the room.

They say you're not supposed to put the pad directly on your skin, but I do it anyway and curl up on my side. I'd gladly take my flesh melting off over the pain in my gut.

A knock at the door. I grunt and Mom pushes her way in, holding a bottle of naproxen and a glass of water. "When was the last time you took painkillers?"

"Lunch," I lie. I popped four before tryouts.

"You can have two more, then." Mom perches at the edge of my bed. She might as well be a mile away. It's really obscene, how big the bed is.

I groan and pull my legs up tight to my body, into the fetal position.

"I told you that you should have stayed home today." My mother taps the naproxen bottle to her palm, shakes two pills out.

"Coach would have cut me from the team." I accept the pills. Swallow them greedily.

Mom is quiet. She drums her fingers—the nails rounded and coated with clear polish—on my comforter. Her anxious tic. Finally: "Have you told Matt?"

"No."

I can't tell what she's thinking—whether she actually *wants* me to call Matt at college and tell him.

"He could support you," Mom says, after a beat. "You don't have to go through this alone."

"It wasn't his anyway."

I stare straight ahead so I don't have to see the look on her face.

When she stands up, her profile comes into focus. She looks sad for a moment before she catches herself. "I hope you learn something from this pain."

My mother shuts the light off on her way out—or at least, she tries to. She can't find the switch at first, because it's opposite where it used to be in my old room. Finally, she gives up, leaving me under the glow of the top-of-the-line energy-efficient LED bulbs.

She's wrong, I think. Pain isn't supposed to teach you anything. It only exists to hurt you. And she should know that better than anyone.

I'm camped on the porch, rain plinking on the overhang, staring at the house across the street when Rachel pulls up in her cherry-red Volkswagen Beetle the next morning. No one lives there. The contractors had to abandon construction inside the house because the people who bought it ran out of money. Since we moved in, the empty house has been the subject of my mother's bitching. All the house is doing is existing, not bothering anyone. It's exactly the type of thing that offends my mother.

Rach and I have been best friends since we were kids. She turned seventeen in July, which means she got her license over six months before I will. Rachel had to repeat kindergarten, and kids used to make fun of her, because what kind of moron can't pass kindergarten? Then in the eighth grade she got her braces taken off, discovered a hair straightener, and grew B-cups, and everyone shut up.

Rachel lowers her sunglasses to look at me as I duck into the passenger seat.

"Do you feel okay?"

"I'm fine," I lie. "I woke up too late to do my makeup."

"I hope the list is up," Rach says, putting the car into

reverse to back out of my driveway. She actually sounds nervous.

Of course we'll be on the list. Rachel, our friend Alexa, and I were the only freshmen to make the dance team two years ago. Rach's mom drove us all to school that morning so we could look at the list together. Arms linked, knees knocking under our new jean skirts for our first week of high school.

Seeing our names on that list made us feel unstoppable. I was naïve and thought being one of the dance team girls meant I wouldn't be known as the sister of one of the cheerleaders. But our particular tragedy isn't the type people forget easily; being Jennifer Rayburn's sister is like having an enormous scar I have to dress every morning to hide.

A shot of nerves twists my stomach. Or maybe it's the naproxen. My sloppy performance at tryouts yesterday is reason enough for our coach to drop me, if she felt like it. Coach is not known for doling out second chances. Forget your dance shoes? Go home, and don't bother coming to practice tomorrow.

I wonder if I'll even care if my name isn't on that list. I tilt my head against the window. Rachel rolls to a stop at the sign at the end of my street. She looks both ways, counts silently to herself, ever the perfect, cautious driver, always looking twice at my house to see if Tom is watching.

Tom is the sergeant of the local police department. Having him for a stepdad is a really easy way to figure out how many people you know have a deep-rooted fear of law enforcement.

6

Rachel pulls into Alexa's driveway, and of course she isn't ready; she never is. I'm about to text her, ask why she has to make us late every damn morning. But her front door swings open, and she flounces down the driveway, wearing her Sunnybrook Warriors hoodie with skinny jeans.

Alexa pours herself into the backseat and immediately whips out her compact. She starts applying her Merlot-red lip stain.

"Seat belt!" Rachel yells.

I catch Alexa's eyes in the side mirror. "What do you even do all morning," I ask crabbily, "if you always have to do your lipstick in the car?"

Alexa rakes a hand through her hair, shaking out her freshly ironed waves. "Well, Monica's obviously getting her period."

I almost make Rachel pull over so I can walk.

We get to school with a few minutes to spare before the first bell. The side doors by the gym are propped open and we step into the hall and right into chaos. There are buckets scattered on the floor, catching steady drips of water leaking from the ceiling. A custodian is on a ladder, attempting to tape a trash bag over the hole. I hear him mutter something about all the goddamn rain this year so far.

"This place is so ghetto," Alexa announces, and I want to hit her, because she has no idea what the word actually means. Besides, we're one of the wealthiest school districts in the county.

A bunch of trophy cases outside the locker room have

been moved into the center of the hall. We sidestep them, but not before I see her. My sister.

She smiles at me from the largest photo in the biggest trophy case. She's posing for the camera with four of her friends. Their mouths are painted cherry; their cheer pleats are blue and yellow. The photo is from the first home game of the season, five years ago when there was still a cheerleading squad.

A wave of nausea ripples through me. Every day after gym, after dance team practice, I go out of my way to avoid this picture.

I knew all the girls in it, some of them better than others. Juliana Ruiz and Susan Berry were Jen's best friends and fixtures in our house for as long as I could remember. When they made the cheerleading squad their freshman year, they became friends with two sophomores: Colleen Coughlin and Bethany Steiger.

They all smile at me: Jen, Juliana, Susan, Colleen, and Bethany. It really is a beautiful picture.

By the end of the season, everyone in it was dead.

Chapter Two

A small crowd is gathered outside the main office, where Coach said she would post the list this morning. As we approach the bulletin board, a pack of freshman girls walk away, dejected.

Next to me, Rach sucks in her breath. We step up to the bulletin board. I scan the candy-colored papers tacked to it—a list of people who got callbacks for the fall play, a flyer advertising the girls' soccer team car wash, information for a weekend SAT prep course.

"There's nothing here," Alexa says.

"Yeah, there is." A familiar voice. I turn around; the Kelseys are behind us, iced lattes from Dunkin' Donuts in hand. Kelsey Butler rattles the ice in hers. She points—her nails, painted apricot, popping against her dark skin.

I look where Kelsey is pointing—a sheet of paper tacked to the bulletin board. On it, a single line:

DANCE TEAM LIST WILL BE POSTED AT NOON

Kelsey Butler's best friend, Kelsey Gabriel, sidles up next to her to get a better look. Kelsey G's usually fair hair is sun-streaked even lighter, and her skin is freckled. "Ew. Why?"

"More people tried out this year," Kelsey B says. "Maybe she needed more time to decide."

The Kelseys walk off together. They'll be on the list; they're seniors, and both of them were in classes with me at the Royal Hudson Dance Studio when we were younger. The Kelseys, with their inhumanly high leaps and whip-fast pirouettes, are the closest things Coach has to favorites.

My friends and I stay close together and head for the second floor—we're Rayburn, Santiago, and Steiger, and homerooms are assigned in alphabetical order. As we file onto the stairs, I catch a glimpse of Rachel. She's picking at the corner of her mouth, where her lipstick is flaking.

"It's fine," I say, softly enough that only she can hear. "You've got this."

She's no doubt thinking about what Kelsey B said. Rachel is haunted by the triple pirouette she hasn't mastered—the one Coach threatened to put in our competition routine this year.

Before I can find my seat in homeroom, my teacher says my name. "You're wanted at guidance."

My stomach plummets to my feet. "Why?"

"Dunno. I'm not your secretary," he drones.

I take the slip from his grasp, eyeing my guidance counselor's almost-illegible scrawl.

I choose the longer route to the guidance office so I can pass a bathroom. I dig out the plastic baggie of naproxen my mother left on the counter next to my Tupperware of veggies and ranch this morning. She's doling out the pills to me four at a time, as if they're Oxys or something. I open the baggie and knock them back with a sip of water from my bottle.

Mr. Demarco is sitting with his back to me when I rap on the doorframe of his office. He swivels around in his chair, his face brightening when he sees me. He's in an ice-blue polo that makes his matching eyes pop. Rachel and Alexa call him a silver fox.

"There she is." Mr. Demarco sets his Starbucks cup, marked *PSL*, on his desk. "Sit, sit."

He drags a chair next to his desk. He moves a box of pamphlets off his seat; I catch a glimpse of a campus quad, bright with fall foliage. I sit down, pressing my chem textbook into my abdomen.

"So." Demarco smiles without showing any teeth. "How are you?"

"Fine." I grip the chem textbook. Press harder. Does he know? There's no way he could have found out. Not unless my mother told him, and I made her swear, my nails digging half circles into her arm, that she wouldn't even tell Tom.

Demarco takes a sip of his coffee. "I'll cut to the chase. Mrs. Coughlin is trying to put together a memorial ceremony, in the courtyard."

Mrs. Coughlin, the health teacher. Colleen Coughlin's mother.

Mr. Demarco doesn't give any further explanation; he doesn't need to. Colleen Coughlin was in the passenger seat of Bethany Steiger's car when she hydroplaned during a storm and drove into a tree. The car was so mangled that supposedly the coroner had trouble figuring out which girl was which. One of the paramedics at the scene vomited.

The first two cheerleaders to be killed that year.

"A memorial." I take off the ponytail holder on my wrist and wrap it around my fingers, cutting off the circulation in the tips. "Like a religious thing?"

"No, not at all," Demarco says. "Just a small ceremony in the courtyard. Mrs. Coughlin asked if you'd like to be a part of it."

At my stricken expression, Demarco picks up his empty cup, taps the base of it against his desk. "Obviously you don't have to say yes. Mrs. Coughlin did pick out some poems she thinks would be nice for you to read."

He hands me a stack of paper held together by a butterfly clip. I don't look at it. "It's just . . . ," I mumble. "It would feel weird. I didn't even know Colleen and Bethany."

"Oh no, we'd honor all the girls at once. Everyone thought it would be best that way."

In other words, get the memorial out of the way before homecoming, because my sister's two best friends died five years ago the night before *their* homecoming. It wouldn't be very nice to remind the crowd about the horrific way Juliana Ruiz and Susan Berry were killed when everyone just wants to watch some football. "Wow. Okay. Thanks. I actually think I have a quiz next period."

"Of course. I'll write you a pass."

12

While Demarco fishes around in his drawer for his stack of passes, I let my eyes wander. There's a Sunnybrook Warriors pennant over his desk, right next to a New York Giants calendar. Right above a framed photo of the Sunnybrook football team from six years ago, posing with the state championship trophy. We haven't won it since.

If you look at pictures of my family, you might wonder whether my sister was adopted. Mom, Petey, and I all have shocks of brown-black hair and blue eyes. Jennifer was blond, like our real father, and had his green eyes.

I remember a time when she liked me. There's proof: photographs of us trick-or-treating dressed as sister Disney princesses and videos of us putting on plays on the back patio, starring ourselves and Mango, our Jack Russell/rat terrier mix.

But we were four years apart, and once Jen started middle school, it seemed like my very existence offended her.

"That's just how it is with sisters," Mom would tell me when I was still small enough to climb onto her lap, face stiff with tears after a fight with Jen. Feel her fingers grazing over my ear as she played with my hair. "Aunt Ellen and I didn't become friends until we were in college."

Before homecoming her sophomore year, I gave Jen strep throat. It wound up saving her life. For a little while, at least.

Susan's parents were in Vermont for her cousin's wedding the night before the game, and Juliana and Jen were going to stay at her house with her. Susan refused to miss homecoming, even for the wedding, and besides, someone needed to be at home with Beethoven, the Berrys' beloved Saint Bernard.

Mr. Ruiz was going to pick them up in the morning so they could grab breakfast at the diner before the homecoming game. It was a tradition Juliana had with her family—pancakes before she performed.

It wasn't supposed to be a big deal, a bunch of fifteen-year-old girls spending the night by themselves. Sunnybrook was one of the safest towns in the country, and on our street, everyone looked out for each other. But when Juliana's father arrived to pick the girls up the next morning, both of them were dead.

They'd been strangled. Juliana's hands were sliced open, and one still held a shard from the broken mirror that hung in the foyer. She had fought like hell.

Susan hadn't seen it coming. She was on her back at the top of the stairs, staring at the ceiling. Across the hall, the shower was still on. She must have run out when she heard Juliana's screams.

If my sister hadn't been too sick to sleep over at Susan Berry's house that night, Susan's deranged neighbor would have murdered Jen too.

Lucky, everyone called her. *Blessed*.

In the end, though, it didn't make a difference.

Some people say a curse fell over our town five years ago. What else could explain the tragic deaths of five girls, in three separate incidents, in less than two months?

Some people think Jen's death was the most tragic of all.

Jen was in the top three in her class, beloved by

everyone who was lucky enough to know her. She wanted to spend the summer before her junior year in South America, volunteering for Habitat for Humanity. She was planning on going to veterinary school, because as much as she loved helping people, her heart belonged to animals—especially the horses she used to ride as a child.

Jen wouldn't have done it. That's what they don't understand. My sister, with her pages-long to-do list of everything she wanted to do in life, never would have killed herself. Maybe it makes sense to them that she would do it, once they put themselves in Jen's shoes. Would living every day having to imagine what Jack Canning would have done to her if she'd been at that house be much of a life at all? Was life even worth living if all of her friends were dead?

I don't know if we're cursed. All I know is that my sister wouldn't have killed herself. And if she did, why didn't she leave a note explaining why?

Chapter Three

I need to make another stop at the bathroom, so I head for the faculty ones by the main office, because everyone knows teachers aren't disgusting pigs like the rest of us. You have to ask the secretary for a key, but Mrs. Barnes is married to one of the officers who works with Tom. She lets me in all the time.

There's someone in the women's room, so I lean against the wall opposite the front doors while I wait, watching the stragglers file into the building. When you show up late for school, you have to sign in with the security guard sitting at the desk by the door.

A brown-haired guy is bent over, scrawling something in the security guard's notebook, laughing at something he's saying. The guy isn't a student; he's too tall, too not-high-school-looking . . .

What the hell is he doing here?

A slick of sweat breaks out on my palms. I whip around to face the bathroom door, away from him, but it's too late. A quick glance over my shoulder and I know he saw me.

I want to kick down the faculty bathroom door, yell for

whoever is taking her time in there to let me in. Instead, I swivel and take off down the hall, in the opposite direction he's heading, even though I'm moving away from the science wing and my chemistry teacher Mr. Franken's room.

I speed-walk, biting the inside of my lip to distract from the stabbing in my abdomen. Straight down the hall, where there's a pair of student bathrooms. *Don't stop—*

"Monica! Wait up."

It's not Brandon's voice. Of course it's not Brandon calling out to me—why would he act like he knows me here?

I turn to face a guy wearing a Sunnybrook cross-country jersey. Jimmy Varney, one of Matt's best friends. He smiles and nods at me. "Hey. How was your summer?"

"Good," I murmur, afraid I'll puke in his face if I open my mouth any wider. Jimmy's eyes refocus on something—someone—over my shoulder. He raises a hand. "Coach! Yo!"

Jimmy rests a hand on my arm. "I'll catch up with you later?"

I nod, and Jimmy darts off. Brandon is trapped as Jimmy descends on him. I pick up my pace and don't stop until I hit the bathroom, where I shut myself in the first stall.

Brandon is the new cross-country coach.

I don't even make it to my knees before I vomit into the toilet.

———

None of this would have happened if it weren't for that white dress.

I got the job at New Haven Country Club in June. When I told my mom I needed a ride for my first day of work, she blinked at me and said, "God, Monica, if you wanted money, you could have *asked* me."

But it wasn't about making money, not really. I'd wanted something more than summer days spent in Rachel's backyard, practicing straddles and aerials on her trampoline. I wanted a way out of evenings at the lake, Matt's beer breath in my ear and hand on my thigh.

The members of the New Haven Country Club have the type of money that they can shell out eighty bucks for someone to watch their kids while they play golf and sit in the spa sauna all day. My title was Kiddie Camp Counselor, but all I had to do was accompany the kids to the pool and the tennis courts and make sure they didn't die in the process.

On my first day, I saw Brandon hanging out at the lifeguard hut, swinging his lanyard around his wrist.

I knew where I'd seen him before: at Matt's cross-country championships in New Jersey in the fall. Matt's family had let me ride in the car with them so I could watch him compete. Laura, Matt's older sister, noticed Brandon first.

"Damn," she muttered, nudging me until I spotted him at the bottom of the bleachers. I had to look away, afraid Matt might catch me staring at the other team's hot coach.

By the end of my first day of work, I had a name for him: Brandon.

By the end of June, Matt and I had broken up. We both knew it was coming; he was leaving for college in Binghamton at the end of August. But the thought of not seeing him waiting at my locker on the first day of school sucked so much, I asked for extra shifts at the country club just so I wouldn't sit around the house thinking about it.

Rachel and Alexa thought the perfect place to debut Single Monica was at Jimmy Varney's Fourth of July party, since Matt wouldn't be there; he and his family were at their lake house upstate for the weekend. Rachel had just turned seventeen and passed her road test, so she and Alexa planned to pick me up when my shift at the country club finished at six.

That morning, when I packed the white dress to change into after work, I thought of Brandon.

He was skimming the surface of the pool with a net when I got out of the employee bathroom. Brandon looked up at me, his lips parting. His face went pink and my skin went warm under the dress.

I thought about the look on his face throughout the entire party that night.

That look made me feel like I could do anything. So I started to use my breaks to talk to him. At lunch, I sat in the empty chair next to the lifeguard stand, eating my mother's chicken salad while Brandon told me about what I'd missed on my days off. A six-year-old girl who screamed and refused to get in the water until Brandon fished out a dead beetle from the bottom of the pool.

He never asked how old I was and I never asked how

old he was. We both understood it would ruin whatever was going on.

A week later, when six o'clock came around and it was time to close up, I texted my mom that I had a ride home. I offered to stay late and help Brandon clean the pool. After, we sat on the edge, thighs almost touching, watching the waitstaff set up for a wedding inside the country club.

"That was cool of you to help," he said. "I'm sure you'd rather be hanging out with your boyfriend."

He nudged my knee with his, and I kept my head tilted down so he couldn't see the flush in my cheeks. "Who said I had a boyfriend?"

"Sorry," he laughed. "I'm sure you'd rather be hanging out with the guy you wore that white dress for the other night."

I sliced my foot through the surface of the water. I didn't say anything. Didn't want to give it away that he was the guy I wore the dress for.

But he must have figured it out, because he asked if I wanted a ride home. He stood and extended a hand, helped me to my feet.

When he started up his Jeep, classic rock blasted from the speakers. Something about a blue-eyed boy and a brown-eyed girl. We were the opposite.

He really was going to take me home. I'm the one who told him where to turn, and when we reached my street, I told him to keep going and he did. He kept driving until we reached Osprey's Bluff.

"Monica." He swallowed, shut his eyes. I undid my

belt and climbed into his lap, facing him. I held his hands on my cheeks for a little while, studying his face. He stared back at me in a way Matt had never looked at me, stroking his thumb along my jaw.

Brandon said my name again. "This is a bad idea."

"I'm not going to tell anyone."

He didn't push me away when I kissed him. He wanted it, I could feel how badly he wanted it, and when he asked, "Are you sure? Are you really sure?" I nodded. He leaned over and opened his glove compartment, tracing stubbly kisses around my neck the whole time.

It happened two more times before the beginning of the last week in August, when my mom took me for my annual gynecologist visit and the doctor asked when my last period was, and I said I didn't know because I honestly didn't remember, and she frowned and made me pee in a cup.

I called in sick for what was supposed to be my last shift at the country club, three days before school started. Brandon didn't text me to see what had happened—why I never said goodbye.

Friday, I swallowed the first pill in Dr. Bob's office. I spent Saturday curled up on my side on my bed, sobbing into my pillow and praying I wouldn't throw up from the second pill, because then it wouldn't work.

In the morning, I had a text from Brandon, asking if we could talk. I'm so stupid, I thought maybe he wanted to see me again.

But he was trying to warn me that he'd gotten a job at my goddamn high school.

Mom doesn't speak to me as she collects me from the nurse's office, signs us out, and leads me into the parking lot without uttering a single word.

The rain has turned to a light mist. I tilt my head back and let it cool my face as Mom unlocks the car.

I keep my eyes on my lap as I buckle my seat belt. "I'm sorry. I threw up."

I watch her from the corner of my eye, searching for any indication she might ask me if there's something else going on. She starts the car and flicks on the wipers. "You can't keep taking painkillers on an empty stomach."

The truck in front of us stops short. Mom slams on the brakes and all I can think is *pain*. I'm sweating, ears ringing. Her voice breaks through—she's saying my name over and over. Shaking me.

I blink away the black spots clouding my vision. We're pulled over, and my mother is staring at me. "Did you just pass out?"

"I don't know." Pressure builds behind my eyes. "Mom. I just want this to stop."

"I know." Her hand lingers on my shoulder. Her touch is light. I imagine her cool fingers brushing my hair behind my ear like she did when I was little, before my sister died and my mom stopped touching me. As if I'd become breakable.

She withdraws her hand and doesn't say anything else until we get home.

Mom is the manager of a playhouse—it's too small to be called a theater—in town. She has to pick up booster forms for the upcoming production of *The Importance of Being Earnest*, but she drops me off at home first and makes me chug Gatorade to get my blood sugar back up.

From my bedroom, I hear her on the phone with Dr. Robert Smith. I wonder if his name is actually Bob Smith, or if he changed it to something so generic no one could find him and pipe bomb his house.

"Naproxen can make people sick to their stomach. He called you in some nausea medication," my mother says when she sticks her head in my doorway. "It should be ready by the time I leave the playhouse—I'll pick it up on my way home."

As she's shutting my door, I call, "Mom?"

"Yes, Monica?"

My heart is still racing from the sight of Brandon this morning. The adrenaline is the only explanation for the fact that I have the urge to tell my mother the real reason I asked her to pick me up.

My mom and I don't exactly have an open relationship; she had to find out that Matt and I broke up by running into his sister at Starbucks. Even if I did tell her things, it would be totally demented to admit that I had a summer fling with the new cross-country coach.

I'm not seventeen. Brandon is in his twenties. Tom is a cop. I tamp down the thought as quickly as it comes to me.

"Thanks," I say.

"You don't need to thank me."

She studies me for a moment before shutting my door.

It almost hurts, how taken aback she looks at my acting the slightest bit grateful. It makes me wonder why anyone would ever want children. I can't think of a more thankless job.

When I hear the front door slam downstairs, I sit up in bed. Flinch at the fresh swell of pain in my lower body. I haven't had a painkiller since before I went to Demarco's office this morning.

Every second my mom is gone feels like an eternity. When I can't bear it any longer, I drag myself out of bed and head downstairs.

The naproxen bottle isn't on the kitchen island where my mother left it this morning. I don't even know half the places in this house that she could have hidden it.

I pause outside the downstairs bathroom, eyeing the door to Tom's office. Tom's back has been messed up since his car accident last year; some dumbass kid stole an ATV and led Tom and his partner, Mike, on a chase through Sunnybrook. The kid blew through a stop sign and hit a BMW, which then hit Tom and Mike.

My mother made Tom stop putting off the surgery in the spring. The doctor gave him Vicodin for his recovery; on a bad pain day this summer, I saw Tom sneak a couple pills from the bottle in his desk drawer.

The pain has destroyed my ability to think straight. It must have, because I've convinced myself that if the bottle still has pills left, Tom won't notice one missing. I just need one.

Tom doesn't lock the door to his office. He and my mom shared one in our old house. Their desks were practically on top of each other's, and when their work-from-home days overlapped, they didn't do much other than snipe at each other. Now Tom's office just looks like he didn't know what to do with all this space.

I pad over to his desk and tug at the handle of the top drawer. Rifle through the detritus—Post-its, a tipped over tray of paper clips and thumbtacks, dried-up Wite-Out pens.

I shut the drawer and move on to the one below it. When I yank, the contents rattle. Mango starts barking and trots into the office to investigate.

"No. Bad dog." I nudge him away with my foot and paw through what's inside the drawer. No Vicodin prescription.

A stack of envelopes, bound together by a rubber band, catches my eye.

They each have a printed label, all addressed to Tom Carlino, at our old address: 13 Norwood Drive, Sunnybrook, NY.

I run my finger over the tops of the envelopes, counting them. There are four. Every one is postmarked the same date—November 7—each one a year apart from the last.

I set the envelopes down on my lap, trembling.

November 7 is the day my sister killed herself.

I throw a glance over my shoulder. Mango is lying across the threshold of Tom's office door, watching me.

I unfold the piece of paper in the first envelope, revealing a black-and-white picture. The quality is crappy, like someone printed it off the Internet. It takes me a moment to process what I'm looking at.

The photo of my sister and her friends. The one in the trophy case at school.

I scan the page, hands trembling when I read the words at the bottom. I cast the picture aside and tip the next envelope so the contents fall out.

Every envelope contains the same thing. Four pictures total, each with the same message typed at the bottom.

I KNOW IT WASN'T HIM. CONNECT THE DOTS.

Chapter Four

November 7 was the worst day of our lives. And apparently, every year since the first anniversary of Jen's death, someone has been sending my stepfather anonymous letters.

Does my mom know? Are the letters the reason she and Tom wanted to sell the house so badly—to get away from them?

I know it wasn't him. Connect the dots.

I turn the letters over, inspecting every envelope inside and out. They're all postmarked from Newton, the next town over. There's no return address, and our old address is typed onto a label.

I replace the letters exactly as I found them. Suddenly the Vicodin isn't so important. The next drawer down doesn't budge when I tug on the handle. I give it another jangle to confirm: it's locked, not stuck.

Key, key. I rifle through the rest of the drawers. There's a ring of tiny keys in the top drawer. I don't even know what I'm looking for. There has to be something else here that could explain these letters. Why Tom would keep them—and what the hell they mean.

My phone buzzes with a text from Rachel:

we're safe 😊
Where are you?? There's a
meeting at 2:30 today

I fire off a response:

went home sick. Tell coach I'm
sorry

In the doorway, Mango sits up straight and lets out a throaty growl. Moments later, a car door slams. My mom is home already.

I shut Tom's desk drawer. Scramble to my feet and rush Mango out of the office. He takes off for the front door, barking, sliding around on the hardwood because he's still not used to not having carpet. I close Tom's office door and slip up the stairs before my mom's key turns in the lock.

It's almost midnight, and the rain has picked up again. It sounds like quarters being dropped on the roof. I'm in bed, watching the droplets run down the skylight. Next to me is a fraying copy of the novel I'm supposed to be reading for English. I've barely touched it.

Some weirdo could have sent those letters to Tom. An anonymous creep. Juliana's and Susan's murders had made national news, briefly, before the headlines were

28

consumed by a trifecta: a sex scandal involving a congressman, a terrorist attack in Europe, and a brutal wildfire in California. Jen's suicide barely registered on the media's radar. People kill themselves every day.

I open my browser and type in *Sunnybrook NY deaths*. The top result is an article from the *Westchester Courier*, dated the January after Juliana and Susan were killed.

OFFICER CLEARED IN DEATH OF MURDER SUSPECT

An internal investigation has determined that a Sunnybrook police officer acted reasonably when he shot Jack Canning, 38, the suspected murderer of two teenagers in October of last year. Mr. Canning died in his home after a confrontation with two Sunnybrook police officers, Thomas Carlino and Michael Mejia.

Even after all these years, the sight of Jack Canning's name twists my guts. Tom and his partner, Mike, had just started their shift that morning when Mr. Ruiz found the girls and called the police. They were the first officers to arrive on the scene.

As the ambulances and backup were arriving, Jack Canning stepped out onto his porch. When he saw Tom, he went white in the face, ran back into his house, and slammed the door.

Tom and Mike went after him; when they cornered Jack, he pulled a gun on them. Tom shot first. While he was bleeding to death on his carpet, Jack Canning grabbed Mike by his shirtsleeve and muttered the words *I'm sorry.*

Later, when the police were processing the scene, they tossed Jack Canning's bedroom and found several pictures of Susan sunbathing by her pool.

My brain circles back to those months after the murders, while the investigation was ongoing. They were the worst of our lives; Jen was dead, and we didn't know if Tom would face any charges in the shooting. I can still see Tom sitting in the dark in our den every night, beer bottle wedged between his knees. Killing Jack Canning was the only time my stepfather had ever discharged his weapon.

I force myself to read the rest of the story.

Jack Canning lived next door to Susan Berry, 15, one of the teenaged victims. Court records show that when Mr. Canning was 20, he was arrested for a lewd act with a minor. Due to the victim's refusal to cooperate with police, the district attorney's office decided to drop all charges.

Many in Sunnybrook feel that this oversight cost two young women their lives. "This was a preventable tragedy," says Diana Shaw, who lived across the street from Mr. Canning and his mother. "We should have known that a predator was living in our neighborhood. The justice system failed, and now two beautiful girls are dead."

According to officers Carlino and Mejia, they pursued Mr. Canning into his home upon seeing him behaving suspiciously near the crime scene. The officers claimed Mr. Canning barricaded himself in his bedroom. Upon breaking the door down, Officer Carlino found Mr. Canning removing something from his dresser drawer. When Mr. Canning refused to show his hands, Mr. Carlino fired. Mr. Canning died at the scene. Later, investigators found a revolver in Mr. Canning's dresser drawer and several photos of Susan Berry, including ones of her sunbathing by her pool.

I sit back in my chair, an odd thrumming in my body. Something isn't right.

This article says that Jack Canning was reaching into his dresser drawer before Tom shot him.

I read the paragraph again, searching for any mention of Jack Canning pointing a gun at Tom and Mike. When I don't find one, I double back to the search results and narrow the hits to ones that mention Tom and Mike by name.

This can't be right. They all say the same thing, that Jack Canning was reaching into his dresser, where he kept a gun, when Tom killed him.

So why, in the version of the events I have in my head, was Jack Canning pointing the gun at Tom and Mike?

In the weeks that followed, my mother shielded me from the news. She said Tom had to shoot Jack Canning, or Canning would have shot Tom and Mike. Everyone else in town was saying it too—that Jack Canning murdered two girls and would have murdered two cops as well if Tom hadn't taken him down. In public, and especially when the cameras were rolling, they all spoke about what a tragedy that night was. In private, I heard people whisper about how glad they were that my stepfather had killed the pervert and how they hoped Jack Canning suffered in his final moments.

I bring my feet up to my chair. Hug my knees to my chest. If Jack Canning hadn't really been reaching for his gun . . .

My door creaks open, sending my stomach into my throat.

I slam my laptop shut. Tom is standing there, his shape illuminated by the glow of the hallway sconce outside my door.

"Jesus," I say. "Can't you knock?"

Tom cocks his head at me. Mango rockets past him and crouches at the base of my bed. He tries to jump, but he's not used to the height of my new bed. The result is him pathetically bouncing on his back legs.

"I thought you were asleep," Tom says. "The dog was scratching at your door to get in."

I push myself away from my desk. Scoop up Mango and deposit him on the bed.

Tom is still watching me. "What are you doing up?"

"Nothing. I couldn't sleep."

Tom eyes my laptop. "Staring at your screen will only make it worse."

I try to imagine what his reaction would be if he knew what I'd been reading.

I know it wasn't him. Connect the dots.

I want to ask him what it means, but I can't tell him I know about the letters. *Hey, Tom, I found something weird when I was snooping through your desk for drugs.* I can't form any words at all.

"I know," I say. "I might take some melatonin."

"That's a good idea," he says. As he's shutting my door, I think I see him look at my laptop once more.

I have to make up the chem quiz I missed yesterday. I finish with ten minutes left in the lunch period. On my way to the cafeteria, a security guard spots me.

"Where we going, hon?"

"Lunch," I say, and he nods and leaves it at that. No one ever says shit to me. For being in the hall after the bell, for being in the newspaper office without a pass. I've seen how security hassles some of the other kids—groups of black girls, the guys who speak to each other in Spanish, the rowdy football players. I've done worse things in one summer than all of them have probably ever done combined.

Rachel spots me from across the cafeteria; she waves with one hand and gives Alexa's shoulder a shake with her other. Alexa looks over at me and clamps her mouth shut. A wave of paranoia hits me.

They can't have figured it out. They don't even know I've been with a guy since Matt and I broke up.

Rachel moves her bag off the seat next to her so I can slide in. I hold back a wince.

"We were just talking about the seniors," Rachel says in a voice that suggests they totally were not talking about the seniors. "Coach didn't pick captains yet."

"Isn't it going to be the Kelseys?"

"That's the thing," Alexa says. "They showed up late

for the meeting yesterday because they went to Dunkin' Donuts."

"I didn't show up to the meeting at all," I say.

Alexa's expression darkens. "Well, you had an *excuse*. You were sick."

"Who else made it?" I ask, eager to shunt aside thoughts of what Coach will do to punish me for missing the meeting.

Alexa takes a noisy pull from the dregs of her iced tea. "Everyone from last year, plus these two freshmen."

"And that girl Ginny or whatever her name is," Rachel says. "The one in our grade."

Obviously Rachel knows exactly who Ginny Cordero is—our class only has two hundred kids, so it's virtually impossible to go ten years without learning everyone's name. But we pretend we don't know, because it makes us feel important.

"Her," Alexa says.

I look over at the lunch line. Ginny Cordero is buying a Snapple. She keeps her eyes down as she takes her change from the lunch lady and tries to slip out of the cafeteria. Joe Gabriel, Kelsey's twin brother, stumbles back to catch a Nerf football and nearly knocks Ginny over.

Ginny Cordero isn't a loser or anything. People just don't think about her much at all. She's pretty in that untouched way—pale skin dotted with freckles, sun-streaked strawberry-blond hair she never cuts.

Sometimes I think about her.

When Jen was thirteen, she wasn't in high school or on

cheerleading yet, so she was still taking tumbling classes at Jessie's Gym three nights a week. Whenever Tom had to work late, my brother and I had to ride along in the car with Mom when she went to pick Jen up.

Jen was always talking about how annoyed Jessie would get with Ginny Cordero's mother, who was always late picking her up. Class ended at 7:00 p.m., and sometimes Ginny's mom didn't show up until 7:40, and Jessie would have to wait until she did to close the gym.

One night, my mother pulled into the parking lot, and Jen wasn't waiting outside with the other girls. Petey was next to me in the backseat, straining in his car seat, fussy because it was approaching his bedtime.

Through the gym's front window, I spotted my sister sitting next to Ginny in the waiting area. She refused to come outside until Ginny's mother arrived at twenty after seven.

Now Ginny's eyes connect with mine for a moment before she slips out of the cafeteria.

I wonder if she remembers that night—if it's why she's always avoiding looking me in the face.

"She was really good," Rachel says. I don't even remember seeing Ginny at tryouts on Monday.

"You're really good," I say. But I can tell she's thinking about that triple pirouette—her Achilles' heel.

When Alexa stands, announcing that she's buying a cookie, Rachel turns to me, her voice low. "Why did you get called to guidance?"

"Coughlin wants me to help with a memorial for the cheerleaders."

"She asked me too," Rachel says. "After health yesterday."

Bethany Steiger was Rachel's cousin. Rach hated her; Bethany only ever wanted to hang out with Rachel's older sister Sarah, and she would make fun of the gap between Rachel's front teeth.

I look down at the PB&J I've barely touched. I tear off a piece of the crust. "Did you say you'd help?"

"I couldn't say no. She put me on the spot." Rachel eyes me. "Are you going to do it?"

I don't answer. Part of me itches to tell Rach about the letters, just like I wanted to tell her about Brandon this summer. She and I tell each other everything; two summers ago, when Matt told me he loved me for the first time, under the porch light of my old house, I called Rachel immediately, even though it was almost midnight. I'm the only one of our friends who knows that her parents were separated for a year when we were kids and that she doesn't remember losing her virginity to a senior on the soccer team last year at one of Kelsey Gabriel's parties. She made me swear I'd never tell, and I know she'd do the same for me.

But when I think about telling her why I was in Tom's desk, and what I found there and what I read online last night, something in me screams not to. And I don't know why.

"Monica." Rach waves a hand in front of my face. "Did you hear me? Are you going to help with the memorial?"

"I don't know." After a moment, I say, "Do you ever wonder if we know everything about what happened that year they all died?"

Rachel gapes at me. "What do you mean?"

"I don't know." I pick up my sandwich. "Never mind."

"No, seriously. Tell me what you mean."

"It's like . . . the accident, and the murders . . ." I have to swallow. "And Jen. Sometimes it feels like they're all dots that no one ever tried to connect."

Rachel almost looks scared. "Monica, what are you talking about?"

"Nothing. Forget it, okay?" I grab my empty water bottle and stand, aware that she's staring at me the entire walk to the recycling bin across the cafeteria.

Rachel doesn't bring up what happened at lunch again for the rest of the day. In the first fifteen minutes of dance team practice, it becomes clear she has bigger problems.

Our warm-up is a series of stretches, leaps across the floor, fouetté turns, and pirouettes. Moments before the song is supposed to end, the music stops abruptly.

We all turn to Coach, trying to suppress our panting. She's standing by the speakers, arms crossed in front of her chest. Coach is only five foot three, but somehow that makes her scarier.

The sophomores in the row in front of me glance at each other. *Which one of us is it?*

My stomach sinks; I know who it is.

"Steiger," Coach barks. "Get the triple by Monday."

Coach starts the music from the top. I spot Rachel blinking rapidly as we move back into formation. In the row in front of us, Ginny Cordero looks over her shoulder. When our eyes meet, she looks away.

When it's time for a break to rehydrate, the Kelseys plop themselves by Coach's feet. *What are you doing this weekend, Coach? Are you going to the game?*

It's been three years, and they haven't given up on needling her for signs that she is, in fact, human. There's a photo of her son—a doughy blond kindergartener—on her desk, but we have yet to confirm that he actually exists.

She's been the coach for four years now, taking the team all the way to nationals every February. Before she arrived, the dance team was all glorified ass shaking to the sorts of rap songs that suburban white girls have no business dancing to. Anyone with talent was a cheerleader, until the girls died and their coach quit and Principal Heinz thought it was way too painful to keep the squad together.

Coach ignores the Kelseys and turns to the rest of us, who are chatting in our groups. Ginny Cordero is off in the sidelines, eyes on her water bottle.

"Hate to interrupt your riveting conversations," Coach says. "But your new uniforms are here."

Some squeals of delight as everyone gathers around the box Coach drops at her feet. Alexa picks up a package labeled SMALL. She looks at her chest and sighs, exchanging the uniform for a medium. We each grab our proper sizes and head off to the locker room.

Last year's uniforms had V-necks, and apparently they were too scandalous, because now we have sleeveless triangle tops that cover everything but our arms and shoulders.

Coach shouts into the locker room, asking what's taking us so long, and we trickle out, tugging at the waistbands of our pants, smoothing the spandex over our butts. The uniforms, slick as a seal's skin, show every lump, every roll, and no one wants to be forced to try on the next size up.

At the end of the hall, there's a series of smacks and squeaks of rubber on linoleum. A pack of cross-country guys is running toward us; they can't run outside in the thunderstorm, so Brandon must be making them do laps inside the building.

My stomach twists. I angle myself behind Rach as the pack of guys flies by. Kelsey G preens, stretching her arms over her head. Some of the seniors whistle; Joe Gabriel slaps one of them upside the head.

"That's my sister, dumbass."

"Keep moving. No gawking at the ladies." Brandon. He's trailing behind the guys, a small smile of amusement on his face.

"Hi," Alexa shouts, and I want to strangle her.

Brandon doesn't look up from the stopwatch in his hand. "Hi, girls. Better not keep your coach waiting."

When he's out of earshot, Alexa lifts her ponytail off the back of her neck. "He is so hot."

"He's got a girlfriend," Kelsey B says, bored with us all.

My shoes stick to the floor. I lurch forward.

Alexa eyes Kelsey. "How would you know?"

"I saw him at the mall," Kelsey G says. "He and some girl were looking at coffeemakers in Macy's."

I force out a single word: "When?"

"This weekend." Kelsey shrugs. "Kels was with me."

We all look at Kelsey B, who nods. *It's true.*

This weekend. While I was under the covers, heating pad smashed into my abdomen, pillow over my mouth so Tom and Petey wouldn't hear me crying, Brandon was playing house with his girlfriend.

Girlfriend. Brandon has a girlfriend.

After practice, I tell Rachel I have to get something from my locker and that I'll meet her and Alexa by the car. Once the halls have emptied of the after-school athletes, I pause outside Brandon's office door. Inhale. Rap on the doorframe.

His eyes go wide when he sees me. "Hey."

"I need to talk to you."

"Okay. Come in." Brandon steps aside. He motions to close the door but promptly drops his hand to his side, realizing what a bad idea that would be.

I shoot a glance into the hallway. No one's there. I whisper anyway. "Do you have a girlfriend?"

Brandon's lips part. He clamps his mouth shut.

"Okay," I say. "Great. Good to know."

"Monica, wait," he says, even though I haven't shown any intentions of leaving. "She and I weren't together over the summer. I swear."

She. The word lands like a kick in the gut. *She* confirms that she exists. A girlfriend. Brandon has a girlfriend.

"I'm sorry I never asked you why you stopped texting me," he says softly. "She moved back from Boston a couple weeks ago. We broke up when she took a job there a year ago. It just kind of happened."

"It's fine. It was done. Whatever we were doing." Pressure builds behind my eyes. "I'm going to go now."

He says my name, but I don't turn around. Two hard blinks and a look at the light overhead in the hall. Foolproof tear quelling.

Ginny Cordero is sitting cross-legged on the ground, her back against her locker. She looks up from her copy of *The Grapes of Wrath* as Brandon steps out of his office.

My stomach goes hollow. Ginny looks from Brandon, to me, then back down to her book. Cheeks pink. Brandon steps back into his office and closes the door, but it doesn't matter; it's too late. She knows I was in there, alone with him.

"I missed the bus," she blurts. "I'm waiting for my mom to come get me."

I don't say anything. I just haul ass out of there, too ashamed to look at her for some reason.

The locked drawer in Tom's desk has been haunting my thoughts.

My brother has soccer on Wednesday evenings, so the house is empty when Rachel drops me off after practice.

I close and lock the front door behind me. Mango runs circles around my feet. I sidestep him and make my way into the kitchen. He gets on his hind legs and scratches my calves until I relent and dig a Milk-Bone out of the pantry for him.

Mango loved Jen more than he loves any of us. He slept in her bed every night, and every afternoon, he would sit on the back of the couch, looking out the bay window, waiting for her to get home from cheer practice.

While the dog spreads out on the kitchen floor and crunches his treat, I eye the dark hallway leading to Tom's office.

Petey's practice started at five, so he and my mom won't be home for at least another hour, and Tom's shift ends at seven. I head up to my room and peel off my sweaty dance tights, replacing them with cotton pajama bottoms.

Back downstairs, Mango is scratching at the back door. I let him into the yard, leaving the door open so he can come back in when he's done, and pad down the hall to Tom's office.

Like always, his door isn't locked. I push it open and head straight for the desk. I pull on the second drawer again before revisiting the top drawer. No key. The pull-out tray under Tom's keyboard is empty, save for a pen and a few stray rubber bands and paper clips.

I've seen Alexa pick the lock on her parents' liquor cabinet with fewer tools. I grab a paper clip and bend it into a hook shape. Bite my lip and feed the paper clip into the lock.

I can feel where the bolt meets the desk. I just need to wedge something between them. The house phone rings; I ignore it and wipe away the sweat forming at my hairline. Somewhere around my hundredth attempt, Mango wanders into the office and scratches my knee, asking to come onto my lap. I nudge him away. "No. Bad dog."

Another paper clip. I untwist the second paper clip so it's straight as a needle. While that's wedged between the bolt and the lock, I stick the hooked clip in and twist, nearly jumping out of Tom's chair when the lock clicks.

Inside the drawer looks innocent enough. There are several file folders; I thumb through them—pages of account information for the power company, the mortgage on the house.

I replace the folders; something at the back of the drawer glints, catching my eye. The screen of a cell phone.

A foul taste comes into my mouth. I've seen the movies about cheaters. I know what a second phone means.

It's an older model—the kind I used to have a few years ago. Smaller than the version my whole family owns now. I pick it up and turn it over.

Juliana's, Susan's, and my sister's faces smile up at me.

My fingers go numb. Juliana had this case made as a Christmas gift for my sister; the photo was taken at their first football game. The girls are huddled together, arms draped over each other's shoulders. Hair partless, slicked back and shiny, blue ribbons tied around their ponytails.

I hold down the power button, but nothing happens. Of course it's not charged—my sister has been dead for almost five years.

So why the hell does Tom have her cell phone?

In the hall, Mango is going berserk. Barking, nails sliding on the hardwood floor. I shut the drawer at the same moment a car door slams in the driveway.

My foot snags on the carpet as I stand up. *The drawer.*

I don't have the key to lock it back up. I survey the office, panicked, as Tom's voice calls out.

"Monica?"

I step out of the office and shut his door, quietly, my pulse pounding in my ears. I round the corner of the hallway at the same time Tom steps into it.

"You're home early," I say.

Tom frowns. "Guy who's supposed to fix the AC unit is running early. Mom said she called you to let you know I was on my way."

"My phone is upstairs." Jen's phone weighs down the thin material of my pajama pocket. I put my hand over it. If Tom knows that my mother called the house line as well, he doesn't say anything.

He gives me a curious look before eyeballing his office door. My pulse stills; Tom's gaze sweeps over it, and seeing nothing of interest, he heads back toward the kitchen. "I'm gonna throw in some pizza rolls, if you're hungry."

I'm the opposite of hungry. The thought of Jen's phone locked away in Tom's desk drawer all these years has me deeply unsettled.

"I'm okay. I have homework to start." I head upstairs without looking back at him.

I don't like doubting Tom. He's always been more of a father to me than my real dad, who I hear from only on Christmas and my birthday. I was three when he moved out and then in with the professor from his university he'd been having an affair with. They bought a house in Iowa when he accepted a teaching position at a college there, and not long after, my mom met Tom.

For as long as I can remember, Tom has been there. Installed in his armchair from nine p.m. on, watching those shows my mom hates about people treasure hunting in abandoned storage lockers. Tom is the one in the family photos from trips to Disney World, the one who showed up to my dance recitals with an armful of roses. Around the time Jen died, Tom was teaching her how to drive.

Even though she wasn't his real daughter, Tom was as devastated by Jen's death as the rest of us. Sometimes I think it's possible it was worse for him than for the rest of us. He saw Colleen's and Bethany's bodies at the crash site, Juliana's and Susan's at the murder scene; when Jen wouldn't answer her phone the morning she died, Tom was the one who went to check on her and had to break down her locked door.

Tom loved my sister like a daughter. It makes sense that he'd want to go through her phone after her death; Jen didn't leave a note. When a child kills herself, isn't every parent desperate to know why?

But I can't think of a single good reason why he'd hang on to her phone all these years.

I pick my way through the storage tubs in my room, Jen's phone jangling in my pocket. Somewhere in this mess is a box of crap from my old nightstand. I know an outdated phone charger that will fit Jen's phone is buried among it.

I lift a box of my winter clothes; in the tub below it, I can see a charger, coiled and fraying. I dig it out and sit back, my heart pounding like a jackrabbit's.

I know it wasn't him. Connect the dots.

Is that why Tom has her phone? Did he try to connect the dots? The alternate scenario sends a chill through me. Tom was the responding officer to the scene of Bethany and Colleen's accident. He shot Juliana and Susan's killer.

Tom found Jen's body.

Tom is what connects the dots.

I scoot over to my nightstand and plug the charger into the outlet behind it. Plop onto my bed and sit cross-legged, the phone on my lap. When I stick the charger into the phone's port, the screen stays black, and I think maybe the phone is actually *dead* dead.

Then, movement. A lightning bolt icon pops up on the screen.

I wait for what feels like an eternity, but when the screen flickers to life, the time shows that only two minutes have passed. Jen's wallpaper loads; it's a photo of her cradling Mango, his heinous underbite on full display as he accepts a belly rub.

Something isn't right. I shouldn't be able to see Jen's home screen. My sister kept her phone locked; I know because I was a little snoop, and whenever she left her phone within reach, I would try to guess her passcode.

Tom must have found a way around the passcode and disabled it. I take in a breath that's sharp in my nose and open Jen's text messages.

There's nothing there.

Did she delete all her texts? Did Tom?

I switch to her call log and exhale. It's intact. The calls end the morning of November 7.

My mother called her every hour from work that morning to see if she was okay. I still remember she was only working a half day. Jen had woken up nauseous and my mom let her stay home.

Sandwiched between two of those calls is a number I don't recognize.

It's not stored in her phone under a name. The skin on the back of my neck prickles. I scroll through the rest of the call log.

The number isn't there. Whoever the number belongs to only called Jen once, the day she died. The conversation was seventeen minutes—too long to be a spam call or a wrong number.

The conversation ended around 10:20 a.m. Not long after, my mother called Jen three times. She must have sent Tom to the house to check on her after that.

This room is too hot. I strip off my sweatshirt, panting in my dance tank top.

I copy the number into my phone and address a text to it. Stare at the screen, thumbs hovering over my keyboard.

This is absurd. There's nothing I can say to the owner of this number that won't sound totally absurd.

> Hello, I found your number in my sister's phone, and I was wondering—did you know she was about to die when she talked to you that morning?

I hit SEND and swallow and type out:

> Who are you?

My whole body tenses as I press SEND again. I stare at my screen, palms sweating. The delivery message flashes to *read*. An ellipsis appears. A few seconds later, a text pops up.

> Uh . . . who are YOU?

My pulse ticks in my ears. I respond:

> Jen Rayburn's sister.

The read receipt appears. I stare at the screen, waiting for the ellipsis to pop up, to signal that he or she is typing. My stomach sinks lower with every moment that goes by and the screen is still blank.

I reach over to my nightstand. The second I set my phone down, the screen lights up.

> How did you get this number?

> Her phone. Who are you?

My fingers are flying over the keyboard so quickly I screw up the message twice and have to retype it.

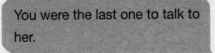
You were the last one to talk to her.

I hit SEND. Lean back into my headboard, holding out the phone in front of me with one hand and covering my mouth with the other.

Five minutes go by without a response. I blink, warding off tears of frustration, and text him or her again.

Please just tell me. Who are you?

I watch the screen, desperate, but this time an answer comes quickly.

That doesn't matter.

Then:

Be careful.

Jennifer

Jen never wanted to be on top. The top was for petite girls, like Juliana, or pea-shoot-thin girls like Susan, muscles toned from years of tennis. Jen, who'd shot up like a sunflower the summer before eighth grade, knew she was forever relegated to being a base. And she was fine with that—she'd accepted her position as one of the hazards of being a tall girl. Flying was simply a thing she'd never be able to do, like wear high heels or date a guy under six feet.

Her sister, who had just started middle school, was going through her own growth spurt. Monica'd already had several meltdowns about her new body. She towered over all the girls in her ballet class, and the boy who sat behind her in math asked to switch seats because her head was blocking the chalkboard.

Jen wanted to grab Monica and shake her sometimes. *The boys will go through puberty soon! There are worse things in life than being tall!*

50

Mom was always telling Jen to chill. Monica was only eleven, and Jen had also been the worst when she was eleven.

Jen would kill to be eleven again.

"Five, six, seven, eight!" Allie—she refused to let the girls call her Coach—singsonged the numbers. Jen cupped her hands over her partner's, knees bent so they could lift Juliana.

Juliana's hands barely seemed to touch Jen's shoulders as she popped up. The other fliers put all their weight on the bases' shoulders, the girls buckling under the weight. Juliana, who was barely five-one, had a rare mix of grace and athleticism.

The other girls only had one of the two, if they were lucky. The truly cumbersome girls were sidelined during the stunts, left to do the pom-pom waving and actual cheering.

Jen knew she was more athletic than graceful. She'd wanted to be a gymnast as a kid but lacked the focus or discipline of the girls who trained at Jessie's Gym six days a week. She'd played softball and basketball in middle school; it had been Juliana's idea to try out for cheerleading the summer before high school.

Jen was grateful for her arm strength as she launched Juliana into a perfect toe touch. Juliana landed in the girls' outstretched arms, legs together and feet pointed.

"Nice, Ruiz!" Allie clapped her hands. "Take five and we'll run it from the top."

Jen stole a look at Susan's face as the girls broke formation, moved into their clusters. Susan divided her ponytail in two and yanked to tighten it, eyes cast down. No doubt feeling the sting of Allie not complimenting *her* performance. Susan was programmed that way—to believe she was a failure when she wasn't the best.

Jen wondered how much Mrs. Berry had to do with that. Susan's mom was always there at the end of practice, always asking how you were doing, offering everyone rides home with a smile that made Jen wonder if she was secretly a psycho.

"What's wrong, J-Ray?" Juliana flicked Jen's bun.

Jen moved a hand to her neck, disoriented by the nickname Juliana had given her this summer. "Nothing."

Juliana's gaze swept past Jen as quickly as it had landed on her. Jen turned to see what Juliana was staring at. Or rather, *who:* Carly Amato, who had transferred to Sunnybrook at the end of last year.

Juliana gave Jen's forearm a squeeze. "Be right back."

Jen thought of the county fair, only a couple of weeks ago. She was waiting in line for the bathroom trailers, while Susan and Juliana were getting refills on their sodas. Whoever was in the bathroom was taking forever; just as Jen was about to give up and find a bathroom somewhere else, two girls stumbled out, helping each other down the steps.

One of the girls locked eyes with her.

"Hey." Carly drew out the word. Her friend giggled. Jen forced out a smile.

Carly's eyes weren't bloodshot, like she was drunk or stoned. But her pupils were black holes, her spidery lashes blinking manically.

The girls stumbled off. Jen watched them link arms, sidestepping a couple pushing a double stroller. The father looked over his shoulder, shaking his head at Carly and her friend.

They wound up at an ice cream truck, talking to two guys. One was tall and lanky with tanned shoulders and thick brown hair that curled around his ears. The other was shorter, more muscular, blond, his eyes hidden behind a pair of Ray-Bans.

Carly laughed at something the blond guy said, reaching over and giving him a playful shove. Jen wondered how they could be so easy with guys they just met. She thought of the look in Carly's eyes. The way she'd wiped her nose.

She hadn't told anyone, but watching Juliana tot off toward Carly, Jen wished she had.

Susan appeared at Jen's side, squeezing the empty water bottle in her hand as if it were a stress ball.

"When did Juliana and Carly become best friends?" Jen asked.

Susan stopped squeezing her water bottle. "Cheer camp, probably. Why? You jealous or something?"

Jen knew Susan was messing with her, but she still felt a tug in her chest. The past summer had been the first she, Juliana, and Susan had been apart. Susan had forgone two weeks away at USA Cheer for an SAT prep course, while Jen spent most of her days entertaining her younger siblings for ten bucks an hour so her mother could go back to work full-time now that Petey was in kindergarten.

Susan and Jen eyed Juliana and Carly. Juliana said something that sent Carly's head back in laughter. Jen felt unease settle over her, followed by a primal urge to yank Carly away from Jules.

"I don't trust her," Jen said to Susan. What she really meant was *Carly scares the shit out of me,* but Susan didn't even seem to be listening. The gears in her brain were probably turning over the homework she had to do when she got home, mentally organizing her binders with those colored tabs Jen and Juliana made fun of her for getting excited about.

"Please, Allie." Carly's manufactured baby voice carried across the gym. "Just let us show you!"

"Show what?" Jen found herself across the mat from Juliana, Carly, and a pocket of seniors who had Allie surrounded.

"A swan dive." Carly's gaze raked over Jen like she'd never seen her before in her life. "Our group leader at camp taught us how to do one."

"Well, that was super irresponsible of her," Allie said. "They're illegal at the high school level."

A chorus of *just let us try it/it's not like we'd do it in competition/come on, Allie, pleeeeease* from the rest of the girls. Allie, fearing mutiny, held up her hands.

"We can *maybe* try it after we run through the routine."

"Yaaaaaas!" Carly grabbed Juliana, bouncing on the balls of her feet. "Juju was *so* good at it."

Juju? What the hell? Jen tried to catch Juliana's eye, but the other girls were already crowding her.

"What even *is* a swan dive?" one of the seniors asked.

"I'll show you guys," Carly said. "There's videos on YouTube."

Allie sighed in defeat, backed away to let the girls scramble onto the mat. Carly lay down at the head of the pack, holding her phone so everyone could see the video she'd pulled up.

The cheerleaders in the video formed a basket. At the end of the line, a girl climbed onto the shoulders of two of the bases. Launching herself forward into a front tuck, she dove Superman-style and landed in the outstretched arms beneath her.

"This is so dangerous," Allie muttered, over gasps of *Holy shit, that was insane.*

Juliana was beaming, sitting cross-legged on the mat with her shoulder touching Carly's. Jen pictured Juliana sailing through the air as if she weighed nothing, and her stomach knotted up.

She thought of Susan standing behind her, living in a world devoid of basket tosses and swan dives and filled with applications to Brown and Stanford.

Jen thought of her friends slipping away from her and how it felt like she was hurtling toward the edge of something they couldn't be pulled back from.

Chapter Five

When I wake up, my last message is still unanswered.

Be careful of what?? Read at 9:03 p.m.

I rub my eyes and look at the time. I stayed up too late, staring at the screen of my phone, waiting for a response. The faint sound of the shower from the master suite next door means I slept through my first alarm; Tom gets into the shower every morning at 6:30 on the dot.

I throw a clean pair of dance clothes into my gym bag and stuff myself into a pair of jeans. The SUNY Binghamton T-shirt Matt gave me before we broke up is at the top of my dresser drawer; I grab it and guide my arms through the long sleeves, fumbling my way into the bathroom to brush my hair.

Once I'm dressed, I sit on the edge of my bed and unplug my phone from the charger. I don't have time to be dillydallying, but I pull up my thread with the mystery number and reread the messages. I tried searching the number online last night, but all Google could tell me was that the cell phone was registered in Ulster County— which I already knew from the area code.

I can't get the owner's name, but Tom definitely can.

Did. Tom must have had Jen's phone for years. He would have seen that Jen spoke with someone the morning she died, and he would have used his omnipotent cop powers to look up the number's owner. If he didn't already know who it was.

But why did he keep Jen's phone in the first place? Did he also think there was more to her death than the coroner's conclusion—a nonsuspicious suicide?

Or is there a more fucked-up reason?

My mother's voice carries up the stairs. I open my bedroom door and shout back. "What?"

"Rachel is here."

I glance at my phone; Rachel is ten minutes early, today of all days. I grab my stuff and fly downstairs.

Chaos is waiting for me. Petey forgot about a sheet of math problems in his homework folder, and he flips a shit over his Cocoa Puffs.

"I'm gonna get a demerit!"

Mom is supposed to be at the playhouse early today, but she drops her toast and coffee and sits down next to Petey to help him with multiplying by six. Upstairs, Tom is stomping around, yelling about how Mango peed on the carpet and he's going to be late for work. The whole scene makes me wish Jen could come back just so I could ask her why she left me with these people.

Even though she's early, I don't want Rachel to wait, so I grab my breakfast to go and head outside, travel mug of coffee and a cider doughnut in hand.

Once I'm buckled in, I take a greedy bite of the cider doughnut, feeling Rachel's eyes on it.

"What is that?" she asks.

I imagine her breakfast of black coffee and half a cup of fat-free yogurt. The Unofficial Dance Team Diet. "A doughnut," I say.

"Oh," she says, like she's never seen one before. In her cup holder, there's a water bottle filled with something that looks like pee. Her quarterly cleanse of dandelion tea, cayenne pepper, and maple syrup. It's supposed to make you drop ten pounds in a week. No doubt this was prompted by the way her chest strained against her new uniform top and the scorching look Coach gave her.

There's a bus stop at the corner; the driver must be super late today, because a girl is still waiting. An oversized cardigan hangs off her slender figure. She nibbles on her thumbnail, eyes cast down so she doesn't have to look at us.

Ginny Cordero.

"Pull over," I tell Rach. "We should give her a ride."

Rachel's nose twitches. "Are you sure there's room . . . ?"

"Why are you being so weird? She's on dance team."

"I'm not being weird. I just . . ." Rachel doesn't finish her thought. But she pulls up to the curb where Ginny is waiting. I lower my window.

"Hey," I say. "Do you want a ride?"

"Oh." Ginny looks at me, then at Rachel. The note of surprise in her voice and the mistrust in her eyes make me sad. Like she thinks this is a trick or something. Us being nice.

"That's okay," she says. "The bus will be here any minute."

My stomach clenches. Is she thinking about what she heard—or didn't hear—outside Brandon's office yesterday? Does she think I'm being nice because I want to figure out what she knows?

"Thank you, though," Ginny adds. "I'll see you at practice today."

"Yeah. See you then." I raise the window. When we reach the light where my street meets the main road, Rachel massages her thumb until the joint cracks.

"You know my dad fired her dad?"

I relax a little; it's natural Ginny would feel awkward around Rachel. "No. I didn't even know he worked for him."

Rachel's dad owns Steiger's, the auto body and tire shop in town. The business has been in their family for years; Rachel's uncle—Bethany Steiger's father—was co-owner.

Thinking about Bethany makes me think about the cheerleaders, which makes me think about my sister, which makes me think about the unanswered text message. All the thinking makes my head fog. As we pull up to Alexa's house, I slip my phone out of the side pocket of my backpack.

While Rachel is busy texting Alexa to tell her we're outside, I text the number again:

> Just tell me one thing. Do I know you?

Rachel's voice draws my attention away from my screen. "She's running late. What a surprise."

"Well, we're early," I say. I set my phone on my lap so I can open my travel mug. While I'm taking a sip of coffee, my phone shimmies.

"Is that Alexa?" Rachel asks. "Is she complaining about me for telling her to hurry up?"

I snatch it up before Rachel can look at my screen. "It's my mom."

While Rach is scrambling for her own phone, probably to hound Alexa again, I open the text.

No.

Alexa climbs into the car and wrinkles her nose at the water bottle. "Is it this time again?"

"Leave me alone," Rach says. "Not all of us can eat whatever the hell we want."

Alexa rolls her eyes. "I don't know how that doesn't give you the shits."

"I never said it doesn't."

Alexa gives the back of Rach's headrest a playful smack. My phone vibrates; I have another text from the number, even though I never answered their last message.

My turn to ask a question. How did you get Jen's phone?

I try to tune out Alexa's manic cackling at something Rachel has said while I figure out how to respond. I decide there's no reason not to go with the truth.

> I found it in my stepdad's desk.

He/she texts back immediately:

> Don't you think it's weird that he had it?

Alexa leans forward, resting her chin on my shoulder. "Ooo, who ya texting?"

I wiggle away from her and turn my phone over. "No one."

"Bitch, do you have a secret lover?"

"Bitch, it's none of your business."

"Knock it off," Rachel says, and even though Alexa yawns and leans back in her seat, I suspect she's straining to get a look over my shoulder. I slip my phone into my backpack.

We get to school five minutes before the first bell. I head straight for the bathroom, away from my nosy-ass friends, and shut myself in a stall. Grab my phone and reread the last message.

> Don't you think it's weird that he had it?

> He must have kept it for a reason. What did you and Jen talk about that day?

A whole minute goes by. Outside my stall, I hear Mrs. Brown, the hall monitor, doing her daily sweep of the bathroom, barking at the girls by the sink to finish doing their makeup and be on their way; the first bell is about to ring any second now.

I swallow a grunt of frustration and fire off another text:

> Can't you tell me anything???

The bell rings; I stick my phone in my jeans pocket and flush the toilet for show. Hurry past Mrs. Brown and upstairs to my homeroom. As I'm sliding into my seat, my phone vibrates.

> Don't trust anything your stepdad says.

It feels like all the air has been sucked out of the room. Out of me. The second bell rings and Mrs. Barnes's voice comes over the loudspeaker, asking us to stand for the pledge of allegiance.

Anything he says about what? I reply.

"Monica," my homeroom teacher snaps. "Put the phone away before I take it away."

I hide my phone in the hem of my shirt, my fingers

trembling around it. When I sit back down, I steal a glance at the screen, at the one-word response.

Everything.

I check my phone every free moment I get for the rest of the day, but my message—*What is everything?*—dangles there, unanswered. After last period, my phone vibrates.

I whip my phone out, but the text isn't from him/ her: It's from Kelsey Butler. She says practice is canceled; Coach's son is sick.

Rachel texts Alexa and me to tell us she has to stay for extra help in pre-calc, which means I have to take the bus for the first time this year. I don't even know what number my bus is, and by the time I get it from Mrs. Barnes and run out to the parking lot, the bus has started to pull away.

"Goddamn it." I run toward the bus, waving my hands. "Hey! Wait!"

The bus slows; the door swings open and I hop on, ignoring the filthy look the driver gives me. She doesn't wait for me to sit down before hitting the gas; I lurch forward, grabbing ahold of the seat next to me.

There's someone sitting by the window, but the space next to her is free. I plop down and drop my backpack at my feet. I glance at my seatmate; Ginny Cordero is staring out the window, hands folded on top of the messenger bag on her lap.

I tap her on the shoulder. When she turns her head, she doesn't look surprised to see me, which makes me think the staring-out-the-window thing was her way of avoiding eye contact and hoping I wouldn't sit next to her.

"Hey," I say.

"Hi." Ginny nods at the backpack wedged between my feet. "Do you need more room? I can move over—"

"No, you're fine."

"Cool." Ginny looks down at her hands. Laces her fingers together more tightly. On her left hand is a scar on the knuckle of her middle finger, small as a grain of rice.

The bus hits a speed bump, and we lurch forward. At the back of the bus, two guys are shouting out the window; the driver yells at them to sit their asses down or she's pulling over.

"It's nice to have a day off from practice," I say to Ginny, when I can't stand the awkward silence between us any longer.

She comes alive a bit at my mention of dance team. "Yeah, it was lucky for me. I forgot my uniform money."

I don't tell her that *lucky* is an understatement. "You're really good. How come you didn't try out sooner?"

"I did," Ginny says. "When we were freshmen. I didn't make it."

I don't even remember Ginny being there. "You used to do gymnastics, didn't you?"

Ginny nods. "Yeah."

"Why did you stop?" I ask.

"My dad— My parents separated and my mom

couldn't afford it anymore. The travel teams are expensive. . . ." Ginny's cheeks go pink, and I hate that I made her feel like she has to talk about this.

"Anyway," she says. "I have dance team now."

She's wearing the same expression she had when she saw me leaving Brandon's office. Does she think I'm being nice to her as an intimidation tactic to keep her quiet?

I swallow. "Yesterday, in the cross-country coach's office . . . that wasn't—"

Her voice is gentle as she cuts me off. "You don't have to tell me. It's none of my business."

I know it's different with her than with my friends, and it's not fair to compare them. But for once, I'm thankful not to be hounded.

The bus driver slows to a stop at the intersection of Lennox and Wilson Streets.

"This is me," Ginny says quietly. I move to let her get out.

She catches my eye as the bus is pulling away. Holds up a hand and smiles.

My mother's car is in the driveway. Twice a week, she leaves work at noon. I head down the hall, stopping short of her office door, which is open. She's facing the other direction, leaning back in her chair, turning a pen over in one hand. A man's voice emits from the speaker on the phone cradle on her desk.

"I just don't think we have the budget for that," my mother interrupts him.

I tiptoe past her door and up the stairs. Once in my room, I deposit my backpack on my bed and sink into my desk chair, digging my phone out of my pocket. I re-read the last messages the unknown number sent to me.

Don't trust anything your stepdad says.

Anything he says about what?

Everything.

I don't know what *everything* means, so I decide the most logical place to start is with the murders. Since I found those letters in Tom's drawer, I've already discovered one detail that contradicts the story I've accepted all these years:

Jack Canning never pointed a gun at Tom.

All I really know about the murders is what the police say happened, and I never had a reason to doubt what the police say happened.

They say that Jack Canning killed Susan and Juliana. They say he was a predator, that he was obsessed with Susan, that he saw the girls were alone and vulnerable and he pounced. They say the pictures of Susan, taken without her knowledge, only supported their theory.

I blink at the blinding white home page on my laptop. The search bar is accompanied by the message *What are you looking for?* It feels like a taunt.

There are several Jack Cannings in the world. I refine my search to include only Sunnybrook, NY.

At the top of the page are several hits for pictures.

Juliana Ruiz, her hair in a high ponytail and silver hoops in her ears. Susan Berry standing next to her, wearing her slightly robotic smile. Her normally pin-straight blond hair is crimped, and she's wearing pearly pink lipstick. The caption says this photo was taken during Spirit Week, on Time Travel Tuesday. Every grade was assigned a decade; the sophomores got the eighties.

I click through the images, a lump in my throat. More pictures of Juliana and Susan. There's only one of Jack Canning—a blurry, unsmiling driver's-license photo. His hair is dirty blond and his glasses take up half his face.

There are no other pictures of Jack Canning, no childhood shots of him snuggling the family dog or showing off a medal at a high school robotics competition. None of the usual pictures of murderers that the news likes to flash as they report that "he seemed so normal!"

I double back to the search results and scroll down. One headline jumps out at me: WHEN DEATH COMES TO TOWN. It's hosted on the Crunch, a website we all used to dick around on in the library before the school blocked it. Calling the Crunch "news" is generous. It's mostly garbage quizzes and celebrity gossip; it's hardly a hub for serious journalism.

Yet, three years ago, someone there decided to write about the Sunnybrook cheerleader deaths.

I glance at my door to make sure it's shut. Like I'm looking at porn or something. I gnaw on my thumbnail and pull up the article. I skim the profiles of Bethany Steiger and Colleen Coughlin and the horrific details of their car accident. The writer must have spoken to someone in Sunnybrook; their account is eerily accurate, down to the part about the paramedic vomiting at the scene.

The first mention of the murders is several paragraphs down. It starts with the night before homecoming, describing Juliana's and Susan's excitement for the following day's festivities.

My chest grows tighter. The details of the murders read like a horror novel: The killer had draped a bath towel over Susan's naked body. I skip the rest of the description of the crime scene, unsure how much more I can stomach.

To many, it was an open-and-shut case, one without the media circus that accompanies a drawn-out trial. Jack Canning was dead, taking his reasons for killing the girls to the grave with him. The elderly Mrs. Canning was moved to a nursing facility and died shortly after.

And yet, many who knew Jack Canning are still unable to reconcile their perception of him as a child-like, gentle giant with the man police say viciously killed two teenaged girls. One has to wonder if the circumstances surrounding the murders created a perfect storm for a hasty investigation. The town was still reeling from the gruesome deaths of Colleen Coughlin and Bethany Steiger. Almost everyone who worked for the Sunnybrook Police Department had a personal connection to the girls. Were the police wearing emotional blinders?

By the time I'm done reading, nearly an hour has

passed. At the bottom of the page is a headshot of the author of the article: Daphne Furman, blond and serious. Probably in her early thirties.

There's a contact email for Daphne in her bio. I open my inbox and begin writing.

> Hi, Ms. Furman. I'm Jennifer Rayburn's sister. I read your story "When Death Comes to Town" and I have some questions.

I hesitate for a moment before sending the message off. I sit back in my chair, gnawing at my chipped pinky nail. Turn my computer off, swallow two Motrins with water from my bathroom tap, and go to bed.

When I wake in the morning, I have a response.

> Hi, Monica. Call me Daphne. What are you doing Saturday morning? We should talk. I can come to you.

In my head, I break down the agonizing wait for Saturday. Twenty-four hours; nine class periods; one dance team practice; one awkward Friday family dinner at Ristegio's, the Italian restaurant in town; and one restless night's sleep. All hurdles to clear before I can talk to Daphne Furman.

I've been Googling her obsessively since she emailed me back. Daphne graduated from the University of

Virginia eight years ago with a dual major in English and journalism. (She also played lacrosse.) Until a few years ago, she wrote exclusively for the local paper in her hometown of Westchester. "When Death Comes to Town" was her first piece published on a major website.

At some point, a long-dormant memory lights up in my brain. Rumors, three years ago, about a reporter harassing the families of the dead girls. Murmurs among my parents' friends about *that reporter*. People said it with a tone usually reserved for child molesters and animal beaters: *that reporter*.

Daphne Furman has to be *that reporter*. And now I'm meeting her for coffee to discuss my dead sister.

Saturday morning is mid-sixties, with not a cloud in the sky. I told Daphne I could meet her at the Sunnybrook Starbucks at ten. My bike is one of those old-fashioned cruisers, with a mint-green body and peach wheels. I dump my phone and wallet in the basket and head off for town as soon as my mom and Petey leave for his soccer practice.

I ride past the gazebo on Main Street, past the sign welcoming me to Sunnybrook in gold-painted letters. Beside it is a town directory boasting our annual craft festival and award-winning microbrewery.

Leaves crunch under my tires, and a breeze knocks loose some of the hair I pinned away from my face. I turn down the alley next to 2nd Street and leave my bike in the rack outside the post office; no one ever locks anything around here because no one ever steals.

Every year the businesses on Main Street try to outdo each other with a scarecrow dress-up contest. On the telephone pole in front of the day spa, a scarecrow wears a bathrobe and has fake cucumbers for eyes. Outside Starbucks, a hipster scarecrow in a flannel shirt sips a latte from a paper cup.

A blonde with her hair in a stubby braid is seated at a two-person table by the window, a laptop open in front of her. Daphne looks younger than she does in her picture on the Crunch's website. A black Under Armour jacket is zipped up to her chin, and she's wearing pearl earrings.

She looks up. Spots me and waves. "Monica?"

I nod. Consider the empty chair waiting for me. An untouched scone sits on a napkin next to Daphne's laptop, which she shuts.

"Thank you for coming," she says, as if *she's* the one who reached out to *me*. "Do you want anything?"

"I'm okay." I slide into the chair, eyeing Daphne's cup of water. What kind of journalist goes to Starbucks and orders water?

Daphne gives me a disarming smile. "I'm guessing you want to talk about my story on the cheerleaders and not the one about the five best videos of cats knocking things off tables."

I flush. Return her smile. "How on earth did you guess?"

Daphne seems to clam up. She taps a finger on the lid of her water. "I spent six months working on that article. I never expected the reaction that it got."

"Well. I think people may have resented some of the things you suggested," I say. "About how the police did their investigation."

"I didn't write the story in a vacuum, Monica.

71

Everything in there—I got that information from talking to people."

"But you didn't talk to the police directly."

Daphne's fingers move to the surface of her laptop. "Not for a lack of trying. The thing is, I didn't set out intending to cast doubt on anyone. It was supposed to be a profile of the girls and Sunnybrook. Then days after it was published, people were emailing my editor accusing me of attacking the police."

Yet somehow she wound up implying that the police didn't do a thorough investigation—that it was impossible for them to be objective when they knew and cared about the girls.

"Emotional blinders," I say. "That's what you accused the cops of having."

"I didn't accuse them of anything." Daphne leans forward, resting her forearms on the table. Lowers her voice. "There are lots of details about that night that don't line up."

My stomach sours. "Like what?"

"There weren't any signs of forced entry at the Berrys' house that night. If the girls were so creeped out by Jack Canning, why would Juliana open the door for him? The door had a peephole. She would have seen it was him on the porch."

"How do you know the door had a peephole?"

"I told you. Some people were willing to talk to me."

I pinch the fleshy area between my thumb and my forefinger. A trick to get rid of nausea, my mom always says. "But Jack Canning was basically a sex offender. Or he should have been."

Daphne's mouth forms a condescending little smile. "Do you know what he did?"

"No."

"He was caught in a car with his girlfriend by her father," she says. "He was twenty, and she was seventeen. Her father almost beat him to death."

Four years. The age difference between Brandon and me is twice that.

I pinch the space between my fingers harder. "He had pictures of Susan in his bedroom. She was fifteen, and he was in his thirties. That's totally different."

"You're right." Daphne sips her water. "But the police never found bloody clothes at Jack's house. Juliana had cuts all over her body. The killer would have gotten her blood on him."

"But he would have had plenty of time to get rid of them," I say. "It doesn't prove anything."

"Also true. Like I said. I didn't have an agenda to prove he didn't do it. In all likelihood, he *did* do it. But facts are facts, and not all of them support the police's conclusion."

I think of the other details in "When Death Comes to Town." Throwaway lines about the other girls, gleaned from comments from friends and family who were willing to talk to Daphne.

The students at Sunnybrook High remember Bethany Steiger as a party girl, but a responsible one; she would never drink and drive. Her family has vehemently denied rumors that Bethany was texting at the time of the crash.

73

Jennifer Rayburn was always smiling. At the beginning of that year, if you told anyone who knew her that Jen would take her own life, they would have thought you were insane.

My mouth has gone dry. "That part in your article about how no one could believe my sister would kill herself—who told you that?"

Daphne's face softens. "Everyone who would talk to me. Jen was very loved."

"I know," I say, my throat tight. "I have to go."

Daphne reaches into her laptop bag. Fishes out a card with her email and phone number and hands it to me. "If you need anything, give me a buzz. I'd be more than happy to talk again."

I don't look back at her as I stand and push my way out the side door. There are too many thoughts pinballing in my head. Too many awful, awful scenarios to consider.

The worst is that Jack Canning might not have killed Juliana and Susan. Tom may have killed an innocent man, and a guilty one could be walking free in Sunnybrook.

But if Jack Canning didn't kill Susan and Juliana, why did he have pictures of Susan in his dresser drawer?

If Jack Canning didn't kill Susan and Juliana, why were his last words *I'm sorry*?

Chapter Six

I promised Rachel I would come over and help her run through our routine. No one wants to say it, but we all know that if Rachel can't land the triple pirouette by Monday afternoon, Coach might pull her out of the competition routine.

The Steigers' basement is not like normal people's basements. Alexa, Rach, and I have spent many nights down here, lounging in our bathing suits in the Jacuzzi tub, sipping the virgin strawberry daiquiris we made behind the bar. A few years ago, Rach's dad installed a full gym with equipment more expensive than the Planet Fitness my mother and Tom go to. Rachel and I have dragged the treadmill to the corner to make room for her to dance.

My phone is synced with the Bluetooth speaker. I back up the music to the 1:20 mark in the song, to the prep for the pirouette. She's anticipating it too much, trying to overcompensate with speed when it's all about keeping the turning leg straight.

Rachel runs through the routine from 1:20, and I don't realize that the music has stopped until she joins me by the speaker. She drags the back of her hand over her sweaty forehead. "Was that better?"

Truthfully, I hadn't even been paying attention that time. "You're getting there," I say, and Rach seems content.

"I need a break," she says, fanning her face with her hands.

I grab my phone and close out of the music player. My heartbeat picks up when I see that there's a text from the last person my sister talked to.

> Have you thought any more about
> what I said?

I shoot a glance at the open door; in the other room— her dad's "man cave"—Rachel has turned the TV on. I type out: *Which part?*

"Mon! What are you doing in there?"

I keep one eye on my phone as I head into the other room, where Rachel is on the leather couch. She's lying on her back, hands folded over her stomach, which rises and falls to match her rapid breathing. "Do you wanna get pizza?" she asks.

"I thought you were cleansing."

"Eff that." Rachel tilts her head back to look at me. "Are you still sick? You're kind of pale."

My phone buzzes in my hand. "I have to pee," I say. "Be right back."

Once I'm shut in the basement bathroom, fan on, I sit on the edge of the Jacuzzi tub and open the most recent text.

The part about your stepdad creepily keeping your sister's phone in his desk.

I feel a surge of irritation.

Why should I trust you? I don't even know who you are.

I was friends with your sister.

Then why didn't she even have your name in her phone?

The person is typing; the ellipsis disappears, as if they've deleted their response. I may have struck a nerve. A knock at the bathroom door makes me jump. "Monica? Are you okay in there?"

"Yeah. Coming." I flush the toilet and wash my hands for show, resting my phone on the edge of the sink. As I'm drying my hands, a text lights the screen.

I can prove it

How?

You'll see.

Rachel and I split a veggie pizza and watch an unfunny comedy on HBO before she drives me home. As she's pulling into my driveway, my phone buzzes.

> Check inside the unfinished house across the street.

I sit up so straight I hit my head on the ceiling of the car. Rach puts the car into park. "What's the matter?"

"Nothing." I turn to look across the street; the driveway to the unfinished house is still empty, the woods on both sides completely still. "I thought I saw a deer."

I palm the ceiling and climb out of the car. "Thanks for the ride."

"Sure. See you Monday."

I watch Rachel pull away, itching to cross the street to the unfinished house. But I'm not stupid; I've considered the possibility that this is a trap and whoever is texting me may be a psychopath.

A psychopath who definitely knows where we moved.

When I look up, I spot movement in our kitchen window. My mother, probably, prepping dinner. Keeping an eye on the driveway, awaiting my return. Even if she weren't already up my ass, she'd have questions if she caught me lurking around the property across the street.

We keep the front door locked all the time, and I don't have my key on me. I input the code for the garage and take the door inside that leads into the kitchen. Mom is over the stove, using a spatula to break up the hunk of pink meat crackling in the frying pan. The menu chalkboard on the fridge says that tonight is turkey chili.

She doesn't turn around. "You're home late."

"It's not even five."

Mom calls into the living room. "Petey, what are you doing?"

Petey shouts that someone just burned his entire village to the ground, and Mom shouts back that he needs to put down the game, change out of his soccer uniform, and read a few chapters of *Where the Red Fern Grows* before dinner. I want to tell him not to waste his time, that the dogs die at the end and everything sucks.

When my mom's back is turned, I cross the kitchen to the sink and peer out the window. The house is still there, existing in an entirely nonthreatening manner.

"What are you looking at?" My mother's voice sounds behind me.

"Nothing. Do I have time to walk Mango before we eat?"

My mother's eyebrows knit together. "Why do you need to walk him right now?"

"Because he's put on weight and I don't want him to die."

She blinks and shakes her head. "Be back in fifteen minutes."

I grab the leash from the key rack and call out to the dog. "Walk? You wanna go for a walk?"

Mango trots into the kitchen at once, sitting at my feet obediently. I attach the hook through the loop in his collar and leave out the front door. The second we step outside, he bolts forward, dragging me down the driveway, tail bobbing up and down like he can't believe his luck.

He hooks right, and I tug on his leash. "No. This way."

My dog is not the brightest or fastest, but he has impeccable hearing, and he can bark like a motherfucker. If there's anyone lurking in the house, Mango will hear him or her and go berserk.

The leaves on the lawn crunch under my feet. Once every two weeks, the owners come and mow the grass to placate my mother. I cross onto the driveway and climb. It slopes hundreds of feet up to the house, and Mango gets lazy halfway through our hike. By the time we get to the front door, he's lagging behind by a good foot, resisting every tug I give his leash.

The outside of the house is complete, but there's no door to the garage. The hair on my arms pricks. Anyone can get inside. I swallow and head through the door off the garage, which matches the one on our house.

A thin layer of sawdust coats the floor of the kitchen, and none of the cabinets have doors. A chandelier without lightbulbs hangs from the dining room ceiling, the wiring still exposed.

I spot the outline of footprints in the sawdust.

I straighten, slowly. Trace the footsteps out of the kitchen and into the living room. The footsteps stop at the bay window facing the street. A cigarette butt is inches from my shoe.

The bay window offers a near-perfect view of my house that makes my stomach turn.

Where?

80

Window.

I approach the bay window.

On the ledge, there's an envelope. I almost don't want to touch it. How long has the person I've been texting been coming here? Has he or she been watching us? Two hours ago, he/she texted me saying they could prove they were friends with Jen. Somehow they made it here between sending me that text and before I got home from Rachel's without my mother noticing a car pulling up outside the house and getting suspicious.

Petey's soccer game. He and my mom wouldn't have gotten home until after four. Plenty of time for him or her to come here, drop the envelope off, and leave without being seen.

A piece of loose-leaf paper, folded in half. I swallow away the dry lump forming in my throat and unfold it.

At the top of the page is a sentence written in neat cursive.

I'm not okay.

Beneath it, in block letters formed by a black felt-tip pen:

DO YOU WANT TO TALK ABOUT IT?

Yes.

I cover my mouth. Trace the rise and fall of my sister's handwriting with the tip of my finger.

I don't want to go home, but I can't stay in this creepy-ass house either. I slip out the way I came, nudging Mango toward the wooded area behind the house.

When I get back to my house, I tell her I ate a late lunch at Rachel's and I'm not hungry, that I'll eat the leftover chili in a couple hours. She makes a sound of acknowl-edgment, mid-argument with Petey about how he can't go to his friend TJ Blake's house, because even though there's no school tomorrow TJ's parents still have to go to work.

I sit at my desk and take the envelope out of my sweat-shirt pocket.

I'm not okay.

I think of the furry purple diary with a flimsy lock that I kept under my bed until middle school. The things I scrawled on the pages in a fit of anger. *Jen is sooooooooo mean sometimes. Mom likes her SO MUCH better. Everyone thinks she's perfect and it's so annoying.*

Why wasn't she okay?

Was Jen the diary-keeping type? I don't know.

If Jen had a diary, Mom would have gotten to it first.

No—my mother hadn't even gone through Jen's things after she died. My sister's bedroom door had stayed shut for almost a year before my mom said she was going to hire someone to pack up all of Jen's things and get rid of them. I told her that I hated her. She closed herself in her room, and Tom left the house and returned an hour later with a stack of storage tubs from Walmart and packed up everything himself.

Jen's stuff is in the basement now, which is somewhere

I have no good reason to be. Around ten, when the laugh track of the evening sitcoms Tom watches in the living room quiets, I wait for him to come upstairs.

When his bedroom door clicks shut, I slip out of bed and inch down the hall, down the stairs, and straight down the basement steps off the garage entrance.

The heating system is making noises like fingernails tapping against a tin can. I feel around on the wall for the light switch.

The fluorescent bulb overhead hums to life. I step down.

The storage bins of crap from our old house are stacked in the corner, next to the hot water heater. I climb over the box that holds our fake Christmas tree to reach them.

There are three tubs with *JENNIFER* written on the sides in Sharpie. I take a breath, the loamy smell of the basement filling my nostrils. Pop the lid of the box closest to me.

A cardboard shirt box rests on the surface of the contents. I lift the top off, delicately pushing the tissue paper aside. A white lace dress and a bonnet. Jennifer's christening outfit.

I snap the top back on and move on to the next. Pick through art projects, graded research papers, programs from her honor society induction ceremonies and wind ensemble concerts. Her flute case.

I pull out a marble notebook labeled *English 10H, Mr. Ward*. English, tenth-grade honors. I thumb through it, reading Jen's haphazard script, a writing prompt copied at the top of each page. *Five years from now, I see myself . . . Write a paragraph convincing a friend not to take drugs . . . Which character from a book would you like to meet and why?*

A copy of *Wuthering Heights*. I remember reading this in Mr. Ward's class last year, and my chest tightens. Jen was reading it when she died, and it didn't occur to Tom to return it to the school when he came across it in her things.

I thumb through the book. She was a few pages into chapter fourteen, her place marked with a folded piece of loose-leaf paper. Green writing shows through.

I unfold it.

I WATCH YOU CHEW ON YOUR PEN CAP WHEN YOU ARE THINKING
I WATCH YOU IN THE HALL, LAUGHING, YOUR EYES MISSING MINE
I WISH I KNEW WHAT YOU WERE THINKING
I WISH I WERE IN ON THE JOKE.

The hair on the back of my neck pricks as I skim the rest. It's more of the same. A demented poem. A stalker's manifesto, written in the same handwriting that's on the note resting on my desk.

In the morning, I wait until I hear the clanging of cabinets in the kitchen before heading downstairs. Tom is spooning cereal into his mouth, both eyes on a copy of the *Daily News*.

"I think we should get security cameras," I say.

"Oh yeah?" Tom doesn't look up from his bowl of Cheerios. "Why's that?"

"This house is too big. I don't feel safe when I'm here alone."

My mother shuts the fridge door with a thud. "You're rarely here alone."

Tom and I follow her with our eyes as she exits the kitchen. Moments later, she shouts for Petey to come down and eat or she's taking the iPad away.

When the clomping of Mom's feet on the stairs fades, Tom sets down his bowl and levels with me. "Is this about Juliana and Susan?"

My spine straightens. I haven't heard him use their names in years. "Maybe."

"I didn't know this still scared you."

A flash of me, five years ago, curled up at the foot of my mother and Tom's bed like a dog. Too scared to sleep in my own bedroom after the murders. "Of course I get scared. I can't just forget it ever happened."

"I didn't say you should. You haven't brought the girls up in a long time, that's all. Why are you thinking about it now?"

I don't know if I'm imagining the note of suspicion in his voice. "It'll be five years soon."

"Mon," Tom says. "Nothing like that is ever going to happen again."

"You can't say that for sure."

"I can't say for sure that a tornado won't hit us tomorrow. But it's still unlikely it'll happen."

I wonder how he thinks that's supposed to make me feel better.

"I'll look into cameras." Tom stands and squeezes my shoulder. "Try to enjoy today. It's nice out. Maybe take that fat pig of a dog for a walk."

Hearing the W-word, Mango trots into the kitchen. Tom heads into the living room and tells Petey that he'd really better put the iPad down and eat before Mom finishes her shower.

I sit at the island. My brother plods into the kitchen, eyes glued to *Clan Wars* as he slides onto the stool across from me, where Mom has left an empty bowl next to his box of Cocoa Puffs.

When the sound of Petey's crunching becomes unbearable, I stand up. I need to think; there's nothing I can do about figuring out who wrote that poem to Jen until tomorrow morning, when I'm able to talk to Mr. Ward.

My thoughts settle on the house across the street. He or she said that I don't know them, but he or she knows where we live. He or she is also confident that Tom is a liar, among other things. So there's a possibility that the letter writer knows Tom—and knows him well enough to have our new address.

It's almost as unsettling as the idea that some random creep is stalking us.

The cigarette butt by the bay window. He or she might have left something else behind.

Mango is still splayed out on the kitchen floor like a frog, his tail flicking back and forth. I grab his leash from the hook on the wall.

"Tell Mom I'm walking the dog," I call to my brother as I steer Mango out the door. I stop short when we reach the street.

A van is parked in the driveway of the house. Next to it, a man is leaning against a shiny black SUV, in conversation with the van's driver. Mango starts to bark; the man looks up at me.

I haven't seen anyone outside that house since we moved in; it can't be a coincidence that the owners or contractors or real estate agents—whoever the hell those guys are—have returned the day after I prowled on the property.

Did someone see me?

I bow my head, breaking eye contact with the man, and make a right. Keep walking until the new constructions thin out and less ostentatious houses appear.

In front of a small two-story house with peeling yellow siding, Ginny Cordero is gardening. By herself—she's not helping anyone, like how I used to help my mom weed the front yard at our old house. Ginny is bent over, tugging bent and dead stems out of the dirt, as if this garden is all hers.

"Hi," I say.

Ginny turns around. She holds up a hand in a feeble wave, confusion knitting her brow. Water drips from the can dangling from her other hand.

Ginny meets me at the bottom of her driveway. She looks at Mango, but she doesn't bend to pet him, like most people usually do. "What's his name?"

"Mango." There's a beat of awkward silence. And then

it tumbles out of my mouth: "My sister named him."

Ginny is quiet. But the look on her face says I haven't made her feel awkward; she almost looks sad. "She was really nice. Your sister."

I hesitate. "Do you want to take a walk with me?"

"Sure."

Ginny leaves the watering can on her front stoop. A black and white cat comes up to the glass door. When it sees Mango, its tail goes erect. Mango lets out a howl, and the cat rockets away.

"Sorry," I say.

"It's okay." Ginny rejoins me, and we head down the driveway together. "It's hot out."

"I know." I don't know if I can do this: make painful small talk about the weather. I don't know why I even came here.

"You know, Jen went to the same gym as me," Ginny says. "A long time ago."

Mango stops in his tracks. He sniffs where the lawn meets the street several houses down from Ginny's. He starts circling; if Ginny weren't here, I'd tug at him to keep moving. But I don't want Jen to escape—to disappear into the graveyard of dead conversations.

"I remember seeing you at the gym," I say.

"Your sister was kind. There aren't a lot of kind people."

Her voice trails off, and I'm hit with the memory of ninth grade, sitting in the back of the class in earth science. The girls next to me snickered whenever our teacher called out Ginny's full name during attendance. *Virgin*-ia, they'd say, emphasis on *virgin*—look at her linebacker shoulders and flat chest. She probably doesn't even get her period yet.

And I did nothing, because it wasn't my problem. I said nothing, because Kelsey Gabriel, who was taking the class for the second time, was the one who dubbed Ginny *Man Arms.*

Ginny finally looks at me, her train of thought recaptured. "Your sister deserved better. All those girls did."

"You know that house across from mine?" I ask.

"The unfinished one?"

I nod. "Have you seen anything weird? Like someone who doesn't live around here hanging around the house?"

"No, I don't think so." Ginny's forehead scrunches up. "Why?"

Whatever pressed me to ask her about the house is also telling me not to say I found something weird in the house. If I did, I'd have to say why I was in the house in the first place. Would Ginny even believe me if I told her?

"No reason," I say. "I should get home. Thanks for walking with me."

Ginny nods. As I'm turning around, she says my name. She holds up a hand. "See you at practice tomorrow."

Chapter Seven

The first week of school last fall, Mr. Ward moved my seat across the room from Rachel's because we wouldn't stop talking. We took to texting, and Mr. Ward spent the rest of the year eyeballing our phones under our desks and sighing like he was questioning every choice he ever made in life.

I kind of sucked back then.

Anyway, Mr. Ward doesn't look too psyched to see me standing in his doorway after last period Monday afternoon. He shoves a stack of papers into his briefcase and blinks. "Are you looking for Ms. Axelrod? Her class was upstairs last period."

"I actually wanted to talk to you. Do you have a minute?"

"Sure, sure. Come in." Mr. Ward tugs at his tie to loosen it and cranks open the window behind his desk.

I step into the room, inexplicably nervous. Mr. Ward sits in one of the desks at the front of the room and drags another chair so it's facing him. He gestures for me to take it. As I set my bag on the desk and settle into the chair, I notice a dab of crusted mustard on his tie.

"So what's up?" Mr. Ward crosses his legs at the ankles.

"My sister was in your class when she was a sophomore."

Mr. Ward blinks, like he can't tell if I'm asking him or telling him. "Yeah, she was. Really talented writer."

"This is going to sound weird." I relax the hand that's holding the poem I found in my sister's copy of *Wuthering Heights*. I'd been clutching it so tightly that I'm worried the sweat on my palm will make the ink bleed. "I'm looking for someone. I think they were in your class the same period as my sister."

"Okay. Who is this someone?"

"I don't know," I say. "But I'm ninety-nine percent sure it's a boy."

Mr. Ward's forehead creases. "Can you tell me anything else about him?"

I think of the argumentative text messages and the refusal to tell me his identity. "He was probably kind of a jerk."

Mr. Ward leans far back in his chair, folding his hands behind his head. "Why do you think he was in my class?"

"I found a poem he wrote in her copy of *Wuthering Heights*," I say.

"So a tenth-grade boy who wrote poetry to girls. That describes half my honors classes."

My face must fall, because Mr. Ward pushes back in his chair and says, "Let me pull up my old class rosters."

I drum my fingers against my knee while Mr. Ward moves to his computer. There's some hollering in the hallway, and a guy in a backward baseball cap comes to a short stop in the doorway when he sees me. "Is the newspaper meeting still in here?"

"Yes, at three," Mr. Ward calls out to him. "Come back then."

The kid retreats and closes the door behind him, muting the sounds in the hallway. At the computer, Mr. Ward is tapping his finger against his mouse, eyes on the screen. "System's slow," he mutters.

I don't know where to look, so I study the Globe Theatre fashioned out of Popsicle sticks atop the bookcase in the corner.

"Got it," Mr. Ward says. "Jen was in fifth-period honors English."

He hums to himself as he scans the screen. "Oh."

I sit up straight. "What is it?"

"Ethan McCready was in Jen's class." Mr. Ward frowns.

Ethan McCready. I turn the name over in my head, waiting for a face to pop up. Nothing. I look down at the paper in my hands. Its edges have gone soft from my folding and unfolding it so many times.

I walk over to Mr. Ward, holding the poem out to him. "This is what I found."

He takes the paper from me and studies it. Mr. Ward sets the poem down on his desk, his eyes still on it. "Wow. Ethan McCready. Now that I think about it, he sat behind Jen."

"Did he have a reputation for stalking girls?"

"Not that I know of." Mr. Ward rubs his chin. "He was one of those kids who made everyone uncomfortable, though. Bit of a loner, only wore black, always had to ask him to take his headphones out."

Mr. Ward doesn't need to elaborate. Every grade has a kid like that. "Did my sister ever complain about him?"

Mr. Ward almost looks sad. "No. . . . From what I saw, Jen was always kind to kids like that."

The knot in my chest tightens. Of course my sister would have been kind to Ethan McCready. Sometimes she was kind to people who didn't deserve it.

She couldn't even bring herself to throw out Ethan McCready's poem.

"Do you know what happened to Ethan?" I ask. "After he graduated?"

"He didn't. He was expelled that fall."

"Why? What did he do?"

Outside Mr. Ward's room, the voices reach a crescendo. The thud of a body against the door. Rowdy newspaper kids. I'm holding up the meeting.

"I don't know. I always thought the whole thing was blown out of proportion," Mr. Ward says. "But a girl saw him writing names in his notebook and went to Mr. Heinz."

"Whose names?"

Mr. Ward hesitates. "The names of all the cheerleaders."

"Like a hit list or something?" My stomach turns over.

"That's what the administration decided it was, at least." Mr. Ward glances at the door. "I don't know, Ethan never struck me as violent. But I don't blame them for not wanting to take chances."

He stands. My cue to exit. He starts walking me to the door. "You know, you can stay for the newspaper meeting. We're short on staff writers this year."

"I've kind of got a full plate. But thanks."

Mr. Ward doesn't look at me as he opens his door. The boy leaning against it topples into the room, to laughter from the other kids gathered outside.

"Just a sad year all around," Mr. Ward says.

I have thirty minutes before practice starts. I head upstairs, dodging Rach's and Alexa's texts asking if I want to go to Starbucks. I'll tell them later that I had to get extra help in chem.

The sign on the library door makes me deflate. CLOSED FOR CONSTRUCTION. I vaguely recall Mrs. Barnes chirping over the morning announcements that we got funding for a new "smart learning" station.

I peer through the glass pane on the door. The lights are on, and the librarian is inside, arms folded, deep in conversation with a teacher who has her back to me.

The woman's wiry gray-streaked hair is tied up in a scrunchie. There's only one person in the school—and probably all of Sunnybrook—who wears scrunchies every day.

I back away, ready to haul ass, but the librarian spots me over Mrs. Coughlin's shoulder. She frowns and walks toward me, and I'm trapped. Mrs. Coughlin turns around, eyes narrowing when she sees me.

The librarian cracks the door open. "We're closed, hon."

"I know," I say. "I just need one specific book."

"Which one?"

"An old yearbook."

"Check with Mrs. Goldberg." The door clicks shut in my face.

I sigh. Mrs. Goldberg is the graphic design teacher and yearbook advisor. Her room is downstairs, in the same wing as the photography darkroom and painting and sculpting studios.

The lab door is open. I poke my head in—it's eerily quiet. The handful of kids on the computers work silently, eyes on their screens. I don't see Mrs. Goldberg.

Someone says my name, softly, from the back of the room. Ginny Cordero is watching me from her computer. She waves me over.

"Hey. Is Mrs. Goldberg here?" I blurt it in a single breath. I don't want Ginny to think I'm stalking her or anything.

"She went to use the copier a little while ago," Ginny says. "I didn't know you took graphic design."

"I don't. I need an old yearbook. The librarian told me Mrs. Goldberg has it in her office."

"Yeah, she has all of them. I can get it for you. I'm on yearbook staff, so she lets me in her office. Which one do you need?"

"The one from five years ago." I pause. I'm not sure if someone who was expelled before the yearbook went to print would be in the portraits section. "Maybe the one from six years ago too."

Ginny nods and ducks into the back room. Stuck to Mrs. Goldberg's office door is a giant poster of a galaxy. I peer more closely at it; a bunch of faces are Photoshopped among the stars. WE LOVE YOU MRS. G!!! —5TH PERIOD SENIOR GRAPHIC DESIGN.

When Ginny returns, she's holding two yearbooks. "These are her copies, so you just have to stay here with them, if that's okay."

"Of course. Thanks." I take the books from Ginny and slide into the seat at the empty computer next to hers. She turns back to her work on the yearbook layout, but I catch her eyes flicking away from the screen and toward me as I flip through the pages of the first yearbook.

Ethan McCready isn't in the book from the year my sister died. I set it aside and open the previous year's yearbook, flipping to the freshman portraits. Trace a finger over the last names on the sidebar. *Mackie, Maroney, Maldonado, McCready.*

I count over four pictures, landing on a picture of a boy with dirty-blond hair hanging in his eyes. His shoulders are hunched forward under a Nine Inch Nails T-shirt. His eyes are so dark they almost look black.

When I look up from the pages, Ginny is watching me, a curious look on her face.

I swallow and point to Ethan. "Have you ever seen this guy before?"

Ginny peers at the picture. "I know him."

"Really?"

"Well, I know who he is," Ginny says. "My mom was his mom's home nurse when she was really sick. I went to her wake with my mom. He looked really lonely, like people were staying away from him. My mom told me he got expelled that fall."

"He had a hit list," I say. "The cheerleaders were on it."

I study Ginny's expression, seeing the pieces slide into

place for her—the car accident, the murders, my sister's suicide. And a boy who wanted all of the girls dead.

Supposedly. "He says he was friends with Jen."

"But Jen was a cheerleader," Ginny says. "Why would he put one of his friends on his hit list?"

"I don't know."

Ginny is quiet for a moment. "Does this have anything to do with what you asked me yesterday? About the house?"

My throat goes tight. The note leaver wasn't some innocent friend of Jen's who had a crush on her. He's the guy who was expelled for wanting my sister and her friends dead. And he knows where I live.

"Ethan was there," I say. "He left something for me—a note my sister wrote him."

Ginny blinks at me. "Why would he do that? How did you find it?"

I hesitate. "Can you take a break for a couple minutes? Maybe we could go outside."

"Sure. I was finishing up anyway. One second." Ginny saves her work on the computer and picks up the gym bag resting at her feet. She adjusts its strap over her shoulder.

The courtyard is brimming with people waiting for sports practices to start. I spot Jimmy Varney throwing around a Frisbee with some of the cross-country guys. He turns his head and waves at me; the Frisbee hits him in the chest and falls to the lawn.

I drop my bag on the grass below one of the trees outside the gazebo and sit. Ginny follows suit. Inside the gazebo, a pack of girls is gathered, lying on their backs on the benches, chattering about some invitational meet coming up. The louder it is out here, the better.

"Sorry I'm being so weird," I say. "I just don't want anyone to hear us."

"It's okay." Ginny pulls her knees up to her chest. The moment she does it, a Frisbee flies straight into her shins.

"Sorry!" Jimmy Varney comes trotting over, his face scarlet. In his wake, his friends are laughing; one of them smacks Joe Gabriel on the back. Joe grins and yells, "My bad," his voice anything but apologetic.

Ginny picks up the Frisbee and hands it to Jimmy. He flushes an even deeper shade of red. "I'm really sorry."

"It's okay," Ginny says.

Jimmy gives me a sheepish smile. "Hey, Mon. Sorry."

"It's seriously okay." I don't mean to snap at him, but I just want Jimmy to go away so I can talk to Ginny.

As Jimmy heads back to his friends, locking eyes with Joe and muttering something under his breath, I say to Ginny, "Joe is such an asshole. He hit you on purpose."

"I don't think he meant to hurt me," she says. "He just did it so his friend could come over and talk to you."

I feel a tug in my chest. It hits me, why I like Ginny so much—it's not only because of her connection to my sister. Ginny reminds me of Jen. My kind sister, who always gave people the benefit of the doubt, even if they didn't deserve it.

Ethan McCready's yearbook picture comes into focus in my mind and his role in all this starts to come together—that note, his claims that Tom can't be trusted—it feels much more insidious now. Is he trying to make me doubt

Tom to shift the suspicion from himself? Aside from Jack Canning, Ethan's now the only person who wanted cheerleaders dead.

Ginny is watching me expectantly. I feel like a dam inside me is about to break.

So I tell her everything. I start with the letters in Tom's drawer and how they led me to Jen's cell phone and Ethan's phone number. I recap my meeting with Daphne and all the inconsistencies about the murders. Ethan's warning that Tom is hiding something.

Ginny eyes me while I speak, a look on her face that I can't quite pin down. I think of Rachel's reaction the other day when I asked her if she thought everything that happened that year wasn't a coincidence.

"I know it sounds ridiculous," I say. "But my sister—I never believed it, that she would kill herself over her friends dying. And maybe that makes me sound like I'm in denial or something, but this stuff with Ethan McCready—him calling her the morning she died . . . I don't know." I take a breath. "It can't be a coincidence."

Ginny mulls this over. She rearranges her feet so she's sitting cross-legged. "You know that theory about a butterfly flapping its wings could cause a tsunami or a tornado across the world?"

I nod. "It sounds familiar. Like, something small can happen and set off a bigger reaction."

"Yeah," Ginny says. "The opposite of a coincidence."

I tug at a blade of grass tickling my ankle and wrap it around the tip of my finger. Ginny's simple explanation has parted the jumble of thoughts clouding my brain. I don't know why I didn't think of the possibility sooner—that the deaths aren't a bunch of dots waiting to be connected, but a single series of events, set into motion by something that fall.

But what happened? How am I supposed to find the exact spot where a butterfly flapped its wings five years ago?

And how am I supposed to believe anything Ethan says—how he was friends with Jen, how I shouldn't trust Tom—when according to Mr. Ward, he wanted her dead?

Tom's car is in the driveway when I get home from practice. The spot in the garage where my mother parks her SUV is empty. I remember her saying something about Meet the Teacher night at Petey's school. She left a Chinese takeout menu on the kitchen island.

Ethan McCready was expelled for making a hit list that would have had Juliana's and Susan's names on it. A couple of weeks later, they were murdered.

There's no way Tom wouldn't have made the connection between Ethan McCready and the girls. Principal Heinz would have gotten the police involved if one of his students had made a hit list.

The case against Jack Canning was convincing, but it wasn't airtight. I need to know if Ethan was ever a potential suspect; the problem is that the person who can tell me for sure is probably the last person who wants to talk about the possibility that someone other than Jack was the killer.

Tom's office door is closed. He usually keeps it open while he works. I ignore the paranoia needling me and knock.

"Come in."

I open the door and find Tom hunched over his computer. He's clicking through photos of a Honda Civic with a smashed-in bumper. He minimizes the window and swivels his chair around. "Hey, kid. Wanna call in dinner? I'm getting hungry."

"Sure." I nod to his computer. "What were you looking at?"

Tom rubs his eyes. "A hit-and-run from last month. Been bugging me."

"I thought you weren't supposed to take your work home with you."

"When you do what I do, the work is never done." Tom studies me. "You all right? Mom says you haven't been yourself."

"I don't know," I say, combing over my words carefully before they leave my mouth. "There's something I want to talk to you about."

Tom's eyebrows lift. Whatever he expected me to say, it wasn't that. "Sure. What's on your mind?"

"Do you know a kid named Ethan McCready?"

"Ethan McCready?"

"He was in Jen's grade. He got expelled that fall for threatening to kill cheerleaders."

"You mean the hit list kid? I sent people to his house. He didn't even own a gun." Tom frowns. "I didn't know you knew about that. Your mom and I didn't talk about it around you or your brother because we didn't want to upset you."

"Did you know Ethan wrote Jen a creepy stalkerish poem?" I ask.

Tom stops bouncing the leg crossed over his knee at the ankle. "Did Jen tell you that?"

I hesitate. "I found it in her stuff."

Tom holds up a hand. "You went through Jen's things? When?"

"What does that matter?" Anger flares in me at the tone of his voice—like he's suggesting I dug up my sister's grave to get that poem.

"It would matter to your mother," Tom says. "Monica, this month is going to be hard enough for her as it is."

"You think it's not hard for me? For the rest of us?"

"Don't raise your voice. And that's not fair—you know I didn't mean this isn't hard for you too." Tom looks at his lap, pinching the bridge of his nose. When he picks his head up, he looks exhausted. "I don't see what your end goal is here. I don't know what you want from me."

I bite back the urge to scream: *I want you to stop acting like you're hiding something.* I want to ask him why he had Jen's phone and whether he knows Ethan McCready was the last person to talk to her.

"Don't you get it?" I ask. "Ethan wanted all the cheerleaders dead, and then Juliana and Susan were just randomly murdered?"

"Monica," Tom says. "Ethan McCready weighed a hundred ten pounds soaking wet."

"So?"

Tom leans back in his chair, the leather upholstery farting under his weight. He watches me for a moment before saying, "Susan and Juliana were strangled."

"I know that."

"They were very fit girls. Between them, they had about twenty pounds of muscle on Ethan. Do you know how much strength it takes to strangle someone?"

My stomach puckers as I fight off the instinct to picture a pair of hands wrapping around Susan Berry's neck. "No."

"Ethan had limbs like toothpicks. Susan could have broken his arms with her eyes closed," Tom says. "The girls were overpowered. Their killer was much bigger than them."

"You mean the killer was Jack Canning's size."

Tom's eyes flash with a warning. "This isn't a conversation I want to have anymore."

"Well, I do. Ethan was in love with Jen." My throat goes tight. "What if he decided that if he couldn't have her, he'd go after her friends? What if he knew she was supposed to be at Susan's that night, and he went there and—"

"Monica!" The force of Tom's voice almost blows me back. My stepfather has yelled at me maybe once in the past ten years.

I know he realizes it, too, because he winces. "The person who killed Susan and Juliana is dead. He's not going to hurt anyone ever again. If someone is telling you otherwise, send them to me and I'll set them straight."

My stepfather isn't a stubborn man. It's why it's scary how sure he is that he had a reason to shoot Jack Canning.

"Monica. Look at me."

I do. Tom forces a smile. "Okay?"

The pit in my stomach widens. "Okay."

On my way out the door, he tells me to order him some General Tso's chicken. His voice is measured, cheery. Letting me know that he's willing to forget this conversation, as long as I never say the names Ethan McCready or Jack Canning to him again.

Jennifer

Juliana had big plans for sophomore year. They had shed the label of annoying freshmen; last year's seniors who wouldn't even look their way were gone, replaced with upperclassman boys who stole glances at them even while their arms were around their girlfriends' waists.

Jules didn't seem to notice the looks from the older guys. Not like Susan, who would suck in her stomach and tuck her hair behind her ears when the football and soccer players came to hang out in the gym where the cheerleaders were practicing. Juliana was thinking bigger; the calendar in her room was color-coded: cheer practice, Spirit Night, homecoming. She didn't seem to realize how popular they already were. Jen and Jules had both been voted to the homecoming court last year, and Susan was the class secretary.

Jen realized it, though. The people she grew up with suddenly seemed nervous around her. It was lonely at the top, with people keeping their distance, as if the other

105

sophomores weren't sure if Jen thought them worthy enough to share her presence.

It didn't help that Jules had a different lunch period than Jen did, and Susan cut lunch out of her schedule completely so she could take an extra elective. Jen had to sit with Bethany and Colleen and their junior friends in the cafeteria.

It was a life other girls envied. It was a life she didn't know if she wanted.

Juliana had dropped advanced math and science, deciding the workload would be too much for her to balance with cheerleading and her job at Alden's, the grocery store her parents owned. So the only class Jen and Jules had together was English with Mr. Ward. When Jules got out of gym the period before, she'd meet Jen at her locker and they'd walk to class together.

Today, Jules was late. Jen lingered by her locker, wondering if she should just head for class on her own. She watched another minute tick by on her phone before looking up and seeing her at the end of the hall: Juliana, her forehead glistening with sweat, a bright pink headband pushing her hair from her face.

Next to her, Carly Amato was laughing at something. Jules spotted Jen; she broke away from Carly, waving at her.

"You didn't tell me Carly was in your gym class," Jen said, once Juliana had made her way to her.

"Was I supposed to?" Juliana fanned her face with her English notebook. "What's your problem with her, anyway?"

I'm pretty sure she's a cokehead. It was an awfully heavy accusation to be flinging around.

"I don't have a problem with her," Jen said.

"Whatever." Juliana brushed past her, into Mr. Ward's room.

Jen stood in the doorway for a moment, stricken. Juliana had *whatever*-ed her. *Whatever* was a door slamming in your face; it meant *I am annoyed but I don't care enough to fight with you.* In a lot of ways it was the worst thing you could say to a friend.

Juliana didn't look back at Jen as she strode up to Mr. Ward and flashed him a pass for her vocal lesson in the choir room. Mr. Ward sighed, pointed at the whiteboard where the page numbers for tonight's assigned reading were listed. Jules copied it down into her planner and was out the door by the bell.

Jen's eyes pricked, her lungs compressing with that panicked feeling she got over crying in public. The last time she'd cried in class was after a math test in the seventh grade—the only test she'd ever failed. The boys who sat behind her made fun of her all day; crying in class felt like her body's way of betraying her. She kept her head bowed while Mr. Ward battled with the girls sitting on the ledge by the window, sunning like turtles on a rock.

"Pleeeeeease can we open the window?" Hailey Rosenfield fanned herself with a marble notebook.

"Have a seat," Mr. Ward pleaded.

"We *are* sitting." Hailey nudged her shoulder into her friend's. The girls giggled, whined about how they just

107

came from gym. Poor Mr. Ward looked like he was barely out of college.

Jen tuned them out, looking up from her notebook only to copy the journal prompt on the whiteboard. *Discuss the setting and how it contributes to the mood of the story.* She couldn't think, couldn't even remember what she'd read of *Wuthering Heights* last night.

Juliana was pissed at her. Jen couldn't think of a time when she'd honestly made Jules mad. It was hard to do, which only made it worse that this stupid argument was over Carly Amato, a girl Juliana had only known a couple of months.

I'm not okay. Jen didn't realize that it was all she'd written in her notebook until Mr. Ward asked if everyone was done writing, if anyone wanted to share their response with the class.

When the bell rang, Jen tore the page out of her notebook. Crushed it and tossed it into Mr. Ward's wastebasket.

By the time she got to her locker, she was crying. She buried her head.

A soft tap on her shoulder. Jen found herself face to face with Ethan McCready.

She'd known Ethan since they were kids; she hated that people called him Ethan McCreepy, and she flinched every time one of the soccer guys smacked the back of his head whenever they passed by his seat on the bus.

But if she was being honest with herself, Jen knew that Ethan wasn't making it easy to defend him. In middle school he'd stopped talking to everyone but two of his friends—computer club boys plagued by ill-fitting jeans and cafeteria pizza breath. It was rare to see Ethan not hunched over a desk, the hood of his sweatshirt up and his earbuds in, no matter how many times teachers told him to take them out.

Most damning of all, though, was that Ethan could, in fact, be extremely creepy. The first time Jen saw him, he'd been watching her.

She was in the woods behind her house, scouring the creek for water-polished rocks, when she heard twigs snapping. She stayed crouched, motionless, hoping to see a deer when she looked up. Instead, it was a boy with a bad haircut in a Led Zeppelin T-shirt.

"Hi," he said. "What are you doing?"

Jen held out her palm. Ethan came closer, inspected the rock, which was as smooth and white as a pearl.

After that day, he showed up sometimes. After Jen told him she wanted to be a veterinarian when she grew up, Ethan brought a book from the library filled with glossy pictures of reptiles and amphibians. If they were lucky, they caught toads in plastic beach buckets, but Jen always made him put them back.

Jen thought about inviting Ethan over for dinner, like she did with Susan all the time, but she was too embarrassed to ask her mother. She hated when her mother asked her about boys, and the last thing she wanted to do was admit that she'd been spending time alone with one.

And then Ethan ruined everything.

The summer between fourth and fifth grade, they'd been catching tadpoles. Jen saw a cluster of them, wiggling beside the rock where she and Ethan were crouched.

She cupped her hands and scooped them through the water. "I got some!"

Ethan put his hands over hers to stop the tadpoles from escaping. When Jen looked up, he was watching her, and her gut told her exactly what was going to happen.

His mouth landed on her upper lip, and she thought maybe he'd missed. Before she could blink, his lips found hers. When he pulled away, she tasted Sour Patch Kids.

"I'm sorry," he said. And Jen ran back to her house, leaving her pail behind.

She'd lied to Juliana and Susan about her first kiss. Said it was with Joe Halpern in the dark of a movie theater in the seventh grade. By then she hadn't spoken to Ethan in years—she hadn't gone back to the creek after the tadpole day. She sat far away from him on the bus and avoided his eyes when they were assigned to the same table in art class.

When she noticed the hair that had started cropping up on his upper lip, she got a funny feeling in her stomach.

"You dropped this," Ethan muttered, and then he was gone.

Jen unfolded the paper. Recognized the words she'd written in her journal at the beginning of class. *I'm not okay.*

Ethan had scrawled out a response: *Do you want to talk about it?*

Jen flushed, even though it was impossible for anyone to know what had just happened. She stuffed the note in her pocket and headed to the cafeteria, forgetting that she and Ethan shared the same lunch period.

Her table was already packed; Mark Zhang had his arm draped over Bethany Steiger's shoulders. Bethany rolled her eyes and pushed his arm off her, even though everyone knew they'd been hooking up since the summer.

When Mark saw Jen, his face lit up. Bethany looked like she tasted something foul, and Colleen examined her nails, trying to look as oblivious as possible.

Everyone also knew that Mark Zhang had had a thing for Jen since she was a freshman.

Jen didn't look at them as she settled into her seat. Colleen looked up at her. "Have you been crying?"

Jen lifted a hand to her cheek. Her face was probably still beet red, and the tear or two that snuck out of her eyes in Mr. Ward's class probably smudged her mascara. "No. Just don't feel well."

"You look like crap," Bethany said. Colleen's eyes widened with horror.

"Like you have a fever or something," Bethany amended. Jen wasn't going to take Bethany's bait. She was always doing that—making nasty comments, diamond-knife-thin cuts that you didn't realize stung until much later.

"I know what will make you laugh." Bethany smirked over her iced tea, looking at something at the table behind Jen. "McCreepy is showing a full moon."

Jen's stomach puckered: Mark Zhang howled with laughter. "No way. He broke his belt after gym. Lemme see."

Colleen tilted sideways, crushing her shoulder into

111

Jen's so Mark could lean across the table and gawk. Jen refused to turn around and look.

Mark's laughing reached a crescendo, and his friend, some other jerk of a football player, joined in. "Yo, anyone got a quarter?"

Bethany dug a coin out of her change purse and handed it to Mark. Before Jen realized what he was doing, Mark stood up and lobbed the quarter at Ethan. Jen spun around in time to see it bounce off Ethan's back and onto the floor. Ethan's shoulders went stiff, but he didn't turn to face them.

"Damn it," Mark said. "Come on, Beth, you take a shot."

The rest of the table laughed as Bethany held a quarter between her thumb and forefinger. As Bethany examined it, Colleen buried her head in her food. Jen watched Bethany in horror as she tossed the coin at Ethan.

Mark hooted. "So close! Who's next?"

Jen's throat was closing. She wanted to scream at them, but something was stopping her. And then Ethan stood up. Pulled his pants up and tugged his shirt down. His face was eerily calm as he strode over to the garbage can, holding his empty tray.

He stopped by their table and dropped a quarter in front of Mark. "I think this is yours."

Mark held Ethan's gaze as he reached and smacked the tray from Ethan's hands. What was left in his carton of fruit punch spilled over Ethan's sneakers. He held Mark's gaze. And then he smirked.

"What the hell is wrong with you?" Mark wasn't

smiling anymore. The table was silent. Ethan's smirk seemed to have unnerved them.

Ethan didn't answer. His gaze slid over Jen, as if he didn't see her at all. She watched him walk away, and at the last moment, when the rest of the table had resumed conversation, laughing awkwardly, Jen saw it.

The way Ethan folded the fingers on one of his hands into the shape of a gun.

Chapter Eight

I haven't texted Ethan McCready since I found the note he left in the house across the street. I don't want him to know that I know who he is. He probably didn't expect me to figure it out. He had saved something of Jen's, but how would he know she saved something with his hand-writing and that I had a way of tying it back to him?

I don't want to scare him into doing anything. Especially not when he knows where we live. If I told my parents about Ethan being in the house across the street, about his taunts, Tom would go DEFCON 1 and Ethan would never be able to contact us again.

If I want to keep my family safe and get answers at the same time, I have to keep my mouth shut.

When I get last week's AP chem quiz back on Friday, there's a big fat "52%" at the top, circled in red pen. Practice is no better; Coach shouts at the sophomores for erupting into giggles during warm-up, and midway through our third run-through of the new competition routine, Coach stops the music.

Next to me, Rachel looks like she's going to crap her pants. But Coach locks eyes with me instead.

"Your fouettés are sloppy, Rayburn."

The weekend feels like a small mercy. When I get downstairs on Saturday morning, Tom is coming through the front door, cradling a paper bag from the deli. Mango dances around his heels, smelling the bacon-and-egg sandwich he gets every weekend.

"Oh good, you're up. Got your cinnamon raisin bagel."

"Thanks." My heart is beating in my throat. Tom looks at me, eyebrows pinched together. *Do you know I took the phone?*

As if he'd even say anything if he did. He falls into step with me on my way to the dining room.

"What do you think about coming to the range today?"

Tom brought me to the gun range when I turned sixteen in the spring. My mom almost had an aneurysm when she found out, and there was some shouting and Tom saying I should know how to protect myself.

When I asked Tom the following weekend if I could go to the range with him again, he said to let Mom warm to the idea first.

Neither of us mentioned it again. I know exactly what this is about: Tom thinks I'm having some sort of freak-out because of the security camera and Ethan McCready things, and he figures a refresher in self-defense is the answer.

I follow Tom into the dining room. "I don't know. Mom might get pissed."

Tom looks at me as he sets the deli bag on the table. "Mom doesn't need to know every little thing that happens around here."

I decide that he found the unlocked drawer and knows that I was in his desk. This father-daughter day at the range is a recon mission; he's going to confront me about the phone, ask what else I saw in the drawer. For the first time ever, the thought of being alone with him unsettles me.

"I'm meeting Mike there," Tom says, as if reading my mind. "In case that sways you."

Mike Mejia is Tom's partner. I have no doubt that when he got married, he devastated every woman in his life who isn't a blood relative. All four of us were invited to the wedding in April. Tom let Mike's new stepdaughter, an apple-cheeked four-year-old, step on his shoes while he whirled her around on the dance floor. Even my mother, three flutes of champagne deep, got up from the table to dance when they played her favorite song.

Mike is popular around here. Tom used to tease me about how I had a crush on him when I was a kid. Now the thought makes me want to throw up, because Mike is Brandon's age.

Something lights up in my brain. Mike's first year on the job was the year of the murders. He might be able to give me insight.

"Let me change," I say.

I sit in the backseat of Tom's car so we can pick up Mike. He gives me a "Hey, kid" and a flash of a smile.

"Hi," I say. "How are Anna and Danielle?"

"Good, good. Anna made me sleep on the couch for forgetting the mashed potatoes from KFC, but good."

"I remember those pregnancy hormones," Tom says. "Phoebe threw a glass at me because I made a joke about—" Tom eyes me over his shoulder. "Well, a dirty joke."

"Ew," I say.

They launch into work banter, then gun talk, and I close my eyes, trying to buoy myself against the nausea that comes over me every time we drive on these winding country roads. Triple B Gun Club is twenty minutes north of Sunnybrook, but it may as well be another state, culturally speaking.

The owner of Triple B remembers me from when I was last here in the spring, so she doesn't hassle me too much with the mandatory safety briefing. Tom ushers me through the door dividing the lanes from the lobby.

The *pop-pop* of guns going off sends my shoulders up to my ears. Tom puts a hand on my back and guides me to the lane he's rented for us. He sets me up with his .22 caliber pistol and keeps his eye on me as I adjust my ear protectors and safety goggles.

I assume the proper stance and aim the gun at the paper target, a sickly skinned cartoon zombie. My index finger trembles around the trigger.

"Remember," Tom says. "Don't expect it."

I fire off ten rounds. All hit the zombie's belly and not the bull's-eye on its head.

"Here." Tom takes the gun from me when the chamber is empty. "You have to relax your shoulders. Watch my stance."

I step aside and let Tom take his shots at the zombie. The first round pierces cleanly through the zombie's head.

He fires the rest off in succession, his shoulders taut, eyes laser-focused, and I'm hit with a rush of nausea.

Was it this easy for him to fire his gun at Jack Canning? Did he hesitate?

Did he go into that house expecting to kill Jack Canning?

Tom turns, motions for me to come try the gun again. I shake my head. "I don't want to."

"Why? You were on the right track. You were leaning to the left a bit—"

"I don't want to shoot the damn gun." The sound that comes out of me is guttural. Mike and the woman in the last lane must have heard me, because they're staring.

"I'm still carsick," I say. "Can I please just wait in the lobby?"

"Of course." Tom's forehead pinches, and I tear out of there without looking back.

On our way out, the range owner flags us down and gives us a 20 percent off coupon for the bar and grill next door, which she owns too.

After the hostess seats us in a booth and takes our drink orders, Tom and I head straight for the salad bar. I drop some mixed greens and pale tomato chunks on my plate, keeping an eye on Tom. One of the waitresses, an older woman with a face like a basset hound, has recognized him and pinned him at the other end of the salad bar. Tom nods politely at whatever she's saying, a held-hostage look on his face.

I finish dressing my salad plate and slide into the booth

across from Mike. There's a sweating glass of Diet Coke on the table in front of me; I didn't even see the waitress bring it over.

Mike cradles a bottle of Heineken, eyeing me carefully like I'm a skittish cat. "How the hell have you been, kid? How's junior year going?"

On the quick walk over here, he and Tom seemed desperate to avoid the subject of my behavior inside the range. *What are you doing for the Giants game tomorrow? Man, Beckham Jr.'s been lazy this year.*

"Okay, I guess. I've been busy with dance team and stuff." I hesitate, peeling the paper tie around my silverware into little strips. "Can I ask you something? Without you telling Tom?"

Mike's eyes swivel to Tom at the salad bar. He sets down his bottle. "Depends on how much trouble you're in."

"It's nothing like that. It's about something that happened at school a while ago."

Mike's eyebrows shoot up.

"Do you know who Ethan McCready is?"

Mike nods and sips from his beer. Wipes away a wet spot on his upper lip. "Yep. I'm the one who interviewed him about that little list of his."

"Is it true the whole thing was cheerleaders?"

"And the football team." Mike's face is grim. "What a mess. We had a lot of hysterical parents calling the station that week."

"But he wasn't charged with anything? He was just expelled?"

"There wasn't anything to charge him with. He didn't make any explicit threats. Didn't have any weapons or shooter-worship stuff in his house." Mike shrugs. "He didn't have a lot to say about it."

"What do you mean?"

"I had to question him about the list, and even he didn't seem to know why he wrote it. I thought it was probably an attention thing." Mike sips his beer again. "His mom had advanced cancer, no dad in the picture. Ethan wasn't exactly rolling in friends. Some kids will do anything to get noticed."

My right hand is still sore from clamping around the handgun. I massage the area between my thumb and index finger. "It's a little weird that two of the girls on his list were murdered a week later, and he was never a suspect."

Mike smacks his lips. "There weren't any suspects because it was clear who did it."

Mike was there when Tom shot Jack. Mike and Tom had only been riding together for a couple weeks when he followed Tom into Jack Canning's house, because that's what partners do. They have each other's backs. No cop wants to see his partner get in trouble for making a snap decision.

Five years ago, I was terrified that Tom would get fired or go to jail. I prayed every night that Mike would help the truth come out. Back when I was so sure of what the truth was. That Tom was only shooting a killer.

I want to ask Mike if he still thinks about that day, but

120

he's had a haunted look on his face ever since I brought up the murders.

"I'm sorry I brought it up," I say. "People at school were saying stuff, and I figured I'd ask you."

Mike frowns. Scratches the corner of his mouth with a knuckle. "No, I see why it's unsettling, considering the circumstances."

"What circumstances?"

Mike sets his beer down. "Ethan lived around the corner from you. Tom used to complain about him wandering the neighborhood at night. You didn't know that?"

I glance over at Tom, still trapped in conversation with the waitress. As if sensing me watching, he turns his head. Catches my eye. Frowns.

"No," I tell Mike. "I had no idea."

Chapter Nine

Rachel is in a mood when she picks me up Monday morning. I thought she would be over Coach reaming her out on Friday, but a weekend of stewing must have made things worse. She's actually *scowling* as I get into the car.

I'm buckling my seat belt when my phone vibrates. I have a text from a number I don't recognize, but it's not Ethan McCready's number.

> Can you come to Mrs. Goldberg's
> office during lunch?

As we back out of the driveway, a fine mist hits the windshield. Rachel smacks the handle that controls the wipers harder than she needs to. "So glad I straightened my hair this morning."

I want to ask her if she's aware that there are wars going on in other countries, but she might actually be angry enough to make me walk. Now I wish she'd stew quietly so I could fucking think.

I don't know who would want to meet me in Mrs. Goldberg's room. I'm about to tell the sender that they have the wrong number when another message comes through.

> It's Ginny, by the way. Your number was on the contact sheet Coach gave us.

I exhale a little. I don't know why, but Ginny's message buoys me and carries me all the way to lunch.

Mrs. Goldberg's door is open when I get there, and I spot Ginny at the same computer she was sitting at last week. I settle into the chair next to her.

"I found something I wanted to show you," she whispers.

I follow Ginny's eyes to the computer screen. She clicks on *My pictures* and scrolls down to a folder labeled *Homecoming*, which sprouts more folders: *Prep, Parade, Game, Dance.*

Ginny opens the *Prep* folder. The night before the football game is when everyone gathers in the school parking lot to add the final touches to the class floats.

She tilts the screen of the iMac so I can see what's in the folder. A quick scan, and I feel my forehead furrowing. None of these people look familiar. Ginny points to a group of girls gathered around a giant Pac-Man head. One of the girls is ducking, wriggling away from a boy whose hands are covered in papier-mâché goop.

I sit up straight. I know *her.* In one of the other photos snapped in the same scene, Susan Berry poses over the Pac-Man head, a yellow-dipped paintbrush in her hand.

Lips closed, tight. Susan rarely smiled; even while she was cheering, she always wore the dutiful expression of someone who was performing a task and wanted to get it over with. These pictures are from five years ago.

I turn to Ginny. "How did you get these?"

"People submit tons of photos for the yearbook every year. We keep them all on flash drives, whether they make it into the book or not."

Ginny scoots her chair over and pushes the mouse toward me. I scroll through the pictures. Realize with a pinch in my chest that I'm looking for my sister. But Jen was at home that night, bundled in a blanket in a Chloraseptic and antibiotic haze, pissed off that she was missing everything.

"Scroll down a bit," Ginny says. "Look at the one . . ."

Her voice trails off, because I see it: a picture of all the cheerleaders, huddled together, arms tucked around each other's backs.

Tiny Juliana Ruiz is crouched in front of the group, hands in the pocket of her cheerleading hoodie, mouth stretched in a dizzying grin. Juliana's giddiness was infectious. Jen said Juliana regularly got kicked out of class for her uncontrollable giggle fits. She always cheered the loudest at games, in a way that would be obnoxious if anyone else were doing it.

"Look what happened next," Ginny says, voice low.

The rest of the pictures were snapped in succession, like a flipbook. In the next one, Juliana is retreating from the group of girls. Then she can be seen at the edge of the frame, standing by the fence separating the parking lot from the football field, cell phone in one hand, one finger hooked over the metal link. She's not smiling. She may even be crying; it's impossible to tell from the angle.

In the final shot, Juliana is standing at the fence, still, face in her hands.

I don't know what to say.

"It's probably nothing," Ginny says quietly. "I just thought it was weird that she was crying . . ."

"And a few hours later, she was dead." I bend my head closer to Ginny. "Is there a way I could look at all of these?"

"I can put them on a flash drive for you. Hold on."

Ginny disappears into the back room. The ball of anxiety that's taken up residence in my chest grows, and by the time Ginny returns with the flash drive, I'm so dizzy I have to put my head in my hands.

"What's wrong?" she asks.

I look up at her. "My stepdad lied to me. When I brought up Ethan McCready, he acted like he didn't remember his name. But his partner told me that Ethan lived in my old neighborhood and that Tom used to complain about him all the time."

"You didn't know Ethan lived near you?"

I shake my head. "A lot of kids lived in our neighborhood. I remember there was this group of boys who were kind of sketchy. Ethan could have been one of them but they definitely weren't the type of kids my sister hung out with."

Ginny takes a hamster-small bite of the sandwich she's snuck out of her tote bag. On Mrs. Goldberg's whiteboard, a sign reads NO FOOD IN THE ART LAB!!! in large letters. She chews and swallows. She almost looks as nervous as I do. Her voice is barely above a whisper when she finally speaks again.

"Your stepdad was the one who shot Susan Berry's next door neighbor."

"Yeah. He was."

Neither of us says what I know we're both thinking; something had upset Juliana earlier that night, before she and Susan got home and Jack Canning noticed they were by themselves. It might not be connected to the murders, but if it is . . . it means there's a chance that Daphne was right and Juliana's attacker was someone close to her.

It means there's a chance that Tom killed an innocent man—and whoever did kill Juliana and Susan is still out there.

When I get home from practice, I deposit myself at my laptop. I plug in the flash drive Ginny gave me and sit back as the pictures load onto my hard drive.

Juliana Ruiz and her mom were closer than any mother-daughter pair I'd ever seen. When Juliana and Susan would spend a Saturday night at our house, Juliana would be up first thing in the morning so she could get breakfast with her mother before church.

One of my clearest memories is of Juliana, draped across our living room couch, musing out loud about which of the boys in their grade she'd like to kiss during spin the bottle at Susan's thirteenth birthday party and which boys she'd kissed the year before. Jen clammed up the whole time, cheeks burning, because Mom was in the kitchen, within earshot.

"What?" Juliana said, rolling onto her stomach. "You don't tell her everything? I tell my mom everything."

Mrs. Ruiz might know what made Juliana cry earlier the night she was murdered. It could have been nothing serious—her homecoming date blowing her off, maybe. Either way, I need to know.

Googling Juliana's parents' name doesn't yield anything: no address, no phone numbers, no emails. Just a couple of articles briefly mentioning Juliana's murder. A few months after the murders, Mr. and Mrs. Ruiz sold their grocery store and moved closer to family in West-chester. The Berrys divorced shortly after they finally sold their house.

I step into my closet and dig out Jen's phone; I'd buried it in my jewelry box, just in case Tom noticed it was gone and decided to come snooping up here. I scroll through the contacts, but Jen doesn't have Mrs. Ruiz's number.

My mother's voice carries up the stairs: "Monica, we're eating."

"I'll be down in a sec," I yell. I click out of the windows on my laptop and sit back in my chair.

My mind swivels to the first anniversary of Jen's death. That evening, my mom shut herself in her bedroom; I stood outside her door, listening to her murmurs, trying to figure out who she was speaking to on the phone. Tom had put a hand on my shoulder and steered me away; when I pointed out that Mom had been on the phone for almost an hour, Tom said, "She needs to talk to someone who's been through the same thing."

I slink out of my room and down to the end of the hall, listening for a break in the sound of the pots clanging and the oven timer beeping downstairs.

The door to the master suite is open a crack; I push my way in, the door purring against the carpet. The room is done up in cream—the paint on the walls, the carpet, the silky bedspread. It's so bland, it's disorienting. The only thing out of place is a pair of Tom's jeans strewn across the chaise beneath the bay window.

Tom is not a chaise guy. The jeans on said chaise are from Costco. If Jen were here, she'd find the whole scene hilarious. She'd find this *house* hilarious.

My mother's iPhone is on her nightstand, hooked up to its charger, where she always leaves it. I swipe a finger across the screen and enter her password—Petey's birthday. Same as the security code to open the garage door. At least I know where I stand with my family.

I scroll through her contacts; I notice there is no one with the last name Berry or Steiger or Coughlin.

My mom may have lost touch with the other girls' parents out of self-preservation, but Mrs. Ruiz wasn't just a cheer mother. When Mrs. Ruiz came over to say goodbye before they moved, Mom clung to her and sobbed more than I'd seen her cry since Jen died.

And sure enough, at the bottom, there's Tina Ruiz.

"What are you doing?"

I look up. Petey is in the bedroom doorway, index finger jammed in his ear, digging at earwax even though we're always telling him that's disgusting. I set Mom's phone down. "What are *you* doing?"

"Telling you to set the table." Petey cocks his head. "Were you on Mom's phone?"

"Mind your own business."

I know what he's going to do the second his lips part. I rocket off the bed and cover his mouth with my hand, muffling his cry of *Mah-OM*. "There's a twenty-dollar bill in my nightstand. Stay quiet and it's yours."

Petey shrugs out of my grasp and flounces into the hall. Moments later, I hear my bedroom door click open.

I shake my head and text Tina Ruiz's number to myself from my mother's phone, deleting the outgoing message when I'm done.

When the plates are cleared from the table, stray crumbles of taco meat scraped into the garbage, I head back up to my room. No one questions my antisocial behavior, and that's fine. The more unpleasant my family thinks I am, the more likely they are to leave me alone to do whatever this is that I'm doing.

After I scratch out some answers to my pre-calc problem set, I sit cross-legged on my bed, palms damp with sweat. I rehearsed what I want to say, combed over every word, but it doesn't make calling Mrs. Ruiz feel less wrong.

I stare at the number on my screen for a solid minute, my heartbeat mimicking a metronome. I swallow and hit the call button.

A woman picks up. "Hello?"

"Hi. Is this Mrs. Ruiz?"

"No, it's Maria. Who is this?"

Juliana's sister, Maria, was younger than I was when Juliana was killed.

"My name is Monica Rayburn," I say. "Can I talk to your mom?"

I wait for Maria to decide I'm a scammer, then lie and say that Mrs. Ruiz isn't home. Instead she says, "One second."

There's shuffling on her end. I catch a faint "Who is it?" followed by Maria huffing, "I don't know!"

"Hello?" Mrs. Ruiz's voice is guarded. A go-away-if-you're-selling-something voice.

"Mrs. Ruiz," I say. "Hi. This is Monica Rayburn."

Silence. The quick rush of breathing.

"Jennifer's sister," I add, feeling my insides shrink.

"No, of course. Monica. I'm sorry."

"Is this a bad time?"

"Oh, no, I was just putting the baby down. Hold on one moment."

Baby?

The sound of a door clicking. I picture Mrs. Ruiz shutting herself in her room. Sitting on the edge of her bed, Juliana's photo staring at her from the dresser. I nearly hang up.

"You had a baby?" I say.

"His name is Matthew," she says.

"Congratulations." *Matthew.* The name means "gift from God." It was my ex Matt's favorite fun fact about himself.

"Thank you. We adore him. How are you, Monica?" Mrs. Ruiz sounds brighter. "It's been a while."

"I know. I'm sorry. I should have stayed in touch."

"You were just a kid. It's good to hear from you now."

"I just— I wanted to see how you were doing." I can't bring myself to tell her why I'm really calling.

"That's very sweet of you," Mrs. Ruiz says cautiously. "Is there something else you wanted to talk about?"

Her voice is gentle, patient. As if she'd known that at some point she would get this phone call from me.

"I'm on yearbook now," I lie. "I was looking at some old pictures and I saw one from the night . . . the night before homecoming. Juliana looked really upset."

"Oh," Mrs. Ruiz says. This is new to her.

"Do you know what might have been bothering her?"

Mrs. Ruiz is silent. Probably wondering why I need this information so badly that I had to call her at dinner-time on a Monday night five years later.

"I'm sorry," I say. "I just . . . I don't know. I thought it might have something to do with my sister."

"I honestly don't know," Mrs. Ruiz says. "I hadn't seen Jen in over a week at least."

That can't be right. Jen spent half her weekends at Juliana's house. "Are you sure?"

"I asked Juliana about why Jen wasn't there," Mrs. Ruiz says. "She said that Susan and Jen weren't speaking to each other. Juliana wanted to stay out of it."

My mouth is dry, my skin buzzing. "What were they . . . Do you know why they were fighting?"

"Juliana didn't want to tell me."

"Was that weird for her? Not telling you?"

"Monica. I know why you're calling."

I don't know what to say. When Mrs. Ruiz speaks again, her voice is gentle. "None of it had anything to do with what happened that night. It was a terrible, horrible crime, and I can't imagine how it must have haunted your sister."

"I just have so many questions, still."

"I do too," Mrs. Ruiz says. "But after a while, searching for the answers felt like grasping around in the dark. At some point, you have to choose to live in the light."

Chapter Ten

After I say goodbye to Mrs. Ruiz, promising I'll stop by and meet the baby sometime once I get my driver's license, I turn back to my laptop. All the pictures have loaded by now.

I start with the ones in the folder marked *Sunnybrook vs. Shrewsbury*. The game where the infamous picture of the five Sunnybrook cheerleaders was taken.

I click through them, pausing on a picture of Juliana and a blond girl. Their cheeks are painted with blue and yellow *S*s. They're blowing kisses at the camera. The other girl is about a foot taller than Juliana, her white-blond ponytail so high it looks like it's sprouting from the top of her head. Her upper lip is pierced, and she has an edgy look to her that clashes with her cheer uniform.

I'd forgotten I took Jen's freshman yearbook upstairs with me after I raided her things the other night. I dig the book out and arrange myself among the pillows on the bed. Flip through all the class portraits. Mango trots into my room, sniffing the air. When he sits at the foot of my nightstand, I scoop him up and plop him on the bed. While he's circling, trying to find a comfortable spot,

I turn to the front of the yearbook and search the other photos for the blond girl: team portraits, candid pictures from dances, Spirit Night.

She isn't in any of them. The girl must have been new the year of the murders; there's no way she was younger than my sister.

I eye my phone where it's resting on my nightstand. Before I can talk myself out of it, I call Ginny. She picks up on the second ring.

"Monica?" she says. She doesn't sound surprised that I'm calling; it almost sounds like she was expecting it to be me.

"Yeah. Hi," I say, suddenly nervous. "Is this a bad time?"

"No, not at all." She pauses. "Are you looking at the pictures?"

"Yeah. I'm trying to figure out who else Juliana was friends with, who might know why she was upset when they were building the float." I think about what Mrs. Ruiz told me about Susan and Jen fighting, and Juliana being in the middle, and I hesitate. I feel like some sort of gossip or voyeur, trying to dissect everything a teenager did and felt one night five years ago. "I talked to Juliana's mom. She didn't know why Juliana was crying that night. She thought maybe it was because my sister and Susan Berry weren't talking to each other."

"What were they fighting about?" Ginny asks.

"I have no idea. Jen never said anything." I zoom in on the picture of Juliana and the blond girl. "I found a picture of Juliana with this blond girl, but she's not in my sister's yearbook from the year before. Can I come look at

Mrs. Goldberg's old books tomorrow at lunch maybe?"

"I have them here—at home," Ginny says. "She gave me copies from the last five years so I could compare the layouts. What does the girl look like?"

"She's tall and skinny. Her hair is super platinum blond, like it's dyed."

"Got it," she says. "I'll look and call you back."

Ginny ends the call, but I don't put my phone down. Mango drops his head on my knee and lets out a breathy snort. My heartbeat is gaining speed at the thought of finding the blonde—a Sunnybrook cheerleader who might be able to tell me things I don't know about the girls. Or don't remember.

When my phone trills, I press accept before it gets the chance to ring again. "Hey."

"Hey," Ginny says. "I think I found her in the cheer team picture. Super thin eyebrows, piercing above her lip, right?"

"Yeah. That's her."

"Okay. Her name is Carly Amato. She was a senior."

Carly Amato. I turn the name over in my head, disappointed. I was hoping to recognize the girl's name—for some long-forgotten piece of information to click into place. "I've never heard of her."

"I looked her up already," Ginny says. She sounds embarrassed. "I found a Facebook page for a girl who looks like her. She has dark hair now. And her tan is . . . less fake."

"Hold on." I click my laptop awake and do a Facebook search for Carly Amato. The top result is the girl Ginny described.

According to her posts, Carly Amato is a nursing

student at Orange County Community College. The majority of her posts are about how many exams she has and photos of a Yorkie named Peanut whom she refers to as "her baby."

I keep clicking until I get to her oldest photos and watch her transform in reverse until she's blond and pierced. My heartbeat picks up. "This is definitely the same girl."

"What are you going to say to her?"

"I don't know. What should I say?"

Ginny pauses. "Maybe just tell her the real reason you want to talk to her."

"Yeah. Okay. Thanks."

She makes me promise I'll update her if Carly responds, and we end the call. Ginny makes the idea of telling the truth sound so easy. *Just tell her the real reason.*

I think of the reactions Rachel and Tom had to my questioning the deaths. For a few moments, I stare at the empty Facebook message draft addressed to Carly before I start to type.

> Hey, Carly—you cheered with my sister, Jen Rayburn, at Sunnybrook High. Colleen Coughlin's mom is putting together a memorial at school and we're trying to get some of the old team to participate and I was wondering if you and I could talk.

I slip my thumbnail between my teeth, reading the last sentence over and over. Such a brazen lie could backfire. Everyone who went to Sunnybrook High knows Mrs. Coughlin is a demon; my mentioning her name might make Carly send my message straight to the trash.

I delete the last line, replacing it with just *I was wondering if you and I could talk.*

When I wake up, I check my inbox. It's empty; but there's a check mark next to my message to Carly Amato.

She read it six hours ago.

Tom doesn't have Saturday off, and my mother has to work at the playhouse, so I'm watching Petey, noise-canceling headphones on to drown out the sounds of him practicing his trumpet in the living room.

I'm slathering peanut butter on a slice of toast for his lunch when my phone starts shimmying across the counter, Ginny's name lighting up the screen. I tug my headphones off and accept the call.

"Hey." I try and fail not to sound too eager. But something about Ginny's investment in all this has reinvigorated me, given me purpose. Not only have I told someone everything, but she believes me too.

Ginny's response is drowned out by the sound of "La Cucaracha."

"Hold on a sec," I tell her. I duck out the door connecting

the kitchen to the garage, shutting myself in. "Okay. What's up?"

"I've been watching Carly's Facebook page." Ginny's voice is barely a murmur, as if there's someone near her, listening in. "She just checked into the library at Orange County Community College."

I stand up straighter, my back against the door. "How far is Orange County Community College?"

"Twenty minutes." A pause. "My mom doesn't need the car until seven."

"You have your license?" I ask. "I didn't even know you were seventeen already."

"Since last Monday." Ginny almost sounds embarrassed.

Monday was the day I met her in the yearbook office to look at the pictures. We talked for over an hour and Ginny never mentioned it was her birthday. Sadness slices through me; I wonder how many other things I don't know about Ginny just because I never bothered to ask. She speaks before I can work out what to say next.

"We don't have to go if you don't want. I just thought since Carly's there, and she hasn't responded to you . . ."

My mom isn't going to be back from the playhouse for another couple of hours, and I can't leave Petey here alone. Carly will probably have left the library by the time my mom gets home. "I'm stuck watching my brother."

A faint tapping, as if Ginny's drumming her fingers against her phone. "Can you bring him?"

I hadn't thought of that, but . . . "It'll take some bargaining. Can you be here in fifteen minutes?"

"See you then," Ginny chirps.

I end the call and let myself back into the kitchen. In the living room, Petey has given up on "La Cucaracha" and splayed himself out on the sectional. I come up behind him and rest my hands on the back of the couch.

"I have to go somewhere quick," I say, treading carefully. "I need you to come with me."

Petey turns his head up at me. Blinks. "Why can't I stay here?"

"Because Mom will kill me. You can wait in the car."

"What car?" Petey says. "You can't drive."

"My friend is coming to get me."

Petey's eyes light up. "Rachel?"

"No," I say. "But this friend is nice too."

Petey thinks for a minute. Shakes his head. "I just found something to watch."

I grit my teeth. "You can download *Clan Wars* on my phone and play in the car."

"Mom said no *Clan Wars* today."

"Yeah, well, I won't tell her if you won't."

Petey watches me, calculating. He may be a fifth grader, but he knows a raw deal when he sees one. I sigh. "I'll give you twenty dollars if you come and don't tell Mom where we went."

Ten minutes later, I'm shooing Petey out of the house and locking the front door behind us as Ginny rolls into the driveway. She's wearing her Jessie's Gym warm-up jacket, her hair coiled in a bun.

I climb into the front, Petey into the back. He takes a long look at Ginny. "Who *are* you?"

"Don't be rude," I say. "This is Ginny."

Petey settles back in his seat. Meets Ginny's eyes in the rearview mirror. "Do you play *Clan Wars*?"

Ginny smiles and shakes her head. "I don't know what that is."

I try to be patient as Petey explains the nuances of village building and pillaging to Ginny. Once he falls silent, legs drawn up to his chest, my phone balancing sideways on his knees, I turn to Ginny and speak softly. "Seriously, thanks for doing this."

She shrugs. "It was my idea."

I realize that it's part of the reason I like her so much: Whenever Ginny says something, it sounds like she means it. It's enough to ease my worry that she doesn't really want to be doing this—that I've somehow roped her into a mess she feels like she can't get out of.

We listen to the radio and steer the conversation toward dance team, just in case Petey is eavesdropping from the backseat. When the exit for Orange County Community College appears, we make a right onto campus and follow the signs to the library.

As Ginny is parking, Petey pipes up: "Why are we here, anyway?"

It takes me a beat to come up with something. "I need a book for school. Our library didn't have it."

"Do I have to come in?" Petey asks.

I hesitate; I want Ginny with me, but I can't leave Petey in the car by himself.

Ginny's voice is barely above a whisper when she says, "Maybe your brother and I should wait out here.

So Carly doesn't feel ambushed."

I nod. Once, twice, three times like a bobblehead. "Yeah. Okay. You're right."

I climb out of the car and head for the library entrance. Paranoia hits me as the automatic doors open for me. What if the librarian asks me for my college ID? What if Carly left already?

The library is one floor. I do a lap, heading past the circulation desk and a café. At the far end of the library are several long tables, peppered with people slumped over laptops or open textbooks. A sign on the wall overhead says STUDY AREA ONLY.

I wend my way through the tables, spotting a girl with a long raven-black bob that grazes her bare shoulders. My pulse quickens. Carly Amato turns her head toward me. She yawns and picks up her phone. From where I'm standing, I can see that the screen is full of cracks.

A textbook is open on the table in front of her, displaying a gruesome two-page diagram of the human digestive system. She's not reading, though. She's on her cell phone, playing some sort of bubble-breaking game.

I want to bolt, but Ginny and I didn't come all the way here for me to bitch out at the last minute. I inch toward Carly's table. Rest a hand on the back of the chair across from her, and say, "Hi. Can I sit here?"

She looks up at me. Blinks. Carly Amato looks about twenty years older than her yearbook and profile pictures, even though she's only twenty-two, if I'm counting right.

Carly nods at the chair, as if to confirm it's free. Not looking at me, she leans back and yawns so loudly that the guy next to her sets his book down and gives her a nasty stare.

"Are you Carly?"

Carly Amato looks like the type of girl who would answer that type of question in a smoker's growl: *Who's askin'?* Maybe I watch too many movies, because instead, Carly stops playing her game. Gives me a head tilt. The voice that comes out of her is husky. "Yeah. Do I know you?"

"I'm Jennifer Rayburn's sister."

"No shit." This time Carly actually puts her phone down. She leans back on two chair legs, bumping into the chair behind her. The guy sitting in it turns around and scowls, but Carly ignores him, her eyes focused on me. "You're, like, big now. I remember you from our games."

I don't want to tell her that she's probably thinking of someone else's little sister—that I rarely went to watch Jen cheer because I was always at dance class or at Rach's or Alexa's house. "I think I remember you too," I lie. "You were blond then."

Carly rummages in her purse. Produces a long tube made of bright pink metal. "You wanna go outside for a sec? I need a vape break."

"Yeah. Sounds good."

She leaves her textbook on the table and taps the shoulder of the guy sitting behind her. "Can you watch this?"

He nods, looking grateful for our exit.

Carly leads me out one of the emergency exit doors

142

and leans against the side of the building. Sucks on the tube and blows out a stream of smoke that smells like fake strawberries and vanilla. After a few moments she breaks the silence.

"So, do you cheer?" she asks.

I shake my head. "I'm on dance team." Carly must not remember that the cheerleading team was disbanded. She doesn't look like she remembers what she did yesterday.

"Cool, cool." She takes another drag from her vape, bored of me already. "What brings you out here? You're not in college already, are you?"

"No." I don't know what else to say. I nod awkwardly to her vape: "How is that different from a cigarette?"

"There's no tobacco or tar and shit." Carly considers the device in her hand as if someone stuck it there without her noticing it. "Honestly, I don't know why I bother. I've been smoking since I was fifteen."

"It's hard to quit," I say. "It took my stepdad like twenty years."

Carly eyes me as a white cloud billows around her lips. "So are you checking out the campus or something?"

The look on her face is clear: *What the hell are you doing here?*

"Yeah," I lie. "I recognized you and figured I'd say hi. Were you friends with my sister?"

"I mean, we cheered together. But I was new that year, so I never got to know her or anything," Carly says.

The cold nips at my fingers. I stick my hands in the pockets of my North Face jacket. "What about Juliana Ruiz?"

Carly eyes me. "We went to the same cheer camp that summer. We hung out a bit. Why?"

"I saw a picture of you two at a football game. Were you close?"

"I barely knew her. I mean, I hate to say it, but your sister's friends were kinda conceited."

She doesn't sound like she hates to say it at all. In fact, it sounds as if she's been dying to say it to someone. My annoyance is colored by an unpleasant thought—*were* my sister's friends conceited? I try to remember a time when Susan and Juliana actually spoke to me beyond an obligatory *hi.*

Everyone likes to talk about how adored the dead girls were. I never stopped to consider the alternative—that Juliana and Susan and maybe even Jen herself had enemies.

"Do you remember Ethan McCready?" I ask Carly.

Carly turns and looks at me. "Who?"

"He made a hit list that year and got expelled. The cheerleaders were on it."

"*Oh.*" Carly gives a small shudder. "Him."

"So you know him?" I ask.

"Nuh-uh." Carly brings her vape stick to her lips. "I never said one word to the kid, and then I find out he wants to kill me? Fuck that."

I have to clamp my mouth shut to keep my jaw from dropping, because it seems totally lost on Carly that Ethan wanted to kill *all* the cheerleaders—and five of them actually wound up dead.

"Why would Ethan hate you if he never even talked to you?" I say.

"Kids like that always hate cheerleaders." She moves her vape stick away from her lips, eyes on me. "Except one cheerleader."

My stomach goes all slippery. "You mean my sister."

"Mmm-hmm." Carly's still watching me, her spidery eyelashes unblinking. It's deeply unsettling.

"A lot of guys liked Jen," I say. "Ever since middle school, all the guys liked her."

"Well. I don't know if it was one-sided." Carly's razor-thin eyebrows arch up. "With Ethan, I mean."

My heartbeat quickens. "What are you talking about?"

Carly's eyes sparkle. *I know something you don't know.* I decide right there that I hate her.

"She was the only one who wasn't on his hit list," Carly says. "You didn't know that?"

"That doesn't mean she liked *him.*"

"Well, they were friends as kids. He lived around the corner from her," she says, as if she's forgotten Jen and I were sisters and lived in the same house. "The two of them, like, went off into the woods together all the time."

That's impossible. My sister would have never hung out with someone like Ethan. I never even saw him on our street. "Who said that?"

Carly's mouth pinches, as if she's holding back a smug smile. "Let's just say it came from a reputable source."

I feel another fissure in my patience. "Who?"

"Susan Berry," Carly says. "The same day she saw Ethan writing the hit list, she saw Jen slip something inside Ethan's locker. When she told some senior on the cheer squad, they convinced her to tell Heinz."

Bullshit. The word zips around my head like a pinball. "Susan thought *Jen* had something to do with the hit list?"

"I don't know what she thought," Carly says. "But she told Principal Heinz everything she saw."

"Susan wouldn't do that to Jen. She wouldn't just make up some bullshit story about her helping Ethan write a hit list."

"Well, maybe she didn't make it up." Carly holds my gaze and takes another pull from her vape. Lets the smoke out her nose. "You can't believe everything you hear, though. Girls are always whittling little weapons to stab each other with."

The last part is the only thing she's said that makes sense. "Right." I bite back the dozens of nasty words I have for this girl. This stupid, lying, awful girl who implied my sister had something to do with Ethan McCready's hit list. "I have to go. Sorry I kept you from studying."

"No prob." Carly tucks a lock of hair behind her ear, revealing a cascade of silver studs. Then, as if an afterthought: "Sorry about your sister. She really did seem nice."

"Thanks," I say, anger still swelling in me. I step off the curb, heading for the parking lot as quickly as I can, desperate to escape Carly and the sickly sweet vanilla smell of her smoke.

As I approach Ginny's car, I see her and Petey in an animated conversation. She turns her head to the driver's side window. Her face falls when she spots me. It must be obvious how my conversation with Carly went; I wish

146

I had done a lap around the library to compose myself.

I slip into the passenger seat, Petey's hands already on my headrest, his voice and peanut butter breath in my ear. "Do they make slime at that library?" He turns to Ginny. "At our library, they make slime."

"No, this is a college library," I say. My voice is trembling.

Ginny lifts her eyes to meet Petey's in the mirror. "I saw a recipe for color-changing slime," she says. "You should look it up."

Petey chirps, "Cool!" and immerses himself in my phone. I close my eyes.

Ginny's voice is soft beside me. "Are you okay?"

I nod, my throat tight. "Carly says she wasn't friends with any of them."

When I inhale and open my eyes, Ginny is watching me expectantly.

I can't bring myself to tell her what Carly Amato said about the paper Jen slipped into Ethan's locker. It's complete bullshit—there's no way that paper was a hit list. Her friends were on it. Friends whose deaths completely broke her, she loved them so much.

Mrs. Ruiz's voice knifes its way through my brain. Jen and Susan weren't speaking. Susan went to the principal when she saw Ethan McCready's hit list. According to Carly, Susan saw Jen slip something into Ethan's locker . . .

The note. *I'm not okay.*

A misunderstanding. It explains everything. Jen was simply replying to Ethan's message: *Do you want to talk about it?* Susan saw Jen putting the note in Ethan's locker, the same day she saw Ethan writing the list, and instead of talking to Jen about it, she went to Principal Heinz. Of course Jen would be pissed enough at Susan to stop speaking to her.

"Hey, we should get McFlurries!" Petey yells from the backseat, breaking my train of thought.

My hand moves to my empty pocket with a flutter of panic. I think about my wallet on the kitchen island. Right where I left it after I gave Petey his bribe money. "I forgot my wallet."

"That's okay," Petey says. "I have twenty dollars now. I got you."

I don't say anything. My reflex is to tell him no, but I can't handle the thought of going home right now.

"I would enjoy a McFlurry," Ginny says.

Can she sense it, how I'm not ready to go home? I let myself breathe. "I would enjoy one too."

Ginny and I don't bring up Carly Amato again on the drive back into town. McDonald's is only a block away from the playhouse, but I don't have the presence of mind to be worried about my mom catching us out right now. When Ginny parks, Petey tumbles out of the backseat and darts ahead.

"Wait for us," I say, still too dazed to be irritated with him.

Petey stops at the entrance and holds the door open for Ginny and me.

At the counter, I order vanilla ice cream with Oreo pieces, and Ginny gets Butterfinger.

"That's what Jen always got," Petey says, matter-of-fact,

before asking the cashier for vanilla ice cream with M&M's. I don't have the heart to tell him that he's confusing Jen with me; that Butterfinger McFlurries used to be my favorite.

"Go get us a table." I nudge Petey once he's paid the cashier. I watch him wind his way through the restaurant and plop himself in a booth nearby. He takes out my phone and holds it sideways, which means *Clan Wars*. I forgot he still has my phone. My head is thrumming with so many questions.

"Are you okay?" Ginny's voice is soft, but it brings me back.

"I don't know. Carly told me Susan saw Jen put something in Ethan's locker the day before he got expelled. It had to be the note they were passing back and forth. But Susan must have thought it had something to do with the hit list and told Principal Heinz."

"Do you really think Susan would do that?" Ginny whispers.

"I don't know."

Ginny is watching me as if she can sense there's more. I swallow. "Carly was talking like Jen was involved somehow and that she wasn't the only one who thought that way."

Ginny is quiet. The cashier sets her McFlurry on the counter, but she doesn't move to collect it.

"That's crap," she finally says.

It's the first I've heard Ginny curse and it's like a jolt to my brain, waking me up. "Right?" I look her in the eyes. "It makes no sense."

The cashier sets my McFlurry down. Ginny and I grab our order and join Petey at the booth. I sit next to him, and Ginny slides into the seat across from us.

I let Ginny eat a spoonful of her ice cream before I catch her eye and speak again. "There's something else. Carly says Jen was the only cheerleader who wasn't on the hit list."

Ginny glances at Petey and drops her voice to a whisper. "Are you sure you want to talk about this in front of him?"

"Don't worry about him," I say. "Look."

I say Petey's name at normal volume. Once, twice, three times before shouting: "PETER THOMAS CARLINO."

"What?" He doesn't look up from my phone. With one finger he's building a new settlement. With the other hand, he's spooning ice cream into his mouth.

I turn back to Ginny. "See? We're good."

Ginny swirls the tip of her spoon through her ice cream, nudging at a piece of Butterfinger. "Jen not being on the list doesn't mean anything. Just that Ethan liked her."

"The last thing she wrote to him was *yes*."

Petey's voice finally breaks the silence. He points to my untouched McFlurry. "Are you gonna eat that?"

Jennifer

I don't know. If Jen was being honest, that was how she would answer Ethan McCready's question.

Do you want to talk about it?

Jen didn't know. She *did* want to talk about how shitty she felt, but she didn't want to talk about it with Ethan McCready. And it wasn't because people thought he was a loser and a creep. She couldn't look at him without thinking about that kiss all those years ago.

She wondered if she would like it if he kissed her again; she wondered if he even wanted to.

The day after he gave her the note, Jen had slipped it through a slit in his locker with trembling fingers. *Yes.*

Immediately, she wanted to take it back. Becoming friends with Ethan McCready again was not the most rational response to whatever weirdness was going on with her and Jules and Susan.

But he kept invading her head. Every thought she had over the past few days seemed infused with Ethan.

151

Even now, as she observed herself in the mirror of the dressing room at Addie's Closet, she imagined Ethan seeing her in her prospective homecoming dress.

Everyone wore short dresses to homecoming, which made Jen anxious. Tall girls and short dresses were a recipe for disaster. She'd picked a dress that seemed like it would look the least vulgar on her. It was covered in rose-gold sequins, with a keyhole halter top.

She knew the boys at school thought she was hot. *Hot* was their word: *Jen Rayburn is the hottest girl in our grade.* Jen never knew how to feel about it, though. She had done things with boys; just last year she'd made out with Chase Kenney at the movie theater, eventually having to shrug away from him when he guided her hand into his pants. All she felt afterward was disgust with guys and how they only wanted one thing from girls.

And now here she was, imagining Ethan McCready's gaze running up her legs, to the place where the hem of her skirt met her thigh—

The curtain sectioning off the dressing room opened. Jen jumped back, her face warm, as if she'd been caught doing something gross. "Jesus, Jules."

"Sorry." Juliana stepped into the dressing room with Jen. She was wearing a lacy black-and-gold crop top and a long tulle skirt. It was the type of outfit only Jules could pull off.

"You look *frigging* awesome." Jules stepped around Jen, tugging at the hem of her dress like a seamstress. "You're getting it, right?"

"I don't know."

Addie's Closet was the only boutique in town. Most girls drove forty minutes to the outlets in Ithaca, but cheer practice had been sucking up most of Jen's weekends, and between Monica's ballet classes and Petey's playdates, her mother didn't have time to take her.

Mrs. Berry had dropped the girls off at Addie's and said she'd be back in an hour. Susan was still dillydallying by the sale rack. She was the most indecisive person— Jen knew she'd wind up coming back to Addie's with her mother tomorrow. She watched Susan hold a black sheath dress up to herself and then put it back on the rack.

Juliana finished up at the register and joined Jen at the door. "Suz! Ready to go?"

Susan sighed. "I guess."

The girls filed out of the store and across the lot, waiting until the sign across the street flashed to WALK. The Sunnybrook McDonald's was unnecessarily nice—the façade looked like an old farmhouse, with a giant gold foil M over the doorway instead of those tacky arches. Above, the sky was turning the color of sherbet.

McFlurries and fries obtained, Susan slid into a booth by the window. Juliana and Jen followed, setting their Addie's Closet shopping bags on their laps.

Susan swirled her straw through the top of her ice cream. "I'm not going to find anything."

"Maybe if you weren't so anal," Juliana said.

Susan threw a French fry at Jules. Jen stole one from the packet on Susan's tray while she wasn't looking. Suz could be absurdly territorial when it came to her food.

"So," Susan said. "Anything you want to tell us?"

Jen's insides frosted over. She didn't like the way Susan's voice had cooled. "What are you talking about?"

"I saw you put something in Ethan McCready's locker this morning."

Juliana, who had just had her hand on Susan's tray, froze with a fistful of fries. "McCreepy?"

Jen felt a flare of annoyance. "Don't call him that. You guys can be so mean."

"And *you* can be too nice," Juliana said. "There's something wrong with that kid."

Jen poked her spoon through her ice cream, even though she didn't want it anymore. "It was nothing. I left my book in Mr. Ward's room. He brought it to me. The end."

"Suuuuuuure." Now Juliana sounded as frosty as Susan had earlier—even accusatory, as if she thought Jen was hiding something.

"Why are you guys doing this?" Jen asked. "Teasing me about a boy like we're in middle school?"

Suz smacked Jules's hand as she reached to steal more fries. Suz's eyes were on Jen. "Ethan's always staring at you. It makes me worried."

"Worried that what?" Jen asked.

"That you're going to go missing and wind up stuffed in an oil drum."

"Seriously," Jen snapped. "Stop."

"Jesus. It's not that big of a deal." Juliana eyed Jen like she was a cobra poised to strike. Her eyebrows knit together like Jen was being totally ridiculous, and they hadn't been taunting her just moments ago.

Jen put down her McFlurry. "Whatever. I don't want to talk about this anymore."

Whatever. The word hung between her and Juliana. It felt like it had become a weapon for them to use on each other.

Ethan wasn't in school Monday; by third period, the whole building was in hysteria.

Jen caught pieces of the story in the halls, whispered between people in class: "Some sophomore was going to shoot up the school."

"Yeah, he was going to kill all the cheerleaders and football players."

The knot in Jen's stomach grew when she heard her name over the loudspeaker. She was being called to the principal's office.

Mr. Demarco, her guidance counselor, was there, sitting across from Principal Heinz. Leaning against the bookshelf was her stepfather.

"Jen," Tom said. "Are you okay?"

"Why wouldn't I be?"

"Why don't you sit?" Mr. Heinz tugged on his tie. His collar was spotted with sweat.

"Ethan McCready was expelled this morning," Mr. Heinz said.

Jen's stomach shot up to her throat. *Some sophomore was going to shoot up the school. He was going to kill all the cheerleaders.*

She met Mr. Demarco's eyes. His usually crisp polo

was uneven, as if he'd gotten ready in a rush this morning. "You're not in trouble, Jen. Why don't you have a seat?"

Jen lowered herself into the empty chair next to Mr. Demarco's. She noticed he was holding something—a sheet of lined paper torn from a notebook. He handed it to her. "Have you seen this?"

She felt her eyes racing across the page. In Ethan's handwriting were the names of all the sophomore and junior cheerleaders: Juliana Ruiz, Susan Berry, Colleen Coughlin, Bethany Steiger. Stephanie Kazmark, Ariella Lopes, Chloe Munro.

All except hers.

"I'm not on here," she said, to herself more than to anyone else.

"That's what we wanted to talk about." Mr. Heinz's gaze flitted to her stepfather.

Tom held up a hand. "Jennifer, you don't have to say anything if you don't want to."

Jen looked down at the list. "I don't even know anything about this."

Mr. Demarco's voice was gentle, goading. "It's okay if you do. We just want to figure out what happened."

"Isn't it obvious what happened? Ethan wrote this, and for some reason he left me off. Or forgot me."

Mr. Demarco and Principal Heinz exchanged a look. Next to her, Jen noticed Tom's grip on the edge of the bookshelf tighten. "I think Jen has told us all there is to say."

"Are you and Ethan friendly?"

Jen glanced at Tom. "He lives in my neighborhood. We're not friends."

"Okay. Thank you, Jennifer." Principal Heinz rubbed his eyes.

Once they were in the hallway, Tom pulled Jen aside. "You know you can tell me the truth."

Jen blinked. Was he serious? "I already *did*."

Tom's pained smile made her heart shatter into a million pieces. "I know, kiddo," he said. "I'll walk you back to class."

Something was wrong. By lunch, Jen was positive that there was more to everyone's bizarre reaction in Principal Heinz's office than they were letting on.

She didn't think she could bear going to lunch; they would all be talking about Ethan and how he looked mad enough to kill them all after Mark Zhang had knocked his lunch tray out of his hands and ruined his sneakers. Bethany would be especially hysterical—she was the one who had joined in and thrown the quarters at Ethan.

But Colleen wasn't involved—she had laughed, sure, but Jen had sat there and done nothing. Why hadn't Ethan put her on the list?

Jen knew why, but thinking about it, and what people would say about her if they knew, sent spasms through her chest.

The bell for sixth period rang, and Jen was still at her locker, dodging glances from the people congregating in the hall outside the cafeteria. Stephanie Kazmark had called her mom to pick her up; someone in Jen's math class this morning swore he saw a police officer bring a bomb-sniffing dog to Ethan's locker that morning.

The air around her was charged; it was almost as if everyone was more *excited* by everything going on than they were scared.

She had to talk to Ethan. There had to be some way—

"Out of the hall," Mrs. Brown bellowed, sending a shot of panic through Jen. If she lingered too long, security would make her go to the cafeteria, where Bethany and Colleen and Mark were.

Band room. Jen took off for the auditorium, hurrying through the side door. Onstage, her band teacher, Mr. Garner, was conducting a lesson for the saxophone section. No one noticed Jen as she snuck up the side of the stage and went through the wings.

The door to Mr. Garner's room, which the wind ensemble was allowed to use for practice, was open. Jen shut herself inside, grateful all of the chairs were empty. She tucked herself into the corner and took out her phone. Would someone like Ethan, who wasn't swimming in friends, even have a Facebook page?

Ethan McCready *did* have a Facebook page. In the profile photo, his face was turned away from the camera, the hood of his sweatshirt pulled over his head, but she knew it was him. Her finger hovered over the Add Friend button; she definitely couldn't do that. People would see it, and they'd talk even more.

She swallowed and composed a private message to him.

Are you there?

The ticking in the clock overhead fell into step with the pulsing behind her eyes. A migraine coming on. She got them when she was stressed. When a (1) popped up over her inbox, the pounding ceased for a moment. Ethan had replied.

yeah.

Her heart was speeding; she wanted to ask him if he was okay, how much trouble he was in . . .

An angry voice popped up in her head. *Why would you do that? Why would you ask HIM if he's okay after what he did?*

Blood flowing to her face, she typed back:

Why did you do it?

I didn't mean it.

So then why did you do it?

It took Ethan a few minutes to come up with his response.

I don't know. I was just mad about what happened in the cafeteria the other day.

Jen drew her feet up on the chair, knees to her chest. She stared at her phone, at a loss for how to respond.

When she didn't write back, Ethan sent another message.

> I would never hurt anyone. I really
> need you to believe me.

Jen swallowed. Wrote back:

> Why do you care if I believe you?

> I thought you knew why.

The backs of her eyes pricked. She imagined the look that would be on Juliana's and Susan's faces—on all of the cheerleaders' faces—if they saw this conversation. If they saw *her* talking to Ethan McCready like he was a friend.

Another message from Ethan came through:

> Don't worry. I swore to them all
> that you had nothing to do with it.

Jen's veins turned to ice as she thought of how twitchy Mr. Demarco and Principal Heinz had been. And then that sad look in Tom's eyes, like he wasn't sure whether to believe her when she told him she wasn't involved.

Ethan leaving Jen off the list had a simple explanation: He liked her. He always had, she suspected, and the thought must have occurred to everyone. There had to be something else, some reason for them to suspect—

Jen's hand flew to her mouth. The note. She'd slipped the note into Ethan's locker on Friday morning . . . Ethan was expelled for the hit list this morning . . .

Someone saw her. They saw her slip the note in Ethan's locker—probably the same person who saw him scribbling a list of cheerleaders' names after the scene in the cafeteria.

Jen jumped to her feet. She had to go back to Principal Heinz's office, to tell him that they had it all wrong, that she hadn't done whatever they suspected. Adding names to Ethan's list, maybe? Fantasizing about revenge on her fellow cheerleaders for some unknown misdeed?

She waded through the chairs crowded into Mr. Garner's room, knocking some over on her way into the hall. Immediately, a security guard appeared in front of her.

"Where do you think you're going?"

Jen's body shut down. She couldn't form the words: *Principal Heinz. I have to talk to Heinz right now.*

The sound of a metal door slamming at the end of the hall drew Jen's attention. She turned. Locked eyes with Susan, who was putting her flute into her locker.

Jen's insides went cold. How could she have forgotten that Susan had confronted her the other day, when they were shopping for dresses? She'd seen Jen put the note in Ethan's locker. Did she seriously think it had something to do with Ethan's list?

Susan looked away from Jen and hurried off toward the band room.

161

Friday was class Spirit Night, but Jen had very little spirit to contribute. She hadn't spoken to Susan all week, even though no one could confirm that Susan was the one who told Principal Heinz about the hit list, about how Jen had slipped a piece of paper into Ethan McCready's locker.

The cheer squad bake sale table was smothered in brownies, bags of caramel popcorn, marshmallow fudge. All things the cheerleaders would never eat in front of Allie, who seemed to subsist on almonds and kale juice and five-dollar bottles of water from Whole Foods.

The irony of being assigned the bake sale table hadn't escaped the cheer girls. Jen watched Colleen Coughlin consider a rejected cupcake, its top caved in. Jen herself was nauseous from stolen licks of brownie batter.

The buzzer went off inside the gym, to a chorus of cheers and boos. The cheerleaders were taking turns manning the bake sale table. Jen's event, the relay race, was later. Inside the gym, whoever was emceeing announced that it was almost time for the male kickline performances.

Male kickline was always the highlight of class Spirit Night. Every year, a few girls from each class would choreograph routines for the guys in their grade to perform. Last year, the appointed freshman male kickline captain, Cassidy Burns, had chosen "Like a Virgin"; the boys had squeezed themselves into jean shorts and lacy fingerless gloves, and some had even drawn birthmarks on their cheeks with eyeliner. Principal Heinz's eyes almost popped out when they started rolling around on the floor, gyrating. Mrs. Coughlin wanted to cut them off mid-song. In the end, the guys were disqualified for being inappropriate and Cassidy was banned from choreographing any future class Spirit Night dances.

There was no question this year that the job would go to Juliana. She didn't even have to lobby for it; she raised her hand at the student council meeting and Mrs. Coughlin said the job was hers. Juliana Ruiz was a responsible, respectful girl. There would be no gyrating on Juliana's watch.

Jules had been bubbling over with excitement all week about class Spirit Night—every night the male kickline group met in her basement to practice their routine to "Barbie Girl." Jen had gone over to watch their final rehearsal, and she had to admit, the sophomores would be hard to beat.

Ethan McCready and his hit list were the furthest things from anyone's minds. Actual death was the only thing that could cast a cloud over class Spirit Night. Earlier in the week, Mrs. Coughlin wanted to cancel it, terrified that Ethan would show up and massacre everyone. She was always like that, working herself into a lather over something.

In the end, the administration had compromised on a police officer stationed outside the building. Mike Mejia was currently in the parking lot, having just bought a hunk of candy-corn fudge from the bake sale.

Bethany fanned herself with the paper listing the prices for the treats on the table. The gym was stifling, all those sweaty teenaged bodies bouncing off each other. The heat was making its way to where Jen and the other girls were sitting, just outside the gym.

Bethany swiveled in her chair and poked her head through the gym doors. "Where are those little bitches? I'm not missing the kickline."

Jen rolled her eyes. The freshman girls on the team had drawn the short straw, stuck manning the bake sale table while the upperclassmen watched the guys dance. "Do you have to call them that?"

Bethany snorted. "You want to sit here instead?"

"They'll come." Jen looked away, feeling Bethany's eyes on her still. "What?"

"What's going on with you and Susan?" she asked. Colleen set down the cupcake she'd been fondling, suddenly interested.

"Nothing," Jen said.

"You guys haven't talked all week," Colleen said.

"It's our business, okay?"

Bethany leveled with Jen. "You know she's just jealous of you, right?"

Bethany used shit talking as a form of currency; Jen knew Bethany only wanted her to say something nasty about Susan so she could trade it for something later. *You'll never guess what Jen said at Spirit Night.* Bethany even talked about Colleen, her best friend, constantly, telling everyone what a slut she was.

"Why would Suz be jealous of me?" Jen said. "She's pretty and she's smarter than I am."

"Because she has to work at it," Bethany said. "Does she even sleep?"

A girl bounded through the gym doors and plopped down at the table. Jen jolted, terrified it was Susan and that she'd heard everything. But it was just one of the freshmen; two more followed, ready to relieve Jen, Bethany, and Colleen of their shift at the table.

Jen scanned the bleachers, looking for someone to sit with. Susan was sitting in the sophomores section with the girls she played tennis with. She was looking around the gym, wearing neon pink—the sophomore class color for this year—looking a little twitchy. When her gaze landed on Jen, her lips pinched together and she looked to the girl next to her, suddenly very interested in their conversation.

Hit her. Jen cracked her knuckles, a little disturbed by the thought that had streaked through her head. She'd never hit anyone in her life, not even her little sister, who definitely deserved it. But the sight of Susan sitting there, acting like *Jen* had done something wrong—it was too much.

Jen stalked up the bleachers to where her other friends were sitting—a group of girls she'd also grown up with. Most were in her honors classes; the others had either gone to Jessie's Gym with her as kids or had been on her peewee soccer team.

She didn't even realize that she didn't see Juliana anywhere until the buzzer sounded and Mr. Heinz announced the freshman male kickline team. The crowd went nuts; Jen had to stand up with them to see the center of the gym, where the freshman boys were cartwheeling out.

When their routine was over, and Mr. Heinz shouted, "Let's make some noise for the sophomores," Jen scanned the gym for Juliana, finally finding her on the sidelines, cheering the sophomore guys on as they ran out to the center of the floor.

The guys all froze into different poses. "Barbie Girl" started blasting, and for those three minutes, Jen forgot Susan, forgot Ethan McCready, forgot how much everything sucked. Juliana had outdone herself. The guys were actually kind of good, and their strutting and preening had the crowd whooping and laughing.

Next to her, Christine Verni was giggling so uncontrollably she had to grab Jen's arm for support. Jen smiled, the first real one she'd had in ages, and cheered along, cupping her hands around her mouth and hollering out to her guy friends who were dancing.

And then it was over. Jen couldn't wait to pounce on Jules, to tell her what a fucking fantastic job she'd done. Jen got up from the bleachers and ran down to the floor. She scanned the crowd around her for Juliana's hot-pink T-shirt, but there was only a sea of red-clad junior girls.

When she was positive Juliana wasn't among them, Jen looked at the side door. It was swinging shut; Mr. Heinz and Mrs. Coughlin didn't seem to notice, distracted by the scene the junior kickline was now making in the center of the gym. The guys were dressed as firefighters, suspenders stretched over their bare chests, and Mrs. Coughlin's face was the same shade as their plastic costume hats.

"We specifically told you everyone had to be *clothed*," she was shouting at them as Jen snuck by, hurrying out the side door before anyone could notice and try to stop her.

The rear parking lot was full of cars, and empty except

for two girls hanging out by the soccer field, their backs to the fence as if they didn't want to be seen.

Even though she was hundreds of feet away and it was dark, Jen could see the neon pink of Juliana's T-shirt. A sharp, high-pitched laugh told Jen who Jules's companion was, even though she already knew.

Carly and Juliana didn't notice Jen at the curb; a couple of other kids were there also, waiting around for rides home. Kids with strict ten p.m. curfews. Jen kept her eye on Juliana and Carly and ducked behind an SUV about ten feet away from the fence.

"Your mom won't notice some are missing?" Juliana asked.

"No. Her doctor gives her, like, sixty a month," Carly said.

Juliana fell quiet for a moment. "Should I mix this with alcohol?"

"It's fine," Carly said. "I do it all the time, and that's like the weakest dose."

Jen was still processing what Carly had said when a black pickup truck pulled up to where the girls were standing. Jen craned her neck around the side of the SUV, but the tinted windows of the truck blocked Jen from getting a look at the driver.

"Took you long enough," a male voice from inside the truck said.

"Sorry. Precious Jules had to watch her boy ballerinas perform."

"Male kickline," Juliana corrected her. The driver roared with laughter; Carly joined in, and Juliana started to say something, but the door to the pickup truck slammed, cutting her off.

Pills. Jen took her hand off the SUV, worried she'd leave a streak of sweat on it. Pills: She *knew* it. Carly Amato was a druggie.

She wanted to shout out to Juliana, let her know she was watching. Maybe then Jules wouldn't get into that truck with God knows who, doing God knows what kind of pills. But her throat had locked up, and all she could do was watch her best friend she had left get into a truck so big it seemed to swallow her whole.

Chapter Eleven

Sunday morning, I head downstairs and through the garage. My old neighborhood is about five miles away, and the idea of being alone with my thoughts for however long it takes me to bike there is unbearable. I stick my earbuds in and pull up the last playlist I made and shuffle the songs.

The opening bars of the song about a blue-eyed boy and a brown-eyed girl. I'd made this playlist the night Brandon dropped me off. I yank the earbuds out, suddenly okay with silence. Toss my phone into the basket of my bike and hop on.

There's a chill in the air today, and the sky is pearly gray with low-hanging clouds.

I need to find out what happened to Ethan McCready after he got expelled. He knows where we live, and I want to even the score.

I pedal through town and back down familiar roads, until my old house comes up on the right, and my breath catches in my chest. The new owners have decorated the lawn with fake tombstones etched with names like BARRY'D ALIVE.

A grim reaper dangles from the porch overhang, its cloak rippling in the breeze. I think about knocking on the door. Anything for a glimpse inside.

Norwood Drive was known as the street of horrors after Juliana and Susan were killed here. But I couldn't see it that way—I wasn't home the night of the murders. I insisted on sleeping at Rachel's, away from Jen's strep throat. Even after my sister died, Norwood Drive didn't scare me.

Aside from the Cannings, who kept to themselves, we knew everyone on this street. Norwood Drive was its own little municipality; everyone had a role. Mr. Brenner, a widower who was about a thousand years old, walked the neighborhood every day, stooped over, arms held behind his back. If he stopped you to talk, you'd have to forget about your plans for the next hour. Mrs. Shaw, the neighborhood watch, who would pick up the phone to tell you that your garbage can had blown over from the wind—she saw it from the front window.

Susan lived three houses down from us, which meant we had little interaction with the Cannings. Their house was on the dead end. Jack Canning's mother had a stroke after her son was labeled a murderer, and went into a nursing home; the house foreclosed. A Bank Owned sign is still on the front lawn. Last year, Mr. Brenner died.

New families moved into the Brenners' and the Berrys' and our house. The only people left who might have known Ethan McCready are the Shaws, who were friendly with my family. If I show up at their doorstep, they'll make a phone call to my mom as soon as I leave. That can't happen. Tom can't know I came here to ask questions about Ethan McCready.

I climb back on my bike and make a right at the corner, heading for the next block over. A narrow wood clearing separates Spruce Street from Norwood Drive. My mother never let me play near the stream when I was younger. Before all the terrible things that happened on this block, the thing that scared her the most was one of us drowning in six inches of water.

At the moment, Spruce Street is livelier than Norwood Drive. Two kids about Petey's age are kicking a soccer ball around on the front yard of a two-story house. Across the street, a woman is raking leaves. She looks up, pauses when she sees me.

I glide to a stop at the foot of her driveway. Her house is familiar; I have a flash of trick-or-treating for the last time, in seventh grade. I got a pack of organic fruit gummies from this house. When I got home and showed my mother, she rolled her eyes, the same way she used to whenever I reminded her Rachel's mother didn't let her drink soda.

"Excuse me," I say to the woman. "Can I talk to you for a minute?"

She leans against the handle of her rake. "I've already heard about the good word of the Lord."

It takes me a beat to realize that she's joking. I return her smile. "I used to live around here."

The woman gives me a once-over, the skin on her forehead crinkling. "Thought you looked familiar."

I nod at the trash bag at her feet. "Do you want help?"

She doesn't answer. Just picks it up and hands me the

trash bag. "Hold that open for a sec."

"Did you live in that house on Norwood that sold this summer?" She dumps an armful of leaves into the bag, keeping an eye on me.

"Yeah."

She pauses, her businesslike expression softening a bit. She must know who I am, what happened in my house, but she doesn't bring it up and I'm thankful for it. "Where did your family move?"

"Waverly Estates," I say. *And I hate it.* The thought is automatic. I would rather still live here, because it's where we're supposed to be.

"So what brings you back?"

"I'm trying to find someone who used to live around here," I say.

The woman frowns. "Who? Not many people move away from this street."

"His name is Ethan McCready."

The woman pauses, hovering over the pile of leaves she'd been reaching for. "Why on earth is a girl like you looking for Ethan McCready?"

"I think he knew my sister," I say. "I wanted to ask him something."

"He lived over there." The woman points past the house where the kids are playing soccer, at the ranch-style at the dead end. "His mother was such a doll. It's terrible how quickly the disease took her."

"That's awful," I say. "I heard he didn't have a father either."

"Oh, he had one." There's scorn on the woman's face.

"Left Kathleen when she was pregnant with Ethan. They were never married."

"So where did he go after she died?" I say.

"One of her cousins took him in. Hate to say it, but it was a relief when he was gone. He really put everyone around here on edge."

"Because of why he got expelled?" I press.

"Well, that. And his walking the neighborhood at all hours." The woman picks up her rake. Leans on it, crossing one ankle over the other.

I don't know why, but the thought of Ethan McCready walking around with no place to go depresses me. "Does he still live with the cousin?"

The woman strips one of her gardening gloves off and wipes her forehead with the back of her hand. "He lasted a few weeks there." She points down the street. "He was friends with James Montick, the boy who lived on the corner. His mother caught Ethan sleeping in their basement shortly after that. Told him she'd call the cops. Poor kid. No one ever seemed to want him."

So what the hell happened to him?

"You haven't seen him since then?" I ask.

She shakes her head. "Beats me where he is now. Could be anywhere, I guess."

Something in me deflates. I didn't expect to waltz right into the neighborhood and learn that Ethan McCready never left his dead mother's house and find him sitting in front of his TV watching the afternoon news. And what would I do if I *had* found him here?

"Thank you." I hand the woman the garbage bag,

suddenly desperate to leave. "I didn't mean to take up so much of your time."

"Don't be silly." The woman lifts her free hand. Hesitates. She rests it on my arm and gives me a gentle squeeze. I think maybe she's going to say more, admit she knows who I am, but she turns back to her rake.

I get back on my bike. I pedal past the kids kicking around the soccer ball and keep going until I'm out of sight of the woman, slowing when I reach the house where she said Ethan McCready used to live.

I stop in front. It's small and looks well cared for. There aren't any Halloween decorations up, but a wooden heart hanging in the front door reads BLESS OUR HOME. To the left of the house is a small yard boxed off by a white fence. To the right there's a Dead End sign and a patch of woods.

I walk my bike down the path dividing the trees. When the creek comes into view, I pause, remembering Carly's words: *The two of them, like, went off into the woods together all the time.*

I picture Jen sitting on the rock jutting out of the creek, a book in her lap. She always had a book with her, was always coming out here to read. If I tried to tag along, she'd announce that she didn't want to hang out by the creek anyway.

Was she trying to get rid of me so she could meet Ethan in private? Had Susan seen them?

I hook right and head toward the edge of the woods. After a couple hundred feet, the trees thin out and my old backyard comes into view.

My toes curl in my shoes at the clear view of our

house. On the windowsill of the second-story corner room, someone has arranged a row of stuffed animals in a neat line and painted over the purple walls with dark blue. My old room.

I keep walking, staying close to the edge of the woods. Head all the way down to where I can get a look at the Berrys' old backyard. The renovators tore out the pool and installed a stone patio with a fire pit. Inside the house, at the sliding glass door leading onto the back deck, sits a white cat, its tail flicking back and forth like a metronome. Eyes locked on a squirrel balanced on the deck railing, grooming itself.

I picture Ethan standing where I am now. Prowling through the woods, doing whatever he did back here at all hours of the night. Did he watch Susan and Juliana in the house through the glass door that night? Was he waiting here on purpose ... waiting here, keeping an eye on the house of the girl who got him expelled?

Daphne's words return to me: *There weren't any signs of forced entry at the Berrys' house that night.*

Juliana wouldn't have let Ethan McCready in the front door, and it wasn't like the Berrys to leave the back door unlocked. If they'd been leaving Susan alone, they would have taken every precaution to make sure the house was secure.

I let myself imagine an alternate scenario. One where Ethan never went inside the house that night— one where he was standing right where I am, the whole time, watching a scene on the deck unfold.

Someone coming to the back door to meet Juliana.

Someone she or Susan had been expecting. Ethan would have seen Juliana with the person in the house.

A person who was definitely not Jack Canning.

I know it wasn't him. It had been Ethan all along. Not threatening Tom, but warning him. Ethan thought he saw the real killer that night.

I walk my bike out to the street and hop on. Pedal home as fast as my legs will allow me. I let myself through the garage, propping my bike against the wall next to Mom's car. I'll deal with putting it away properly later; right now I have to text Ethan McCready the message I composed in my head on the ride home.

> I know who you are, Ethan. What did you see that night from the woods?

His response comes right away, as if he were waiting for this moment, for me to put enough of the pieces together.

> This is a conversation I'm only willing to have in person.

176

Chapter Twelve

There's no school Thursday and Friday because of staff development. The holiday starts at sundown on Wednesday, so Coach has to cancel practice.

It's ten minutes to three. Ginny and I are in her mom's car, parked in the lot behind the Millerton Public Library. We sit in silence, watching a girl toss a trash bag into a dumpster with PROPERTY OF COOL BEANS COFFEE & TEA painted on the side.

"I don't think this is safe," Ginny says.

I know exactly what she thinks about meeting up with Ethan McCready, because she's mentioned it about a thousand times since I called her on Sunday to tell her everything I learned in my old neighborhood.

When I told her that he wanted to meet up this afternoon at Cool Beans Coffee & Tea, she was silent for a solid minute.

"I mean, he's obviously not . . . *well*," she'd said. "Saving that note from your sister all these years and keeping track of where you live?"

"He can't do anything to me in a public coffee shop," I said, determined. "And besides, I have to hear what he has to say."

Ginny insisted on coming. I didn't mention this to Ethan when I agreed to meet him. I want him to think I'm coming alone.

We climb out of the car. Ginny locks it and we head down the alleyway. Outside Cool Beans, two guys are standing inches apart, one with his back against the brick wall. Facing each other, hands intertwined.

I can't tear my eyes away from them, warmed by the intimacy of the scene. Two guys engaged in PDA is the type of thing that would raise eyebrows in Sunnybrook, where people still substitute the term *good old days* for *before those liberals took over*. I've heard that at the high school in Millerton, they were allowed to put on a production of *Rent*. At my school, a ninth-grade English teacher got fired for playing a DVD of *Romeo and Juliet* that showed an actor's naked butt.

"Oh, I knew this place sounded familiar," Ginny says as we approach the entrance to Cool Beans. A chalkboard sign out front advertises bubble tea and free Wi-Fi. "My mom works at the hospital up the road. She comes here for breakfast after her shift sometimes."

I pause outside the café, eyes locked on the front window. It's crowded, everyone at the table closest to the window on their laptops. "Can you go first?" I whisper to Ginny, suddenly nervous.

She opens the door and slips inside. I stay at her back, my heart straining in my chest. I can't stop seeing that phone number—*Ethan's* phone number—on my sister's call log from the morning she died.

I have to know why he was the last person she talked to.

Cool Beans is packed. There isn't a single free table in the whole place. I scan each of them, looking for Ethan. It's been five years, and I've only seen his yearbook photo; he could have changed his appearance.

"The barista," Ginny whispers. I look at the front counter; a guy with floppy blond hair is wiping down an espresso machine with a rag. My stomach squirms. When he turns and starts untying the apron around his waist, I see his face. It's slimmed down, making his jaw and nose more striking. His skin, spotted with blemishes in his school photo, is clear save for some sandy stubble. It's him.

I'm ready to turn and run out, but Ethan is staring straight at me. He blinks, unmoving, almost as if he doesn't see Ginny at all. He sets his rag down and emerges from behind the counter, a mug of coffee in hand. He stops several feet away from me. When he speaks, I can barely hear him over the chatter in the coffee shop and the sound of the blender behind the counter.

"You came," he says. Ethan's gaze falls on Ginny. "Who are you?"

"My friend," I say, my voice froggy. I swallow, uncomfortable with Ethan hearing the fear in it. "Ginny."

"There's a free table in the back where we can talk," Ethan says.

Ginny and I glance at each other. Ethan rolls his eyes. They're as dark as they are in his yearbook portrait. "I'm not who you probably think I am, and even if I were, there are other people sitting back there to protect you."

179

The note of mocking in his voice ignites something in me. "Well, at least there's plenty of hot coffee around to throw in your face."

Ginny looks horrified. Ethan's mouth curves into a smile. "Follow me."

We head into the back room of the café, where all but one two-person table is occupied. He drags a chair over so all three of us can sit. It's loud in here; too loud for me to think, or even to be nervous anymore. I just want answers.

No one says anything while we settle into our seats. Ginny's looking at her lap, kneading the knuckle on her thumb.

"You guys want anything?" Ethan finally asks. "Tea? Cappuccino? Hot cocoa?" He glances at me. "To drink. Not to throw in my face."

"I'm good." I look at Ginny. She shakes her head.

Ethan shrugs. "Suit yourselves."

We sit in silence for a few more moments before Ethan says, "You look like you were expecting someone else."

He's right. I was expecting the sullen kid from his yearbook photo. The hunched-over creep who sat behind my sister in English.

Instead, Ethan McCready looks perfectly normal. Striking eyes, soft-looking surfer hair. If I didn't know who he was and I passed him on the street, I would think he was cute.

The thought triggers something violent in me; I suddenly want to reach across the table and choke him.

"Do you realize how creepy it is that you were in that house across the street from me?" I demand. "What the hell is wrong with you?"

Ethan taps his fingers, the nails bitten to stubs, on the handle of his mug. "Where do I start?"

"This isn't funny." I don't realize I'm raising my voice until the people sitting at the window look over at us. Next to me, Ginny has gone rigid.

"No, I don't think it's funny," Ethan says. Calmly. Evenly. "Did you come here for answers, or to yell at me?"

I lean back in my chair. Glance over at Ginny, who is studying her hands. Ethan interprets my silence as concession. "Now that that's settled, would you like to hear what I have to say?"

My face is hot with anger. But I nod.

"I'd like to start with the fact that your stepfather," Ethan says, "is the biggest asshole."

Even though I'm not sure I can trust Tom anymore, I want to get up and leave. Ethan must sense it because he holds up a hand. "I'm sorry. But it needed to be said."

"What did he ever do to you?" I demand.

"I'll get to that," Ethan says. "But I need you to know that even though you're going to be skeptical about what I tell you happened that night, I swear I'm telling the truth."

Dread pools in my stomach. Before I can speak, Ginny clears her throat. "You tried to tell Tom what you saw, didn't you?"

181

Ethan looks from me to Ginny. "Yes. What did you say your name was?"

"I didn't," Ginny says, at the same time as I blurt, "What did you see that night?"

Ethan cracks a knuckle. Holds my gaze. "I was in the woods behind the Berrys' house around ten. There was a dark pickup truck parked across the street, and two people were on the back deck. A girl was yelling at someone. I couldn't tell if it was a girl or a guy because they couldn't get a word in. Whoever it was, was tall and wearing a hoodie over their head."

"Which girl was yelling?" I ask. "Susan or Juliana?"

"I couldn't tell then. Now I know it was Juliana, since Susan was in the shower." Ethan takes a sip of his coffee. "It seemed like a bullshit argument, so I just kept walking."

"What do you mean bullshit?"

"Something like *Don't tell me to calm down*, or *I won't calm down*. I don't know," Ethan says. "It didn't sound serious, and the last thing I needed was for Susan Berry to find me creeping around outside her house and call the cops after I was expelled for a hit list with her name on it."

If she had, maybe the girls would still be alive. I swallow back the thought. "When did you tell Tom what you saw?"

"Not right away. At first the cops made it sound like they knew for sure that the neighbor did it, so I didn't really question anything." Ethan takes another sip of his coffee. "Then a few weeks later, when they released the details to the public, the police said they knew exactly what time Juliana died because of her Fitbit."

"And you realized it was around the time you saw the argument on the deck?"

"Bingo." Ethan plucks a packet of sugar from the holder on the table. Pinches it between two fingers and gives it a shake. "I went to the police department and asked to talk to an officer. They put me in a room with this younger cop. He started taking my statement, until your stepdad busted in. He was *pissed*."

"At what?" I ask.

"My being there? Me existing at all? I don't know. He made the other cop leave the room so he could grill the shit out of me. He fixated on the fact that I was outside Susan's house, like I went there wanting to kill her but Jack Canning beat me to it." Ethan grips the packet of sugar, the tips of his fingers turning pink. "Jen was dead by then. He started railing at me that he knew I called that morning. It was like he was trying to accuse me of convincing her to—" Ethan swallows. "He told me if I kept telling lies about the murders and caused the families more pain, he would beat me into a coma."

"That's not Tom," I say, hearing the rage bubbling in my voice. Having a shooting on his record would follow Tom for the rest of his career and haunt his conscience for the rest of his life. He wouldn't threaten to assault a potential witness to a crime. "Tom wouldn't say something like that to *anyone*."

Ethan opens his mouth. Shuts it. Tears open the sugar

183

packet and tips the contents into his coffee. "Grief makes people lose their shit."

"So you seriously want me to believe Tom interfered with an investigation and never told anyone what you saw?" I demand.

"I don't care what you believe." Ethan's gaze flicks down to the empty sugar packet. He folds it in half. "I assume you want to know why I told you not to trust anything Tom says. Now you have an answer."

Ethan sets his other hand on the table. He's holding a cigarette lighter. He drops it on the table. Gives it a spin. I think of all the boys in my classes. Their restless hands, always tapping, drumming pencils against the desk, taking apart pens and putting them back together like they're puzzles.

Another piece clicks into place in my brain.

I say: " 'I know it wasn't him. Connect the dots.' "

Ethan's fingers go still around his lighter. He looks up at me.

"I know it was you," I say. "You've been sending those letters to Tom."

Ethan traces the rim of his mug with a finger. "How do you know about them?"

"I saw them in his desk." My nerves are thrumming with anticipation. "You send him pictures of all the girls, and not just Juliana and Susan. You don't think the deaths are a coincidence."

Ethan meets my gaze. "And you do?"

I glance at Ginny. Her brow is furrowed, eyes focused on me. I've been waiting for a moment like this for years—waiting for someone to tell me Jen didn't *want* to die. Waiting for the missing piece to prove her death was wrapped up in the others and that she didn't kill herself out of survivor's guilt.

"I don't know," I say. I'm not sure which of them I'm speaking to. My stomach sinks when I see the look of pity on Ginny's face.

I turn my eyes to Ethan. "What do you mean by 'connect the dots'? What dots?"

"Well," he says, "you can start by tying the car crash to the murders."

The force in Ginny's voice startles me. "That's just ridiculous. How could the crash have anything to do with the murders? It was an accident."

Ethan blinks at her. "Do you want to hear this or not?"

I give Ginny a pleading look. She clamps her mouth shut, jaw moving as she chews the inside of her cheek.

Ethan's eyes flick from her to me. "Do you know the details of the crash?"

"Bethany was speeding, and she lost control of the car," I say.

"She was going seventy in a fifty zone," Ethan says. "So technically, she was speeding. But have you ever driven on Osprey Road?"

"Yes. People drive like lunatics on it."

"Exactly. So in relative terms, Bethany wasn't even going that fast." Ethan wraps his hands around his mug. "Cell phone records show she wasn't texting. Tox screen showed she hadn't been drinking or doing drugs."

Next to me, Ginny pipes up: "Still waiting for you to

explain what this has to do with the murders."

"Before the crash, Bethany and Colleen stopped at 7-Eleven," Ethan says. "A bunch of people saw two guys in a pickup truck catcall them in the parking lot. Bethany shouted something at them, and they shouted back, and when Bethany turned out of the lot, the truck followed them."

"Who are these people?" I ask. "The ones who saw what happened?"

"They were friends of mine," Ethan says. At the look on my face, he adds: "Despite what you might have heard, I *did* have friends."

I think of the type of guys who hang out in the 7-Eleven parking lot. Potheads. "So you think some mysterious truck ran Bethany off the road?"

"You make it sound like *I* came up with the idea," Ethan says. "You really have no idea what it was like in the months after everything happened, do you?"

I swallow. "What do you mean?"

"I'm not the only one who was skeptical about the accident and the murders," Ethan says. "You were probably too young to be paying attention, but plenty of people were talking. Five girls, who all knew each other, gone in a matter of a month? It was too wild to believe."

I *was* too young, maybe, but also consumed by grief. All I remember from those days is mourning Jen and worrying about Tom's job. Jen and Tom. Tom and Jen.

Two dots.

"Wouldn't there have been tire marks from the truck?" I say.

He cracks a knuckle. "No. It was raining."

"But tons of people in Sunnybrook drive pickup trucks," I say. "The odds are almost zero that it was the same truck that you saw outside the Berrys' house."

"And what are the odds that five girls from the same school, all friends, would die within a month of each other?" Ethan shoots back.

Ginny makes a small sound in her throat, as if reminding us she's still sitting here. "Sorry. But this sounds like a crackpot conspiracy theory."

"I get that it's hard to believe the crash wasn't an accident," Ethan says, staring back at Ginny. "But think about it this way—isn't it weird that Tom Carlino was the first on the scene in all three cases?"

A sharp pain hits me in the stomach. I have to force out the words: "Do you realize what you're accusing him of?"

"Of being involved in all five deaths and orchestrating a grand plot to cover it up?" Ethan shakes his head. "No, I don't really believe that's what happened."

"Then why send the letters?" I say. "Why taunt him when you have no idea what really happened or whether he's involved?"

Ethan stares at me for a moment. Something in his face softens; I wonder if he's seeing her. My sister. It makes my blood drain to my feet.

He shakes his head, as if he's composing himself. "The only thing I know for sure is that he's the best chance at finding the truth. He just has to want to."

I think of what Mrs. Ruiz said to me on the phone: *At*

some point, you have to choose to live in the light. Is that why Tom refuses to talk about the murders—because he can't bear fumbling around for answers in the dark?

Or is he just afraid of what he'll find in there?

Chapter Thirteen

When we're back in the car and my heartbeat slows down, I turn to Ginny. Her fingers are drumming the steering wheel.

"I don't trust him," Ginny says, letting her words hang in the air for a bit. "I don't think he's reliable. He was obsessed with your sister, and he obviously has a vendetta against your stepdad."

My throat goes tight. "What he said about Tom threatening him—I need you to know he would never do that."

"You don't have to convince me."

A funny feeling settles over me. She's never even met Tom. She must sense my confusion, because she takes a deep breath.

"When I was a kid, I was in the car with my dad one night. He'd been drinking, and your stepdad pulled him over." She picks at a raw cuticle, avoiding my eyes. "He drove us both to the station, and I was embarrassed and crying, like I'd done something wrong.

"My mom couldn't get someone to cover her at the hospital, so we had to wait at the station for a couple hours. Your stepdad . . . he let me hang out in his office.

He brought me some food from the vending machine and showed me all this stuff, like how he filed police reports." Ginny looks at me. "I didn't realize until my mom picked us up that Tom did that so I didn't have to sit in the lobby with people staring at me."

That sounds like the Tom I know. The man who's always nearby to put a calming hand on my mom's shoulder when she's going apeshit on my brother or me. The man I've always felt cared about me more than my own father, a virtual stranger who calls me on my birthday and Christmas for molasses-slow conversations of people who have nothing to say to each other.

"So I don't trust Ethan at all," Ginny says, interrupting my thoughts. "I think all that stuff about Tom not taking him seriously is a lie. He must have had a convincing reason not to believe Ethan."

My throat tightens. "The shooting . . . His job—"

Ginny cuts me off, shaking her head. "I don't think your stepdad is the type of person to let a killer walk free just to save his own job."

Her words have a calming effect on me. The debris clouding my thoughts starts to settle, and another possibility emerges, one where the police and Tom aren't hiding anything.

"Ethan didn't think to go to the police right away," I say. "If someone else saw or heard something that night, maybe they didn't think it was unusual. If that makes any sense."

"It does," Ginny says. "Smaller details could have been overlooked if they didn't fit the bigger picture. Someone

190

other than Ethan may have even seen the pickup truck and told the police."

A funny feeling washes over me. Nerves, maybe, but also a shot of clarity. "There's one way we can find out for sure what the neighbors saw."

Ginny stops tapping her fingers on the steering wheel. Raises her eyebrows.

"Witness statements," I say.

The house is empty when I get home a little after four. My mom won't be home until five, and I know Tom took half the day off to see Petey's soccer game.

Ginny and I are sitting at the kitchen island, a hunk of cheddar on the cheese board between us. Ginny arranges a slice of cheese neatly on a cracker from the box I dug out from the pantry, while I wolf mine down and slice another chunk for myself.

We spent the ride home brainstorming ways to get our hands on the witness statements from the night of the murders. My laptop is on the counter in front of us, next to the cheese board, a PDF about the Freedom of Information Act open on the screen.

Ginny reads off the page silently, lips moving. "It looks like civilians are allowed to request police records, though the police departments have to approve the release of information through FOIA, and the person requesting the information has to provide a compelling reason for needing it."

I deflate. " 'I need witness statements for a five-year-old

murder case because I think you screwed up the investigation' is bound to raise some red flags with whoever is in charge of records at the Sunnybrook PD."

A smile quivers on Ginny's lips. I slice her another piece of cheese, but she doesn't take it. "What about the reporter?" she asks. "The one who gave you some of those details, like Jack Canning getting arrested when he was younger?"

"I don't know. I assumed a cop told her about that," I say. "But I guess there's a chance she saw the record herself."

"It's worth trying," Ginny says, but I'm already unzipping my wristlet. The business card Daphne Furman gave me at Starbucks is wedged between my debit card and the inside of my wallet.

I tap her number into my phone, but hesitate with my finger over the call button. Daphne did say I could reach out at any time.

The line rings and rings, and I'm ready to end it when a harried voice answers. "Hello, this is Daphne."

"Hi. This is Monica."

"Monica?"

"Rayburn. We talked a couple weeks ago."

"Oh, of course. I'm sorry. I'm on a deadline and I can't remember what day it is. What's up?"

"I had some more questions about what we talked about." I hit the speaker button so Ginny can hear Daphne. "The stuff you told me about the crime scene— like the forced entry stuff—did you get that from the police report?"

"Not exactly," Daphne says. "I had a source in law enforcement who was willing to sneak me little bits and pieces."

"I figured." I pause. "Is there any way he can get you the witness statements from my neighbors?"

Daphne is silent for a moment. "After my story was published, the Sunnybrook Police Department realized someone was leaking from the database. My source got fired, and the police sealed the file."

"Wait. Your source was fired from Sunnybrook PD?" I know Daphne will never give me his or her name, but I could easily figure out who it is.

"No, he didn't work for Sunnybrook," Daphne says. "He worked at another department. There's a statewide database, so other departments can share information and work together."

"When you say the file is sealed, do you mean no one at all can get it?"

"I don't know. I'm assuming people who work in that department could access it, if they really wanted to."

"Okay. Thanks, Daphne. Sorry I wasted your time."

"No, no, not at all. I wish I could be of more help."

I pause. "Is there any way your source—"

"Oh, Monica, you know I can't give you his name."

My heart sinks, even though I knew what the answer would be. "Got it. Figured I'd try."

Daphne pauses. "He works as a private investigator now, though. If you ever need info on a specific person, he owes me a favor."

Ginny catches my gaze. Mouths, *Ethan?*

I cover the speaker with my finger. "I don't want to waste the favor digging stuff up on him. We might need a bigger favor down the line."

Ginny nods, and I remove my finger from the speaker. "Thanks, Daphne."

"No problem. Talk soon."

When I end the call, Ginny says, "That police database. How could we get on it?"

I pause with a hunk of cheese halfway to my mouth, taken aback. "I don't know."

"Everything would be on there," Ginny says quietly. "The witness statements, the report, the crime scene . . ."

She stops short of saying "photos." My stomach turns over. Below the kitchen island, Mango is scratching at my calf, his eyes on the block of cheese. I break off a crumb and feed it to him.

"Tom's ID card," I say. "He uses it to get on the database at home. There's a thing he sticks it in—some sort of reader."

Ginny nibbles the edge of her cracker, watching me over it.

"It's a lost cause, though," I say. "He keeps it in his wallet, and he never lets his wallet out of his sight. Even if I got it somehow, I wouldn't be able to access the database and replace his card without him noticing."

At my feet, Mango perks up. A car door slams, and he takes off, barking. I snap my laptop shut. Moments later, my mother calls out to me from the hallway. "Monica? Whose car is that?"

There's an edge to her voice, as if she's worried that

whoever inseminated me has come back for round two. She comes into the kitchen, several strands of hair falling out of her bun.

She stops short when she sees Ginny, who looks equally uncomfortable.

"This is my friend Ginny," I say. "She's on the dance team."

My mother does a little head tilt. "Hello, Ginny."

"Hi, Mrs. Rayburn."

"It's Carlino," my mother says, and even though her voice is gentle, Ginny's face turns a deep shade of red.

It hits me, why Ginny is so embarrassed; she told me my mother had given her a ride home from gymnastics once, when her father never showed up to get her. It looks like my mother doesn't even recognize her.

"I was going to order a pizza," Mom says. "You're welcome to stay, Ginny."

Ginny's eyes flit to me, as if she's asking if it's okay. I give her an encouraging smile, but she says, "I'm supposed to eat with my mom tonight. Thank you, though."

My mother moves along to her office and luckily Ginny misses the way my mother looks her up and down, the ghost of a frown on her face. I walk Ginny to the front door, Mango weaving between our legs, afraid we're going somewhere and leaving him behind. I can't stop thinking about Ginny's face when she talked about getting on the police database. The way she seemed to come alive at considering doing something so obviously illegal, when less than a month ago she was too scared to talk to me on the bus ride home.

"What is it?" Ginny asks. "You're looking at me weird."

"I don't know," I say. "You're good at this stuff. It's like you're secretly a badass."

She just shrugs. But as she waves goodbye and heads down the driveway, I catch her smile before she turns her back.

I watch her walk all the way to her mom's car, wondering what happened to the girl on the bus.

The long weekend is washed away by my teachers' revenge for the days off—five-page papers in both English and history, a take-home test for pre-calc, and several practice quizzes for chem, thanks to my deplorable average. We have a three-hour dance team practice on Saturday to make up for Wednesday, Thursday, and Friday, and Sunday is spent icing a pulled hamstring.

Monday morning, my mother comes into the kitchen while I'm eating breakfast. She watches me as she guides an earring into her ear. "Would you be able to stay at Rachel's or Alexa's Friday night?"

I let my spoon rest against the side of my yogurt container. "Why?"

"Tom and I are going to the PBA annual dinner and we won't be back until late. Your brother is staying with Grandma Carlino. I'm assuming you don't want to go with him."

Tom's mother is nice enough, and she always has her freezer stocked with our favorite ice creams—Rocky Road for me, Cookie Dough for Petey—but I'm too old to sleep on a pullout bed with my little brother while our parents are out partying until two in the morning.

"Can't I just stay here?" I ask. "I'm sixteen. I can handle it."

"You just told us a little while ago that you don't feel safe here alone."

"Fine," I say. "I'll talk to Rach."

"Thank you."

My mother is turning on her heel when I think of something. "Mom. Who's going to be at the station if everyone's going to the dinner?"

"Not everyone is going," she says, still battling with the stubborn earring. "Mike will be around if anything comes up."

I turn back to my yogurt. Use the head of my spoon to put pressure on a stray strawberry until I crush it, staining the surface of the yogurt red. When my mother leaves the room, I text Ginny.

> Have to talk to you. Lunch?

I have a yearbook meeting. Before practice?

> Sounds good.

I send the text off, throw out what's left of my yogurt, and finish getting ready for school.

It's evident during homeroom that homecoming fever is setting in. The game and parade are still more than two weeks away, but people are lobbying for homecoming court already. Campaigning was outright banned when I was a freshman, after a group of seniors on the guys' soccer team made a calendar out of seductive photos of themselves, and one fell right into the lap of Mrs. Zhang, the student council advisor.

Mrs. Barnes announces that student council is having an open meeting for anyone who wants to participate in class Spirit Night, and also, the library is reopened.

At lunch, Rachel is absent from the table. I slide onto the bench next to Alexa.

"Where's Rach?"

"Getting extra help," Alexa says, kneading a pouch of low-fat ranch to get the dregs onto her salad. "She has until Friday to drop pre-calc, and she's freaking out."

Behind us, there's a commotion. A pack of senior guys is horsing around. One of them drops a carton of punch; it forms a red river on the tile. Mrs. Brown shouts at them to clean it up or someone is getting sent to the ISS room.

Joe Gabriel bends down to mop up the fruit punch, but the guys are still hanging close by, sneaking glances at us.

I turn to Alexa. "Why are they hovering?"

"Because Jimmy wants to ask you to homecoming."

I'd completely forgotten that homecoming tickets are going on sale this week. In my periphery, I catch Jimmy Varney staring at me. He gives me a sheepish smile and holds up a hand.

I wave back. Jimmy is cute, and sweet. He's the type of guy who could blunt my sharp edges. But even when I was dating Matt, Alexa, Rach, and I went to the dance as each other's dates.

"I don't want to get involved with anyone right now," I say.

Alexa spears an anemic-looking tomato slice. "Babe, Matt is gone. A really cute guy is into you. Let yourself have fun."

I don't want to tell her that I haven't even thought about Matt in weeks. She'll pry, and there's no way in hell I'm telling her about Brandon. I hate feeling like I can't talk to Rach and Alexa, but there's not a single thing I could tell them about the last few weeks that wouldn't horrify them.

"Jimmy's signing up for male kickline," Alexa says, oblivious to the way I've become overly interested in my sandwich to avoid the looks from the guys. "So he's gonna be at the meeting today."

Shit. I'd completely forgotten about that part of Spirit Night. Last year, Alexa, Rach, and I picked the song "Save a Horse (Ride a Cowboy)" for our class's male kickline routine. The guys ad-libbed in the middle, unbuttoning their shirts and lassoing them around their heads, earning us a five-point deduction, but a raucous reception from the crowd. We came in second to the seniors.

"I don't think I can do it this year," I tell Alexa.

She stares at me like I've told her I have cancer. "Why?"

"I'm failing chem," I say. It's not completely the truth, but it may as well be—my average is hovering at a 70 right now. "I just don't have time, between homework and practice."

"You have time to hang out with Ginny Cordero," Alexa says, eyes on her packet of salad dressing.

"Ginny Cordero knew my sister. Sometimes I want to be around someone who will actually talk about her."

It might be the most honest thing I've said to Alexa or Rach in weeks.

As wounded as she still looks, Alexa doesn't press the issue. When the bell rings, I realize I've only taken a few bites of my sandwich. I miss Alexa and Rach, and I don't know how long I can keep this up, how long I can hide what's been going on.

All I can do is hope that the truth will come out, and that they'll forgive me when it does.

There's an assembly during last period on drunk driving. The juniors are filing into the auditorium, and I decide to break apart from my gym class and wait by the doors for Ginny.

She lifts a hand in a small wave when she sees me, and I nod to the topmost row in the stands by the lighting booth. Usually those seats fill up the quickest during assemblies, but today both the guys and the girls are scrambling for the front rows.

The reason is on the stage: Mike Mejia is setting up a PowerPoint presentation, along with an extremely pretty officer I've never seen before. Tom didn't say anything about Mike doing the assembly. It unsettles me a bit, having Mike close by, considering what I'm about to tell Ginny.

Ginny and I find two seats at the end of the highest row, skipping over one with particularly nasty-looking stains.

"My stepdad is going to a fund-raiser in Westchester Friday night," I tell her before I even say hi. "Most of the department is gonna be there too. Except Mike. That's Mike."

I point to the stage. Ginny's lips part, as if she's having trouble processing everything I just threw at her. But I want to tell her everything before the assembly starts and the teachers tell us to shut up.

"I've been thinking about it all day," I say. "If I can find a way to get the key to Tom's office, I can stop by and pretend I need to talk to Mike. I'll create some sort of diversion, and when he's distracted, I'll take his ID card from his reader and use it to get on the database on Tom's office computer at home."

"You mean steal the card? He'll know it was you. And what if the database keeps track of who logs in? Tom could see that Mike logged in on his home computer and—"

"Okay, okay, you're right," I say, deflating. "I got ahead of myself, I guess. Forget it."

"I didn't say it's not worth trying," Ginny says. "But you can't steal the card. You have to get him to leave the station somehow, like an emergency, and if we're lucky and he leaves his ID card in his computer, you can get on the database and email the files to yourself or something."

Onstage, Mike is speaking with the woman cop, arms crossed over his chest, ignoring the girls leaning against the orchestra pit preening to get his attention.

I turn back to Ginny. "But how do I get Mike to leave for long enough?"

"You mean we. How do *we* get him to leave."

The force in her voice jolts me, just like it did the other day in my kitchen. "Ginny. If I get caught, I'm screwed. There's no use screwing both of us."

"I'm not abandoning you now," she says. "This is too big to pull off alone."

I can't think around the swell of noise in the auditorium. I want to tell her of course I need her, but there's some sort of invisible force pulling me back. A conscience, I guess. "I can't ask you to do this."

"You're not asking. When have you ever asked me for help?" Ginny's cheeks are blooming pink. "I offered help. I *want* to help you."

The area behind my eyes gets tight. "Why, though? Why me? I'm not like Jen."

I stop short of saying *I'm not good like her.* I would sooner die than hear Ginny lie to my face and tell me I am like her, and I am good.

But Ginny doesn't lie. I know that much. She simply looks at me and says, "It's not really you I'm helping. Jen deserved better. All those girls did."

I don't know what to say; I glance down at the stage, where Mike is adjusting the microphone for the assembly. Behind him, the female officer is clicking through a PowerPoint of gruesome accident-scene photos, making sure the projector is in focus.

Mike taps the microphone, sending a shriek of feedback through the auditorium. It draws the entire room's attention to the stage. Principal Heinz steps around Mike to speak into the microphone. "Ladies and gents, quiet down! Officers Mejia and DiBiase were kind enough to give their time—"

He's drowned out by the swell of noise in the room. Mrs. Coughlin, who has stationed herself at the bottom of the upper level, sticks two fingers in her mouth and lets out a piercing whistle that shuts us all up.

"You will give these officers your complete attention," she says, before taking a seat.

Onstage, Mike clears his throat. I keep my eyes locked on him, my head swimming. While he's introducing Officer DiBiase, who elicits approving hoots from the guys in the room, I lean over and whisper in Ginny's ear, "How the hell are we going to get him out of that station for more than a few minutes?"

Ginny is staring at the PowerPoint on the screen, at the image of a mangled car. "Isn't it obvious?"

On Friday night, Petey and I pile into the back of Tom's car. He puts an arm around my mom's seat while he backs out of the driveway; she twists away from him, one hand patting her French twist self-consciously.

Tom's eyes meet mine in the mirror. "Whose house am I driving to? Thing One's or Thing Two's?"

"Neither," I say. "I'm staying with my friend Ginny."

"Ginny? Who's Ginny?" Tom turns to my mother.

"I met her the other day," Mom says. "She's on dance team with Monica. She seems like a sweet girl."

Petey opens his mouth, no doubt to chime in and tell Tom about our excursion to the library with Ginny, and I kick his ankle. "Make a right out of the driveway. She's number eighty-four."

"On this street?" Tom sounds surprised.

"I told Mom I could walk."

My mother is silent; I know she didn't trust me to go straight to Ginny's or even to go to Ginny's at all, but she won't dare say it in front of Tom.

Less than a minute later, Tom pulls over in front of Ginny's house. The sight of the car in the driveway makes me exhale. She's home from driving her mom to work, so my parents won't grill me about whether or not there's an adult home.

"Yup, see you tomorrow, bye." I'm stumbling out of the backseat when my mother says my name.

"Are you sure Ginny's mother is home?" she asks.

"Yeah, that's her car." I hike the strap of my dance bag up my shoulder. My mother chews the inside of her cheek. I know she wants to hassle me, get out of the car and ring the doorbell and see for herself, but Petey is shouting "It's six thirty-three and you told Grandma we'd be there at six-thirty!"

Mom sighs. "Please come home when you wake up tomorrow."

"Got it. Bye." I wave one last time before slamming the door. Tom pulls away and I walk up the driveway, heart battering against my ribs at the close call.

Ginny opens her front door before I can knock. A black and white cat at her feet takes one look at me and bolts down the hall.

"Hi." She ushers me into the kitchen off the hall-way, knocking into a table in the foyer in the process. A picture frame falls over; I reach to right it, but Ginny tells me not to worry about it—to just leave it. I realize she must have been at the window when we pulled up, waiting for me.

Ginny stops short and turns to me, as if she's forget-ting something. "Did you eat dinner? I could make some-thing. . . ."

"I think if I tried to eat something right now, I'd pro-jectile vomit."

She gives me a small smile. "Good, because I feel the same."

I use the bathroom off the kitchen—it's my third ner-vous pee break in the last hour. When I'm done, Ginny is sitting at her kitchen table. The cat climbs the back of her chair and leaps onto the table.

I keep my distance as I take a seat. "What's his name?"

"Panda," Ginny says. "She's a girl."

One side of her face is black, and I can see how she got her name. She sits up on the table and glares at me. Cats don't trust me. I honestly don't blame them.

"I hate using Mike like this," I tell Ginny. "I can't stop thinking about how he'll feel when you make the nine-one-one call."

"It'll be okay," she says. "There might be another officer on duty tonight, and we can't risk someone else other than Mike taking the call. He'll realize soon enough it was a false alarm."

She sounds so sure of herself, but my stomach is a pressure cooker of anxiety. And not just because the idea about putting in a fake 911 call about an intruder in Mike's yard nauseates me.

We've gone over the plan dozens of times this week, and I haven't been able to tell Ginny about the part of the plan that's really worrying me.

Panda nudges Ginny's arm. Ginny stands up and heads to the counter, where a bag of Friskies treats is waiting. Panda leaps onto the counter, beating Ginny to it.

While her back is turned, I take a deep breath. "I'm really nervous about something. Mike might get suspicious if I say I'm just there to say hi."

Ginny's turns to me, her forehead creased. "But that's why you're bringing him dinner."

"I know. But what if he's not on his computer? I need to get him onto the database Daphne was talking about. That eliminates the problem of him potentially not being logged in."

A sigh flutters through Ginny's lips. "I can't believe I didn't think of that."

My heart climbs into my throat as Ginny feeds Panda a treat. *Just say it.*

I swallow. "What if I told him you needed help finding your dad?"

"My dad?" Ginny goes quiet, the bag of treats in her hand. "I know where my dad is."

And this is why I knew I shouldn't have brought it up. The look on her face right now—I've never felt like a bigger piece of shit. "I'm sorry. I thought you said he left and you haven't spoken to him."

"He did. And I haven't." She's retreating into herself, a far-off look in her eyes.

"Look, forget it," I say. "I can come up with another excuse—"

"No," she says. She looks up at me, as if she's snapped out of a trance. "It's fine. You can ask him about my dad. It's not like Mike will know the difference."

She gives me a smile, as if to say, *Really, it's fine*, but when she turns around, I see it dissolve from her face.

By ten after seven, Ginny and I are in the 7-Eleven parking lot across from the police station, twenty feet away from the pay phone Ginny will use when I give her the go-ahead. There's a hefty McDonald's bag on my lap, warming my thighs.

"This could all go to shit very quickly," I say.

"It might." Ginny cracks her fingers at each joint, then

absentmindedly slips her thumbnail in her mouth. I swat her hand away.

"Sorry," I say. "But you have really nice fingers. You should let your nails grow."

Ginny stretches her fingers out in front of her and gives them a wiggle like she's never seen them before. " 'Really nice fingers'?"

"Okay. That was a little creepy."

Ginny breaks into a grin. There's a tiny chip in one of her eyeteeth that I never noticed before. "A *lot* creepy. Who says that?"

I smile in spite of myself, and then we're both laughing, and then a big guy steps out of the 7-Eleven, yelling at the woman trailing behind him. Ginny and I fall silent and I remember why we're here, what we came here to do, and I suddenly want to puke.

"Hey," she says softly. "You don't have to do this."

"It's the only idea I have left."

Ginny nods. "If you change your mind—or if something starts to go wrong—text me a code word or something."

"Like a safe word?"

Ginny's upper lip quivers with laughter. "Yes. Sort of."

I laugh, because I don't know what else to do, and it feels good. "What should it be?"

We kick around a bunch of phrases straight out of an erotica novel before remembering how serious this is and settle on *stop*.

My fingers tremble around the seat belt buckle. As I reach for the door handle, Ginny says my name.

"You've got this," she says. "I have faith in you."

At least someone does. I give her a nod and head through the double doors into the police station.

I've never seen the older woman behind the front desk before, but she knows who I am. "Officer Carlino's gone for the night, hon. PBA dinner."

"Oh, I know. I wanted to say hi to Uncle Mike." I have never once called Mike "uncle." But this woman doesn't know that. I hold up the McDonald's bag and flash an innocent smile. "I brought him dinner."

"How sweet of you," the woman says. "I think he was just about to take his break. You know where his office is?"

"Down the hall and to the left." I smile at the woman again and she grins back, nodding for me to walk on back.

This is going to blow up in my face.

I drop my shoulders, trying to look relaxed and not like I'm about to commit a felony as I push open the counter gate and make my way down the hall. In one of the cubicles in the larger squad room off the main entrance, the officer from the assembly—Officer DiBiase—is drinking a Big Gulp and clicking around her computer. She doesn't notice me.

Shit, shit. I should have known Mike wouldn't be the only officer on duty tonight. I slink past the main squad room down the hall, texting Ginny: *The woman is here too!*

She immediately responds: *Don't panic. Remember the 911 call.*

I inhale. Mike's office door is open. I rap on the frame and wait in the doorway.

Mike looks up from his computer and beams, happy to see me. "Hey, kid."

"Hi. I brought this for you." I set the McDonald's bag on his desk.

Mike's eyes light up as he rifles through the bag. "What'd I do to deserve being spoiled like this?"

"Nothing," I say. I could die from the guilt right now. "I heard you were alone, so I figured you might not get a dinner break."

Mike's eyebrows lift. "You need a favor, don't you?"

I feel my cheeks go pink. "Just a small one."

"I'm a little insulted you felt like you had to bribe me," Mike says, but he's already tearing into the Big Mac. He swallows, a string of lettuce clinging to his lower lip.

"Well." I sit in the chair on the other side of his desk and balance my phone on my knee while Mike is wiping his mouth. "It's the kind of thing I feel uncomfortable asking Tom for."

"In other words, you don't want him to know about this."

I shift in my seat. Mike sets his burger down. "You in trouble or something?"

"No, nothing like that. My friend needs help looking for her dad. He left five years ago and she hasn't heard from him."

Mike steeples his fingers under his chin. Nods.

"And it's just that . . . Tom doesn't know I'm friends with this girl. Her dad had a bunch of DUIs," I say. "I don't want him judging her or anything."

Mike lifts the bun from his Big Mac. Examines the patty. "You remembered the extra pickles."

210

"Of course. So do you think you can help?"

Mike looks away from me. Wiggles his mouse, springing his computer monitor to life. "I don't see you. You were never here."

I exhale and stare at the computer screen as Mike clicks an icon on his desktop. His wallpaper is a picture of him with his wife, Anna, and his stepdaughter, Danielle. Cheeks mashed together, pumpkins in their arms. I think of Mike's little family at home, his pregnant wife giving Danielle a bath.

My palm goes sweaty over my phone, imagining sending the text to Ginny. *Stop.* One word could shut this down.

Mike will be terrified on the drive to his house. It will be the longest drive of his life, worrying about the safety of his family.

But it will only last for ten, fifteen minutes tops. And now that I'm here, I only have two choices: try to get into that file or abandon the plan completely.

I take my hand off my phone.

"Okay. What's your friend's dad's name?" Mike asks. On the screen, he's pulled up the database I saw a few weeks ago on Tom's computer. I look at his computer tower; an ID card with Mike's photo is resting inside the same card reader Tom has at home.

I have to swallow to clear the sound of blood pounding in my ears. "Phil Cordero. How are you looking him up?"

"If he was arrested, like you said, he'd be in the state database. If I can pull a license plate or something, it'll be easier to track him down."

Now that he's on the database, I need to pull the trigger. I push away the thoughts of everything that could go wrong, like Mike taking his ID card out of the reader before he leaves or him insisting I leave his office with him—

I text Ginny. *Do it. Go.*

My ears ring as Mike scrolls through the hits the database gives him for Phil Cordero. "He used to live at 84 Pond Way?"

I nod. "Yeah. My friend and her mom still live there."

My pulse ticks steadily. Mike hums to himself, scrolling, scrolling.

And then the radio on his desk crackles.

"Dispatch, I need an officer on North Howell's Road. Woman walking her dog called in a suspicious person climbing a fence, possibly armed—"

Mike snatches the radio up. "What's the address of the house?"

"She thinks it was one fifty-six . . . she wasn't sure."

Mike shoots up from his chair. Wipes his hands down his face. My stomach sinks to my feet.

"Monica, I've got to go," he says, his face ashen. "I'm really sorry—that's my house."

My voice quavers as I stand. "I hope everything is okay."

When he turns and grabs his coat from the hook behind his desk, I elbow the giant Diet Coke. It makes a slushing sound as it pours onto the tile, ice scattering everywhere. Mike jumps back to avoid the splash.

"Shit, I'm sorry. I'll clean that up," I say.

"Don't worry about it," Mike says, but before he can argue, tell me to leave it, he's out the door. Shouting for the woman behind the desk in the lobby to call his house, to tell his wife to lock the doors and shut the windows.

Then he's gone. The only sound in the office is my heartbeat. I can't remember a time when I felt more disgusted with myself. Not even after what happened with Brandon.

My phone vibrates with a text from Ginny. *Just saw him leave. The other cop went with him.*

I shove my phone in my pocket and sit in Mike's desk chair. A photocopy of Phillip Cordero's driver's license is up on the screen. I click back to the landing page and search for *Juliana Ruiz*.

RUIZ, JULIANA. HOMICIDE.
STATUS: UNSOLVED/INACTIVE

I can't do this. There are things in here that I won't be able to unsee. Pictures of the crime scene. Pictures of them.

But Ginny already made the call. Mike is on his way home, and even though he'll find out there's no intruder in his yard, he and his family will spend the night in fear. If I don't get the file, it'll all be for nothing.

I wipe my sweaty fingertips on my knees and open the file.

There are dozens of subfiles. Folders marked with jargon I don't understand. My heartbeat quickens; I can't possibly go through everything before Mike gets back, or before the woman at the desk realizes I'm still here and comes looking for me.

I scroll down, stopping when I see the label on one of the folders: *Written Affidavits*

There are several PDF files in the folder. Scanned written statements. My breath catches in my throat; I had no idea the police talked to so many people. I get a surge of righteous anger: Of course Daphne was wrong. They *did* do their jobs.

I hit control + P. A prompt tells me there are more than fifty pages in this file and asks if I'm sure I want to print. I glance at the door. Click *yes*.

While the printer in the corner spits out the pages, I comb through the statements on the screen. In a woman's loopy scrawl, I spot the name *Jack Canning*. It's signed *Alice Berry*. By the time I reach the bottom of the PDF, the printer wheezes and goes quiet.

Footsteps in the hall. I click out of the database and leap out of Mike's chair. Grab a napkin from the McDonald's bag and dab at the Diet Coke dripping from the corner of his desk.

The receptionist pokes her head in, eyes wide. "Oh."

"I just wanted to clean this up." I angle myself so I'm blocking her view of the printer.

The woman waves a hand. "Don't worry about that. I'll get some paper towels from the bathroom."

When she ducks out of Mike's office, I grab the stack of papers resting on the printer tray. Shove them in my tote bag and slip into the hall. I hurry toward the lobby.

The security camera hanging over the door blinks red. I keep my eyes down and stumble out onto the street. Power-walk to the corner and lean against the telephone pole, my stomach pumping acid.

Ginny pulls up in her mother's car, her eyes white orbs in the night. I throw open the door and collapse into the front seat. "I got it."

She's silent as she pulls away. I watch the police station recede in the side mirror. When we're back on the highway, I force out the words "Pull over."

Ginny puts her blinker on. Drives onto the shoulder. I stumble out of the still-rolling car and retch, arms wrapped around my stomach.

Nothing comes up. A cold sweat has sprung out over my body. I shut my eyes, letting the thrumming in my ears drown out the sound of the cars roaring past us.

I'm sitting at Ginny's kitchen table, face buried in my hands. I look up and move them when Ginny taps my shoulder. She sets a mug of hot water in front of me.

"I don't know if you want one or two." She shows me a handful of hot chocolate packets. "I always use two," she adds.

I take two packets from Ginny. "I thought I was the only one who did that."

She smiles and slides into the chair across from me. Wraps her hands around her mug, her smile slowly fading. "I gave the nine-one-one operator a fake name and number."

215

"And you're sure no one saw you by the pay phone?"

She's probably so sick of me asking that, but she just nods. "Positive." Ginny eyes me. "Are you okay?"

I take a sip from my mug. Lick a spot of grainy, sweet powdered chocolate from my lip. What we just did to Mike—to his family—is so not okay.

The thump of something landing on the table jolts both of us. Panda winds around the napkin holder. Cranes her neck, sniffing at Ginny's hot chocolate. Ginny and I look at each other and exchange a nervous laugh.

My gaze falls to the stack of papers resting between us. Ginny's follows; the cat sits back on her haunches, tail thwacking against the table. She's looking right at me, beady eyes seeming to say *Well, what are you waiting for?*

I divide the stack in two and push the bottom half toward Ginny. While she examines the size of the stack, I dig a pen out of my tote bag and flip over the cover sheet on the first statement in front of me. Scrawl *Timeline* at the top of the page.

The first page is filled with shaky, slanted writing. Practically unreadable. I skim to the bottom first and see it's signed by Mr. Joseph Brenner—he lived across the street from the Berrys. I flip the page and reveal the next one in the stack; mercifully, someone has typed up Mr. Brenner's statement.

. . . while I was putting out the recycling around 9:45, and noticed a pickup truck parked on the street next door, diagonally from the Berrys' house. A petite, dark-haired girl got out of the vehicle and crossed the street. I waved to her as she headed up the Berrys' driveway, but she appeared not to see me. The pickup truck remained parked next door, the engine on. I went inside and made a cup of tea and straightened up the kitchen. Before I went to bed I looked out the window and noticed the pickup truck was gone.

I blurt: "Someone else saw the pickup truck."

Ginny's head snaps up.

I hold up the paper, a tremor of excitement moving through my arm. "This man—Mr. Brenner—I knew him. He lived down the street from us, across from Susan. He used to give out pennies on Halloween." I scan the statement again. "Have you seen anything about when Juliana and Susan got home from float building?"

Ginny's brow creases. She flips through the pages she's already gone over. Pauses. "This one is from Juliana's dad. He said he picked them up a little after nine and left them at the Berrys' around nine-twenty."

I look at Mr. Brenner's words again. *Petite, dark-haired girl.* It had to have been Juliana. But if Mr. Ruiz dropped the girls off at 9:20, what was Juliana doing getting out of a pickup truck at a quarter to ten? "This can't be right. Mr. Brenner said he saw someone dropping Juliana off around nine-forty-five."

Ginny pushes the paper toward me. "Look. Juliana's dad even said he walked them to the door and asked if they were sure they didn't want to stay with the Ruizes,

217

but Susan said she couldn't leave her dog alone all night."

She's right. Mr. Ruiz said float building ended at nine, and he'd left the girls inside the house no later than nine-twenty.

If Mr. Brenner was mistaken, and it wasn't Juliana he saw getting out of the truck and going into Susan's house . . . it means there was a third girl there that night.

A girl who left alive.

But if it was Juliana . . . "She left Susan's to meet someone," I say. "Whoever was parked by Mr. Brenner's—she probably met him inside his pickup truck."

"He says he saw this happen at nine-forty-five?" Ginny pauses. "Ethan said he saw the argument on the deck around ten."

I take a sip of my long-cooled hot chocolate. "So whoever Juliana was meeting followed her to the house after Mr. Brenner went back inside."

A chill crawls up my back. *He waited. He waited until no one would see him.*

But someone did see him: Ethan.

Ginny says what I've been thinking: "Why wouldn't the police follow up on Mr. Brenner's statement?"

The clock on the stove says it's after ten. We've been at the kitchen table for almost two hours. "He was really old—like ninetysomething, I think. Maybe they thought he was confused about what he saw." I rub my eyes. "Or maybe they did follow up and it turned out to be nothing."

I sit back in my chair, nausea ripping through me. "What if there's nothing here? I could have gotten us both in serious trouble for nothing." I can't even entertain the possibility that we didn't actually get away with it and that Mike will figure out what I did. "I'm sorry," I say to Ginny. "I almost ruined everything."

Ginny taps the handle of her mug. There's a dried streak of blood on her thumbnail where her cuticle meets the skin. "Monica? Can we please focus?"

I nod, my throat tight. We go back to reading, my eyes getting progressively heavier. Around midnight, I look up and find Ginny out cold, using her stack of witness statements as a pillow.

I reach over and poke her arm with my pen. She stirs and blinks at me.

"I think it's time to pack it in," I say. "I haven't found anything useful anyway."

Ginny yawns. "Me neither."

We clean up the piles of paper and stuff them into a spare folder Ginny finds in a kitchen drawer, and I put the whole thing in my overnight bag. I eye the pajamas at the top of the bag.

Ginny spies them and says around another yawn, "My bedroom is upstairs."

I follow her up the stairs, making a pit stop in the bathroom across the hall to brush my teeth and change.

In Ginny's room, a twin bed is pushed against the wall. Christmas lights are strung from corner to corner on the ceiling; between each bulb, a photo hangs from a clothespin. I spot a picture of a group of girls in gymnastics

219

leotards. Next to it, an action shot of Ginny standing on the bottom of the uneven bars, arms over her head, reaching for the top bar.

I stop staring, aware that Ginny is watching me from her closet.

"Do you miss it?" I ask.

She shrugs. "Sometimes I do. Mostly it reminds me of when things were bad."

I swallow, thinking of her reaction to my bringing up her father. Ginny turns back to the closet. Emerges holding a fleece blanket and lays it over her rug. She sits on it, cross-legged, and fluffs the pillow waiting on the floor next to her.

"I'll sleep on the floor," I say.

"It's okay."

"No, seriously. I'm not kicking you out of your bed." I plop down on the blanket next to her.

She sighs. "Well, we're not both sleeping down here. We can fit on the bed, if we lie head to toe."

"Okay. That's a decent compromise."

I climb onto the bed first, getting as close to Ginny's wall as possible to make room for her. She lies down and adjusts, her socked feet inches from me, and reaches to flip off the light on the wall over the foot of her bed. It should feel weird, sharing a bed with someone I barely know, but it doesn't.

"Can I ask you something?" I say, breaking the silence.

Ginny shifts on her pillow. "Mmm-hmm."

"Have you ever done anything you feel like you'll never be able to forgive yourself for?"

Ginny goes still. "You mean like what we did tonight?"

"I don't know." I think of Brandon's lips on my throat. The look on my mother's face when my doctor brought her into the exam room. How she asked what I wanted to do. My answer was reflexive; I'd given more deliberation to haircuts.

I swallow. "Do you think doing something shitty is less shitty if you really believe you had no other choice?"

The whistle of the wind in the trees outside Ginny's window fills the silence in the room.

"Yeah," she says after a beat. It feels like she wants to say more, but I sense her rolling over from her back to her side and I leave it.

When my eyes flicker open a few hours later, my mouth parched from the hot chocolate, I turn over, not sure how I'll be able to climb out of bed to find a glass of water without disturbing Ginny. But the space where she fell asleep is empty.

I pad out of the bedroom and into the hall. The door to the room across from Ginny's is open, the sliver of moon-light coming through the window cast on the vacant bed. Her mom's room.

The floorboards groan under my feet as I creep toward the end of the hall. I try to make myself weigh nothing as I take baby steps down the stairs. I'm halfway to the bottom when I see a silhouette in the living room's bay window.

Ginny is sitting on the window seat, angled away from me. Knees pulled up to her chest, arms hugging them as close to her as possible. For some reason, the sight of her sitting there, staring out at the street, her pale skin almost ghastly under the light of the moon, makes me feel like I've walked in on someone naked.

I head back up the stairs and down the hall to Ginny's bedroom. I've forgotten why I got up in the first place.

Chapter Fourteen

I wake up alone in the bed again. My phone says it's twenty after seven; Ginny's mom's shift at the hospital ends in ten minutes. Ginny would have left to pick her up not too long ago.

I undo my bun and rake my fingers through my hair. My mom said to come straight home when I woke up, and I don't want to give her reasonable cause to doubt that I was at Ginny's all night. Tom might be the cop, but my mother is the one who will interrogate me until my story falls apart.

I stuff my clothes into my overnight bag and head downstairs. A Post-it is stuck to the front doorknob. *You don't have to lock it.* I've never seen Ginny's handwriting before; her small print is neat and unassuming.

My mother is Windexing the hell out of the kitchen countertops when I let myself in at home, which means she drank too much last night. She only gets like this when she's hungover—someone comes to clean our house twice a month.

This morning, she even has rubber gloves on. I plunk my dance bag onto the kitchen island to announce my presence and she spins around. Her face falls when she sees me, like maybe she was expecting someone better.

"How was the dinner?" I ask brightly.

"Painful." She sets the Windex on the counter. "We had to sit next to Heidi Coughlin."

"Mrs. Coughlin?" That woman is like a gnat; I cannot get away from her. "Why was she at a PBA dinner?"

"Her father was killed in the line of duty in the city years ago. She goes every year in his memory."

I keep my eyes on the fruit bowl on the kitchen island. Select the least-bruised banana and begin unpeeling it. Mom never could stand Colleen's mother. She and my sister would cringe every time Mrs. Coughlin's name popped up on the caller ID at home. *I think all of the cheer moms should get warm-up jackets to match the girls'! What are you bringing to the potluck, Mrs. Carlino? All the other mothers have signed up for something!*

The force of my mother's stare is so intense I can't ignore it any longer. I look up. She's watching me, in that frightening way where I can't tell what I've done to piss her off.

"She said she asked you to help plan a memorial ceremony, but she never heard from you."

Of course Mrs. Coughlin said something. She was always a meddling pain in the ass. "She didn't ask me herself. Mr. Demarco did."

Mom's eyes flash. "I wanted to tell her that my daughter would never be so inconsiderate. Should I have?"

"I'm sorry. If you want me to, I'll tell her on Monday that I'll help."

"You can do whatever you want, Monica," she says, like she couldn't care less. I'd almost prefer it if she'd yelled at me.

She goes back to her Windexing, and I feel like I should say I'm sorry again. But I can't bring myself to do it. It never makes a difference anyway.

I'm tired enough from a crappy night's sleep in someone else's bed that I think I can nap, even though my body is still racing from last night. I wake up around ten to my phone ringing. The sight of Mike Mejia's name on the screen plunges me into a panic.

Shit shit shit he knows. I consider letting it go to voice mail, but I know it'll be worse if I do. He'll just call Tom if I don't answer. Maybe I can talk him into not telling him at all. I inhale. Answer.

"Hi," I warble.

"Hey, kid. I'm sorry for running out on you last night."

I exhale so loudly I'm sure he can hear me. "Don't be. Is everything okay?"

"Yeah, yeah. False alarm. Some hysterical-sounding woman thought she saw a burglar. Anyway, everything's fine."

My nerves cool a bit, and I even let myself feel amused at his description of Ginny. "That's good to hear."

"So I ran a background check on your friend's dad," Mike says. "I don't know how much she told you, but I found some heavy stuff."

I sit up straight in my bed. I didn't think Mike would actually look up Ginny's dad. "Oh. Well, she said something about Tom pulling him over for drinking."

A light thump, and static, as if Mike is tapping his fingers against his cell phone. "Maybe she should tell you about the other thing."

Ginny must have known what Mike would dig up on her father when she agreed to use him as a ruse. She had to figure Mike might tell me, and some part of her was okay with it.

"I don't think she wants to see him again or anything," I say. "She just wants to know where he is."

"Well, it looks like the registration on his truck expired. The only address he has on record is his house here in Sunnybrook."

"What does that mean?"

"It means he could be anywhere, pretty much. Must be staying out of trouble, though. He hasn't even gotten a parking ticket in five years."

"Five years?" Ginny hadn't said her dad left the year my sister and the other girls died.

"Yep. Looks like he skipped town before a scheduled court appearance. He never showed."

"When was his court date?" I ask.

"Gimme a sec." The sound of keys clacking on Mike's end mimics my heartbeat. "October thirtieth."

Three days after Juliana and Susan were murdered. I have to sit. "What was the court appearance for?"

"Something he probably would have done some time for. I don't feel right telling you more than that, Monica."

Mike sighs. "Bottom line is, this guy disappeared. And it was probably a blessing in disguise for your friend."

But she says she knows where he is. Either Ginny lied, or she knows where her dad is holed up and she's protecting him.

"Well, I've got to get back to work. I'm pulling a double while everyone sleeps off their PBA dinner hangovers," Mike says. "I'm sorry I couldn't help more."

"No. Thank you." My thoughts are blurring together—I don't want him to hang up. Not when something he said is needling me.

"Wait," I say. "You said Phil Cordero drove a truck. Do you know what type?"

"A 2005 GMC Sierra," Mike says. "Leased."

"Is that a pickup truck?"

"That it is," he confirms. "A crap one too."

"Thanks," I force out, a sick feeling gathering in my stomach.

"I can try to help her if your friend's serious about tracking him down," Mike says. "But it might be best if she doesn't pursue this. When a family member takes off . . . Well, if you look hard enough, you'll probably find something that makes you wish you hadn't."

I don't know what to say. Ginny told me she knew where her father was.

"Monica? You there?"

"Yeah. I've gotta go. Thank you, though."

"No problem. By the way, thanks for spilling a large Diet Coke in my office."

I force out a laugh to match his, and he ends the call.

I open my email and pull up the email chain with Daphne Furman. I open a new page.

Hey, Daphne,
    Do you think your private investigator friend might be able to look someone up for me? His name is Phil Cordero and he lived in Sunnybrook until five years ago.

My fingertips are humming; this is so wrong, doing this without Ginny knowing.

But she lied to me about knowing where her dad is. Either that, or she really does know where he is, and she's covering for him, even though he skipped out on his court appearance.

I close my eyes and comb through every interaction I've had with Ginny. Her words from the other day haunt me. *It's not really you I'm helping.*

What if she already suspected that Jack Canning didn't kill Susan and Juliana? What if she was helping me to clear up the doubt in her mind that her own father was involved, and in the process, found something she wished she hadn't?

I hit send, Mike's voice echoing in my head. *If you look hard enough, you'll probably find something that makes you wish you hadn't.*

Chapter Fifteen

We have another Saturday practice today. My mom drops me off at the school on her way to the playhouse for the two o'clock matinee of *The Importance of Being Earnest*. As she drives away from the curb, Ginny's mom pulls up. She gives Ginny a quick kiss on the cheek, and I'm struck by how young she looks.

Just from watching them for a few moments, you can see that there's no wall of tension between Ginny and her mom, like there is between me and mine. Everything about their interaction looks easy.

As Ginny gets out of the car, her mom catches me staring, and before she drives away, she waves at both of us, smiling like I'm an old friend, even though she has no idea who I am.

I smile back at Ginny's mom.

"Your mom's really pretty," I say, once Ginny has reached me.

"Most people assume she's my sister." Ginny hikes her messenger bag up her shoulder. "She was twenty-one when she had me."

I restrain myself from needling her for more information

about her family, about her dad. I look over at her as we head through the side gym door; Coach left it propped open for us. Ginny is looking down at her hands, rubbing at the scar on her knuckle.

Where did she get it? Who is she, really?

Who the hell am I, for doubting her just because her father drove a pickup truck?

The mood in the gym is somber. One of the sophomore girls stands in front of Coach on crutches. She can't even look at Coach as she chokes out the words: "I f-f-fell."

A sprained ankle, obtained when the boy giving her a piggyback at a party last night dropped her. A week sitting out of practice. A lifetime, in competition prep. Coach barely looks her.

My eyes connect with Rachel's; she's standing in the corner, looking white in the face. I make my way toward her; she grabs me by the arms and whispers, "Alexa texted me. She just fucking woke up."

Coach makes the rest of us pay for it. Fifty sit-ups and several laps around the gym. When Alexa rushes into the gym fifteen minutes later, everyone is shooting daggers at her. This is Coach's MO. Punish the group for the sins of the few. Make us turn on each other.

Coach tells us to take a five-minute break. Even Rachel refuses to look at Alexa as she heads off to fill her water bottle at the fountain in the hall. While Lex practically throws herself at Coach's feet, sputtering excuses, I look for Ginny.

She's sitting on the bleachers, downing Gatorade. I plop down next to her, aggravating a brutal stomach cramp. "Hey."

She swallows her gulp of Gatorade and wipes away the red it leaves on her upper lip. "Hey."

We're both watching Coach, standing by the speakers, arms crossed, surveying us like we're a bunch of particularly disappointing zoo animals. Alexa is on the bench below, lacing up her shoes, despondent. I didn't expect her conversation with Coach to be a very long one. Several feet away from Lex, the sophomore who hurt herself sits on the bleachers, her bandaged ankle propped up on the bench. Next to her, another sophomore is bent over, forearms resting on her knees, looking like she's dry heaving.

I turn to Ginny. "Coach is going to put us all in the grave before we even get to regionals."

She takes another sip of Gatorade. "She obviously does not understand the Geneva Conventions. We're not responsible for their crimes."

Ginny nods toward Alexa and the sophomore. Her deadpan elicits a nervous laugh from me. For some reason, my hands are trembling. I stick them under my thighs.

Ginny pauses, her Gatorade bottle inches from her mouth. "What is it? You're nervous."

Ginny told me I could ask Mike to look up her dad. But emailing Daphne about him crossed a line. I'm not sure she'll forgive me if I tell her.

I take a breath. Opt for the half-truth. "My stepdad's partner, Mike, called me this morning."

Ginny glances around. Lowers her voice: "Does he know what we—"

"No, nothing like that."

Ginny picks at the label of her Gatorade bottle. Waiting.

"He called me about your dad," I say. "He looked him up."

Her fingers go still. "What did he tell you?"

"Nothing." My heartbeat quickens. "He just said he ran his information and he couldn't find him."

Ginny's jaw goes rigid; I realize it sounds like I'm accusing her of lying.

Coach's voice fills the gym. "Two more minutes!"

I'm scrambling to rephrase what I said, when down the bleachers from us, Kelsey B lets her foot drop to the bench with a *thunk*. "It totally hasn't been five minutes yet."

I wince. Watch as Coach looks at Kelsey with an eerily calm face. "Ten more laps."

A groan ripples across the gym. Next to me, Ginny shows no indication she heard Coach. Her voice is barely above a whisper. "What else did Mike say about my dad?"

"Nothing," I say, a little too quickly.

The pickup truck. The date he left town. I swallow. I shouldn't have said anything at all, and I don't get the chance to explain myself. Ginny silently gets up from the bleachers and joins the girls who have started their second round of laps. She doesn't look at me again for the rest of practice.

It's raining again, and it doesn't stop until around ten p.m. I'm at my desk, watching the house across the street, even though I know Ethan won't be back.

My email thread with Daphne Furman is open on my laptop, my latest message to her unanswered.

The light from the streetlamp outside blurs behind the raindrops trailing down my window. *I don't trust him.* That's what Ginny said about Ethan, more than once. She sounded convinced he was lying about what he saw outside the Berrys' house.

Or she wanted to convince *me* that he was lying.

I return to the stack of files Ginny and I didn't make it through. Mr. Brenner couldn't describe the pickup truck, but there may have been someone else on the street who saw it and remembered the make and color.

I flip through the statements, skipping over the ones with familiar-looking handwriting. I pause at a page covered in nearly illegible script. Flip it over, in search of the accompanying typed version.

The statement is from Mrs. Diane Cullen. Address 54 Norwood Drive. I balk at the date on the page: April 19. Six months before the murders. The box labeled *Incident* contains two words: *neighbor complaint.*

The typed version of Diane Cullen's statement is only one paragraph:

```
On the evening of April 18, I came home
around 8:30 p.m. to find my back gate open.
Several of my flowers had been trampled,
as if someone had climbed over the fence
to enter the backyard. Nothing was sto-
len from my house but I believe the in-
truder was Mr. Jack Canning, who lives
```

at 61 Norwood Drive. Several others on my street have reported strange incidents, and we believe Mr. Canning to be behind them. In fact, his neighbors had to install a privacy fence due to Mr. Canning watching their daughter sunbathing by their pool.

I read the statement three times. The Berrys had a privacy fence around their backyard. The new owners tore it down when they redesigned the yard; I'd forgotten that detail while Ethan was telling Ginny and me what he saw from the woods that night.

But Ethan McCready couldn't have seen *anything* from the woods; he wouldn't have been able to see over the fence and into the backyard unless he was ten feet tall.

An uneasy feeling slithers into my stomach. Ethan's story about what he saw is bullshit, and the police would have known it. That's why they never processed his statement—not because of some conspiracy to keep Ethan quiet, but because he's a liar.

I inhale, trying to control my simmering anger. We stole those files because of what Ethan told us. Ginny didn't trust Ethan, and I didn't listen to her, and thanks to my impulsiveness, she's pissed off at me.

I have to find a way to apologize. For suggesting she's a liar, for what I implied about her dad, for almost getting us arrested for stealing evidence—all of it. I'll find a way to make it right.

After I have a few words with Ethan McCready.

Ethan is working a double shift Sunday and can't meet me until Monday night. I insist on Monday morning before school.

Sunday night I tell Rachel that I have to get to school earlier in the morning for extra help in chem, and I tell my mother that Rachel and I have to go to school early for extra help. When Mom heads into the shower around 6:15 that morning, I sneak into the garage and hop on my bike.

Osprey Lake is a mile from my house, and another half mile from the high school. Every morning there are joggers and dog walkers taking the path around the lake. A public place in broad daylight.

I got Ethan to agree to meet me by texting him that I found something weird in my sister's things, and I wanted to show it to him. I knew he would bite; Ethan McCready was obsessed with my sister. As much as it turns my stomach, dangling Jen in front of him is my best chance at getting the truth out of him.

I walk my bike to an empty bench below a sugar maple tree. The sky is shell pink over the lake. I barely slept, but my body is awake and thrumming. I grab the thermos of coffee out of my bike basket and wedge it between my knees as I dig my phone out of my backpack.

It's 6:35. I'm five minutes late, and Ethan still isn't here. The knot in my gut tightens.

Someone sits at the opposite end of the bench and I look up to see Ethan lower the hood of his sweatshirt.

He tugs his headphones out of his ears and rubs his eyes, which are dark-rimmed and pink.

For a moment, neither of us says anything. Then he yawns. Says, "Where's your friend?"

"She's not too happy with me at the moment."

"Bummer." Ethan stretches. I hear the joints in his neck crack. "She didn't seem enamored of me either. What did she call me? A crackpot conspiracy theorist?"

"Do you blame her?" I feel my pulse ticking. "You lied to our faces."

Ethan blinks at me. "About what my friends saw the night of the crash?"

"Not that," I say. "When you told us what you saw in the Berrys' backyard, I forgot about their fence. They put up a really tall one, because of Jack Canning."

Ethan doesn't say anything. Adrenaline racks my body, shortening my breath, making my fingers tremble. I hate how he's played me and how he's mysteriously lost the ability to speak now that I've confronted him. I'm not leaving here until I find out why he lied to me.

A maple leaf, scarlet and veiny, falls onto Ethan's knee. He brushes it away. His jaw is set, his face expressionless. A woman wrangling two large black Labs on leashes trots past us. The dogs stop to pee at the tree a couple of yards away from us. I resist the urge to scream at Ethan. "You didn't see anyone on Susan's back deck. You couldn't have seen them from the woods because no one could see *anything* over that fence."

When Ethan finally speaks, his voice is monotone. "I wasn't in the woods at all. I was leaving your house."

I swallow a bark of a laugh. "You were at *my* house."

"Jen snuck me in," Ethan says. "I left through her bedroom window. The one over your garage. I was on the roof when I saw what was going on in Susan's backyard."

"You were in Jen's room," I say slowly.

There isn't a trace of embarrassment on Ethan's face, but he starts bouncing his knee like he's nervous. "It wasn't like that. She was really sick. I just hung out with her until she fell asleep. I didn't want to wake her up to sneak me back out, so I went through the window. Messed up my leg on the drop from the garage roof."

I close my eyes. I'm back in Jen's room, peering out the window over the garage, trying to get a glimpse of her and Juliana, three houses down, sunning by Susan's pool. Anyone on the garage roof would have had a perfect view of the back deck.

"What color was her room?" I ask.

Ethan blinks at me. "What?"

"Jen's room. So I know you were really in there."

Ethan's knee stops jiggling. He looks out over the lake. "I don't remember the color on the walls. Her bedspread was light pink and puckered or pleated or whatever you call it. And she had pictures of her friends everywhere."

When I shut my eyes again, I can see it all. I remember the feel of that bedspread beneath my knees as I climbed behind my sister and braided her hair for Juliana's wake. Ethan's voice draws me back.

"So now you know why I fudged my statement a bit," he says. "If your stepdad found out I was on the roof outside Jen's room that night, I wouldn't have lived long

237

enough to tell the cops anything, because Tom would have ordered my execution."

"Yeah, but your statement was useless," I say. "The police knew it was impossible for you to have seen anything from the woods behind the Berrys' house. You may as well have not told them anything."

"At the time, lying felt like a better option than doing nothing."

When I don't respond, Ethan sighs. "I planned on telling you what really happened at the coffee shop. But when I saw you, I chickened out. I've never talked to anyone about Jen before."

I think of the note in Jen's handwriting. *I'm not okay.* Sadness needles me. I don't want to go to the place where I imagine what would have happened if Ethan *had* told someone about that note right away. "Why wouldn't you talk about her?"

"Who would believe me? Who would honestly believe that someone like Jen Rayburn and me—" Ethan closes his mouth. Rests a hand on his knee, his leg jiggling again. Jonesing for a cigarette, I realize. Tom did the same thing when he quit ten years ago.

My throat feels tight. "Someone like Jen and you what?"

Ethan shrugs. "I don't know. She was gone before I could find out."

All the way on the other side of the lake, I see the outline of a school bus wind around Osprey Road. I check my phone; it's ten to seven. I need to leave in a few minutes or I'll be late, but I want to keep sitting here, talking about my sister. I came here to find out why Ethan lied about what he saw that night, and now that I know he didn't, I'm right back where I started. Sifting through dozens of pieces that might not even belong to the same puzzle—the murders.

Ethan watches me. "What are you thinking?"

My thoughts are racing too quickly for me to fashion them into words. Ethan saw Juliana Ruiz arguing with the person who killed her, who may or may not have been the owner of the pickup truck Mr. Brenner saw. A mystery guy whose name never came up in the investigation—most likely because no one ever had a reason to suspect him. He could be anyone.

"Juliana Ruiz was on your list," I finally say.

Pink blooms in Ethan's cheeks. "Are we back here again? You think I killed them?"

"No, I don't, or I wouldn't be anywhere near you. But it sounds like Juliana was the real target that night, so I'm just trying to understand why someone would want to kill her."

"I don't know," Ethan says. "She was really popular. Everyone liked her."

"Everyone except you."

"I didn't *dis*like her. I don't think Juliana ever said one word to me," Ethan says. "I can't tell you why I put her on the list. I can't even tell you why I made that stupid list except for the fact that a bunch of cheerleaders and football players humiliated me one day and I made a mistake."

Ethan reaches into his pocket and pulls out his cigarette lighter. He flicks it, but doesn't motion to dig out a cigarette or whatever he smokes. After a beat, he says,

239

"Juliana seemed cool. It always looked like Jen preferred her to Susan."

"Did Jen ever say anything to you about them? Apparently Jen and Susan were fighting and it made things weird with Juliana and Jen."

Ethan sticks his lighter back in his pocket. "Jen didn't say anything specific. Just that she felt like she was losing her friends."

"Do you know who Juliana hung out with other than Jen and Susan?"

"I always saw her with the other cheerleaders. Even the older ones. I had gym at the same time as her, and she was always attached to this weird senior."

"Weird how?"

"I don't know. She was ditzy but always trying to seem tough. She was new."

"Carly Amato," I say.

"Yeah. That's her. You know her?"

"I talked to her a couple weeks ago," I say. "She told me she barely knew Juliana."

Ethan flicks his lighter again, eyes watching the flame dance in the breeze settling over us. "Well, that's bullshit. The two of them were always together."

I'm speechless. Ethan stares at me. "Does that change things?"

"It complicates things." My head is swirling. I want to explain, but I'm really going to be late to school. "I've got to go."

Ethan nods. He watches me sling my backpack over my shoulder. It looks like he wants to say something else.

I return his stare. "What?"

Ethan glances down at his lighter again. His voice sounds far off. "When I called her that morning—I asked if she was okay. She said she was, and I believed her."

I pause, the strap of my backpack sliding down my shoulder. Swallow. "You don't think she did it."

Ethan lifts his eyes to meet mine. "Do you?"

"I go back and forth," I say. "Sometimes I don't believe she would ever do that to us. Sometimes I think, maybe, if I had gone through what she did . . ."

"You wonder if you'd feel like you had any other choice."

I nod. Hearing him say it feels like a gut punch.

Ethan is still studying me as I hop on my bike. "Do you think it would be easier if you found out she was murdered?" he asks.

I think for a moment, the balls of my feet grazing the pavement below me.

"Only if I find who did it," I say, kicking up the stand on my bike and pedaling into the direction of the high school.

The school day doesn't start for another fifteen minutes and there aren't any buses here yet. I lock up my bike on the rack, my nostrils curling at the scent of weed clinging to the air. I can't imagine the stoners being at school this early, and I wonder if the rumors about Mr. Ward and the other English teachers blazing in the parking lot are true. Before I head inside, I pull up Carly Amato's Facebook page and send her a new message.

Hey . . . I was wondering if we could talk again. I have some questions about what you told me.

Ginny is waiting for me at my locker.

"I'm sorry," she says. "For Saturday."

She picks over her words carefully, as if she's not sure she's apologizing correctly. I'm pretty confident it's not something she has to do often.

"You didn't do anything wrong. I didn't listen to you."

"Well, I didn't have to freak out like I did." Ginny inhales and closes her eyes. Opens them. "My dad left us on October eighteenth. That was a week before the murders."

All the blood in my body drains to my toes. When I open my mouth to speak, Ginny holds up a hand. "It's okay. I know how it looks. The week he left, he beat up my mom, and she finally decided to press charges."

My chest constricts. "Ginny, that's horrible. I'm so sorry."

"I know. So I don't like talking about him."

I want to evaporate on the spot. Anything to get away from the sad look on her face. "I never actually thought—"

"It's really okay." She hikes her bag strap up her shoulder. "Let's forget about it?"

I nod. The knot that's been in my chest since Saturday has loosened a bit. "What do you have this period?"

"Earth science," she says. "You?"

"Chem. I'll walk with you."

242

We wend our way through the crowds outside the classrooms. When the clusters of people are behind us, I lower my voice so only Ginny can hear. "I have to tell you something."

"What is it?"

I glance down at my phone; Carly's page is still open. I refresh it, hoping she'll have responded to my message by the time the page loads.

"There's not enough time before the bell," I say to Ginny. "Can we talk somewhere at lunch?"

She nods. "Mrs. Goldberg is out today, but I have a key to her room. We can meet there. Monica? Did you hear me?"

I'm staring at the screen of my phone. The page has reloaded, but Carly Amato's profile has disappeared and been replaced by an error message.

"What's wrong?" Ginny asks.

I look up at her, feeling a little shell-shocked. "Carly Amato just blocked me."

Jennifer

Tom was always saying there were no such things as accidents. He would come home with stories about teenagers driving into signposts because they were texting, elderly people in Buicks putting their cars in drive instead of reverse and hitting every car in the parking lot.

"It's not an accident if it could have been avoided." Tom would share the stories over dinner, while he had a captive audience. He wanted Jen and Monica to know, he said, for when they started driving. He wanted them to understand that even the worst-case scenario could be avoided through skill and by paying attention.

Ever since Bethany Steiger drove into a tree, killing herself and Colleen, though, Tom hadn't said much at all.

No one could explain what had happened. Everyone who had ever been in the car with Bethany had said she was a good driver, and her phone records showed that she hadn't been texting Friday night.

That night, after her mother woke her to tell her about

the accident, Jen had waited up until Tom came home. He walked past the living room couch where she had curled up, listening to her mother on the phone in the kitchen. He walked right past Jen as if he didn't even see her.

She caught pieces of what he told her mother. *Worst I've ever seen. Couldn't even tell which girl was which. One of the paramedics puked everywhere.* She heard sobbing, but it was Tom.

That was Friday. It was Sunday evening now, and Jen was staring into her closet. The only black dress she owned was the one she'd worn to her cousin's wedding over the summer. Could she wear the same dress to both services? Would anyone notice?

Jen didn't know what the etiquette was because no one she had ever known had died. She considered it strange that in fifteen years, she hadn't experienced death. She'd almost started thinking that tragedy couldn't touch her. And then Bethany and Colleen happened.

Allie canceled cheer practice for the week and Bethany's memorial happened first.

Mr. Steiger was Jewish and Mrs. Steiger was Catholic, and Bethany had been raised with neither religion. Her family had chosen to have a memorial service at the funeral parlor instead of a traditional wake and funeral.

Since Petey and Monica had both gotten strep throat over the weekend, Mrs. Berry had called Jen's mother the night before, offering to drive Jen to Bethany's memorial service.

Jen couldn't bear the thought of telling her that she and Susan weren't speaking to each other, so she'd made an excuse about how she and Juliana had to do a project together; she'd take the bus home from school with Jules and get a ride to the service with Juliana and her neighbor, an older girl on the squad.

For her part, Jules played along, even though she made it clear how she felt about being in the middle of Susan and Jen's fight. They barely spoke on the bus ride to Juliana's house; the shock and horror at Bethany's and Colleen's deaths hung over them, but in a way, it felt like they were grieving Susan's absence too.

Now Jen sat on the edge of Juliana's bed, tugging on a pair of stockings her mother had bought at the drugstore that morning. Jules was cross-legged on the center of her bed, jewelry box in her lap, picking through its contents. Her big brown eyes were tinged with red. She had been crying a lot the last few days—much more than the other cheerleaders, even though Susan and Jen were closer to Colleen and Bethany than Jules was.

Juliana held up a pair of gold stud earrings in the shape of bows. "Is it inappropriate to wear jewelry to a wake?"

"No," Jen said. "It's not a wake anyway."

"I've never been to one of these things." Jules put the earrings back and looked at Jen. "I need you to do something for me tonight."

Something slithered in Jen's stomach. "What?"

"Will you talk to Suz? For me?"

Jen picked a pill of fuzz off her stockings. "I don't think tonight is the appropriate time."

"Why? All of this just proves life is short," Juliana said. "What if something happened to her while you guys are fighting? How would you feel?"

Juliana stopped pawing through her jewelry box, settling on a golden cross. She draped the chain around her neck. Fumbled a bit with the clasp before lifting her eyes to meet Jen's. "Help?"

Jen crawled over and fastened the chain behind Juliana's neck.

"You know it's all bullshit, right? The stuff about me and Ethan?"

Jules's shoulders tensed at his name. She was silent a few moments. Just as Jen was about to explode, Juliana spoke. "I know you'd never want to hurt any of us."

Jen's heart dropped. It wasn't good enough. "The other stuff, though. About me and him—it's not true."

Juliana shifted so she was facing Jen. "I know. But, like, you have to see it from Suz's point of view. Being on someone's hit list is pretty freaking scary, Jen."

"I know," Jen said, but of course she didn't. How would she? She wasn't on it. "It was still shitty she didn't ask me about what she saw at his locker before she went to Heinz."

Juliana's eyes moved to the cross at her throat. She fingered the chain. "What *did* you put in Ethan's locker?"

"Nothing." Jen flushed. "It was nothing. The issue is that she assumed the worst without even asking me."

"Maybe she felt like she couldn't ask you."

"Did she say that?"

Juliana wasn't looking at Jen. "I noticed it too. You're just not the same."

"The same as what?"

"I don't know how to describe it."

"Can you just try?" Jen asked.

247

"The old you would have told me the truth when I asked what you put in Ethan McCready's locker."

A knock at the door; Mrs. Ruiz popped her head in and asked if they were ready to go.

Jen didn't have to seek out Susan at the memorial service. Before it started, while Jen was waiting in her chair, Susan sat down next to her. Across the room, where Jules was speaking with Bethany's parents, Jen caught her sneaking a glance at them. She wondered if Juliana had spoken to Susan too.

"I don't like this," Susan said to Jen.

"Me neither."

Jen heard Susan suck in a breath. Then, gently, she rested her head on Jen's shoulder. Susan was rarely affectionate.

"I'm sorry," she said.

"Me too." A messy, mascara-stained tear dripped from Jen's face, onto the front of Susan's dress, but she didn't say anything, or seem to mind at all.

A week had passed since Colleen and Bethany's car accident, and Jen was noticing a shift in the atmosphere at school. Almost like the sky lightening after a storm. With each day since they started again, cheer practice became less serious. The girls began to laugh again, in fits and starts.

Allie had finally rearranged the pyramid to account for the void left by Bethany and Colleen.

It shouldn't be this easy, Jen thought. *Grief isn't supposed to be easy.*

She knew it was different for Mrs. Coughlin, who was rumored to have taken the rest of the year off, and for Mr. and Mrs. Steiger, who were talking about selling their house and leaving Sunnybrook. Jen couldn't fathom how the holes in their lives could be repaired by shifting, re-arranging.

Even her best friends seemed to have moved on from the accident. Susan was back to chewing the erasers off all her pencils in anticipation of getting her PSAT scores.

Thursday was the last practice before the game. Friday night was dedicated to the pageantry of the coming weekend—the float building, the announcement of the homecoming court.

When Allie released them for the afternoon, Jen plopped onto the bleachers with Juliana and Susan. The *rrrip* of Velcro as Susan removed her knee wrap. Jen kneaded her own neck, sore from the swift kick one of the fliers had landed in a botched basket toss.

"So," Juliana said. "There's a party Saturday night at Osprey's Bluff."

Jen's stomach tightened. After homecoming last year, they'd gone to Levi Heckman's house. Levi was number one in their class, and they'd been friends with him since elementary school. His parents didn't care about drinking as long as everyone stayed outside. Jen, Susan, and Juliana had gotten tipsy on wine coolers and fed Cheetos to the horses in the stables.

"I thought we were going to Levi's again," Jen said.

"Everyone is going to be at the bluff," Juliana said.

Everyone you feel is important, Jen felt like muttering.

Susan pumped the water bottle in her hand. "Who's going to drive us to the bluff?"

Susan, always concerned with the mechanics of things.

Juliana shrugged. "Carly said we could ride with one of her friends."

"I'm not getting into a car with some senior I don't know," Jen said. "People get busted at the bluff all the time. My stepdad is a freaking cop."

"It'll be fine," Juliana said. "Why do you have a problem with everything lately?"

Jen's throat sealed up. Susan's eyes were on her sneaker, retying her laces, even though they'd been done tightly a minute ago.

Juliana stood, the bleacher groaning beneath them. "I have to pee."

When she was gone, Susan leaned forward, elbows on her knees. "I don't get what's happening."

"She's changed." Jen fought off the sting of tears.

"Don't you see?" Susan said. "We're all changing."

Jen's lips parted, but the sound of something slamming against a locker made her clamp her mouth shut. Next to Jen, Susan jumped like a skittish cat. There was the sickening crack of a slap, followed by a yelp: "Bitch, get off of me!"

Some girl was getting her ass kicked.

Jen hopped over the bench and ran toward the shouting, never looking over her shoulder to see if Susan was following. She skidded to a stop by the lockers outside the athletic office.

Carly Amato had Allie by a fistful of her hair. Jen threw herself between them, yanking Carly off of Allie. In the fray, one of the girls' elbows smashed into Jen's jaw.

Jen ducked back, her eyes watering at the pain. Allie lunged at Carly, landing both hands on her shoulders and shoving her. There was a sickening crack as Carly fell backward, her blond head bouncing off the locker like a rubber ball.

Behind Jen, Susan's voice was breathless, warbly. "Should we call someone?"

Allie turned to look at the girls, as if finally noticing that she and Carly weren't alone. The adrenaline pumping through Jen's veins slowed. She felt like she might puke. Jen rounded on Carly, who was slumped against a locker, massaging her jaw. A dribble of blood leaked from the corner of her mouth.

"What is wrong with you?" Jen shouted.

Carly jerked her head toward their coach and winced in pain. "*She* came after me."

Every pair of eyes in the room swiveled to Allie. Up close, Jen could see that Allie had fared far better in the fight. Her ponytail had come undone, and the skin on her forehead was red from where Carly had pulled her hair, but there wasn't a scratch or a gouge on her.

Allie's labored breathing filled the silence, making it clear she wasn't going to deny Carly's accusation. Instead, she opened her clenched fist, revealing something that glinted in the light. A silver hoop earring. Allie threw it at Carly; it bounced off her chest and skittered across the locker room floor.

Jen stepped back, nearly stepping into Susan, as Allie pushed her way past them. The locker room door slammed, making Jen flinch so hard that her arm, as if on instinct, shot up to protect her face.

The room was silent as Carly picked herself off the floor. Licked the bloody drool from the corner of her mouth.

Before Jen could say anything, before any of them could part to get out of her way, Carly stormed off, in the opposite direction of where Allie had just left.

Sleep eluded Jen that night. She drifted off after midnight, only to wake a few hours later in a cold sweat. Jen touched her throat; for a moment she thought she was in the locker room, and Carly Amato had her hands around her neck, squeezing—

Jen tried to swallow. Her head was cottony and it felt like there were razor blades in her throat. She stumbled out of bed and into the bathroom she shared with her sister. One word broke through the haze in her head: *sick*.

She couldn't be sick. Not today.

Jen blinked against the lights above the vanity mirror and opened her mouth wide. The back of her throat looked like raw meat.

The pep rally was after first period, only a few hours from now. Jen was a base; without her, Allie would have to rearrange the pyramid. An image fought through the pounding in her head. Allie, storming out of the locker room. Carly Amato sprawled on the floor, blood leaking from her mouth. There was the ghost of pain at Jen's

252

jaw from where one of them had rammed her with an elbow.

Jen fumbled through the contents of the vanity cabinet until she found a box of cold medicine. She popped a horse-sized pill out of the foil. Her body struggled against swallowing it.

Her mother was shaking her awake. Jen rolled over, the back of her neck and pillow slick with sweat. She didn't remember coming back to her bed or falling asleep.

"You're burning up," her mother said. Jen opened her mouth to speak; her throat was gummy.

"The pep rally," she forced out.

"Sweetheart, you're not cheering today. I'm calling Dr. Ramdeen."

Jen felt the fight leave her body. She drifted into a hazy sleep, groaning when her mother flipped the light on, gently coaxing her to get up.

She wore her pajamas to the doctor. Dr. Ramdeen's hands were cool around Jen's throat as she massaged her swollen lymph nodes.

Dr. Ramdeen stripped her gloves off and deposited them into the waste bin. "I'll send the cultures to the lab, but it looks like strep."

"How long," Jen croaked, "until it goes away?"

"Homecoming is tomorrow," her mother said from the chair in the corner of the room. "She's on the cheerleading squad."

Dr. Ramdeen squeezed Jen's shoulder. "I'm sorry, love. You're contagious, and in no shape to fly."

I'm a base, Jen wanted to say. *I can perform. I don't need to shout the cheers—*

As if sensing mutiny, Jen's mother stood. "How long until the antibiotics are ready?"

"I'll send the prescription in right now." Dr. Ramdeen gave Jen's shoulder another squeeze. She paused, seeing the devastation in Jen's eyes. "There will be other homecomings."

The sting of tears followed Jen to the car. After she'd buckled herself in, her mother reached over and tucked a lock of hair behind Jen's ear. "Honey. It's just a football game."

"And the pep rally and the dance."

She could sense her mother's patience eroding. "Jennifer. You're very sick, and contagious. Do you want to give Susan and Juliana strep?"

The sleepover at Susan's house. Jen had forgotten; the Berrys were in Vermont for a wedding, and Jen and Jules were staying with Susan tonight after float building.

Now Juliana would be staying alone with Susan tonight. Jen should have felt sick at the thought of her friends hanging out without her. What would they say?

Instead, Jen felt a bubble of relief.

The pep rally would be over by now. Jen's phone had blown up with texts while she was in Dr. Ramdeen's office. Several of them were from Juliana.

Where are you??
Allie says you're sick??
Answer meeeeeee

Jen tapped out a reply:

> Sorry. Was at DR's. She says it's strep

Whaaat? Are you still coming tonight?

> Even if I start antibiotic ASAP I'll still be contagious until Sunday

WHAT!! You're not coming to the dance or the bluff tomorrow either??

> I wasn't going to the bluff anyway Jules

I just don't get why

> Seriously?

seriously

There was the threat of tears again. Jen was so sick of crying, of fighting with her friends, of dancing around all of Juliana's lies.

> Because Carly is sketchy and I don't want to be around her.

The little ellipsis that signaled Jules was typing appeared and disappeared. Jen thought she wouldn't respond at all, until:

> That's why you've been acting so ridiculous?

> I'm ridiculous?

Seconds after she fired the message off, Jen started typing again, blinking away the spots of anger in her eyes. The dam had finally broken.

> I saw you after Spirit Night, getting into a weird car with her. You're doing pills with Carly Amato now??? Jesus Christ, Jules, who even are you anymore?

Adrenaline pumped through Jen's veins. When she saw that Juliana was typing, it felt like an ice cube sliding down into her gut. She expected Jules to shoot something equally nasty back. Maybe an accusation that Jen was stalking her and Carly.

She never saw Juliana's response coming.

> There's so much I have to tell you.
> It's not what you think.

> Really? Because I saw Carly come out of the bathroom at the fair and it totally looked like she was doing coke.

> PLEASE. I'll tell you everything.

> Then tell me.

> Can you sneak out later and come to Suz's after float building?
> It has to be in person

The car blipped. Jen jolted; her mother climbed into the driver's seat, holding a paper bag from the pharmacy. Jen flipped her phone over and rested it on her lap.

Even after she settled in at home, swallowing the antibiotic with a glass of Powerade, at her mother's insistence, Jen didn't text Juliana back. She had no intention of staying up until Juliana got home from float building. If Jules really wanted to talk, she could come to her.

Jen opened up her conversation with Juliana and sent her a text telling her as much. It was barely noon now; Jules would see the message and stop by after school.

She'll come, Jen thought as she drifted off. *I know she will.*

Jen awoke with a start. The sky outside was indigo streaked with gold. She fumbled around her sheets for her phone. It was almost eight o'clock.

Why had her mother let her sleep so long? Jen swallowed, massaging her lymph nodes. Her throat still hurt, but the pain in her head was gone, and her skin was cool to the touch.

Jen got out of bed and headed downstairs. The house was oddly quiet for a Friday night. The kitchen was empty, lights off. It was quiet except for the swish of the dishwasher cycle.

Her mother was in the living room, e-reader in one hand, a glass of white wine in the other.

"Where is everyone?"

Her mother turned her head, looking surprised to see Jen. "Monica is sleeping over at Rachel's, and your brother is asleep. Tom's at work. How are you feeling?"

"A little better," Jen said.

"Do you think you can eat? I'll make you something." Her mother moved to set her glass of wine on the coffee table.

"No. I'll grab an ice pop." Jen didn't want her mother to move. There was something so odd about the scene— her mother, without Monica or Petey hanging off her. It was like stumbling across Mango sitting next to a cat, calmly. Jen didn't want to disturb it.

"Let me know if you want anything later," her mother said.

When Jen got back to her bedroom, she moved to the window. She could just make out Susan's place down the street, three houses over. The driveway was empty, and the timers hadn't turned the porch light on yet. Susan and Juliana would still be at school for float building.

Juliana had never texted Jen back.

At the end of the street was a tall figure. Ethan.

Jen's heart scrambled into her throat. She opened the window next to her desk. Tapped on the screen until it made a warbling noise. The person looked up. The glow from the streetlamp bathed Ethan's face in orange light.

Jen waved. Ethan returned it, cautiously.

Jen held up a finger. *One minute.* She tugged open her desk drawer, searching for a permanent marker. She uncapped it and scribbled something on two pieces of computer paper.

She held the papers side by side in the window, hoping the numbers were big enough for Ethan to read from the street. Ethan blinked; the confusion on his face dissolved. He removed something from his pocket. Moments later, Jen's phone vibrated from her nightstand.

Hey.

Jen texted back:

Hi. Where are you going?

Nowhere really.

Jen swallowed.

259

Do you want to come inside?

Ok

Jen thought of her mother, immersed in her book. She gave Ethan instructions to meet her at the side gate.

Jen slipped her feet into a pair of moccasins. She snuck through the kitchen, quiet not to alert Mango, and unlocked the back door. The grass in the yard tickled her ankles.

Ethan was on the other side of the gate. Jen undid the latch and let him in the yard. His hands were in the pocket of his hoodie.

Jen held a finger to her lips as she led Ethan through the door into the kitchen, then up the stairs. Her heart hammered against her ribs when they came to her bedroom door. What the hell was she thinking? If her mother caught them . . . if *Tom* found out—

A calm settled over her as Ethan stepped into her room. She closed the door behind them and popped the lock in case her mom came up to check on her. Ethan was looking around her room; Jen tried to see it through his eyes.

Did he only see the cheer trophies, the uniform folded neatly on the chair next to her full-length mirror? Did he notice the dozens of pictures of the friends who were barely a part of her life right now?

Ethan began to lower himself onto the other side of the bed.

Jen pulled her knees up to her chest, inching back into

her headboard. "I have strep throat."

"I'll stay over here," Ethan said. He sat at the edge of the bed, looking at the few feet of space between him and Jen. "Is this okay?"

Jen nodded, even though she wished he could come closer. She studied Ethan's face. Up close, under the lights in her room, he looked so much less brooding and serious. His hair flopped almost playfully across his forehead. "Why do you walk around at night?" she asked.

Ethan hesitated. "My mom. She's dying."

"I'm so sorry."

"It's okay. She's been sick for a really long time. Sometimes it's hard to watch."

Jen didn't know what to say, but Ethan seemed eager to change the subject. "What about you? Are you okay?"

Jen shrugged. "I don't know."

"You can talk to me about it, if you want."

"It's stupid compared to what you're going through."

Ethan caught her eye. "You don't have to do that."

"Do what?"

"Everyone goes through shit, and there's always someone somewhere who has it worse. It doesn't make what you're feeling any less real or any less shitty." Ethan shrugged. "You can tell me what's wrong."

"I feel like I'm losing my friends," she said.

Ethan was watching her, waiting for her to explain, but now that Jen had said it aloud to someone, she didn't want to talk about her friends. She didn't want to admit that she'd creepily followed Juliana into the parking lot or that sometimes she hated the hypercompetitive robot

Susan was turning into. Jen didn't want Ethan to see the ugliness inside of her.

So she nodded to the headphones dangling out the neck of his hoodie. "What are you always listening to?"

Ethan tugged at his headphones, as if he'd forgotten they were there. "Books."

"Can I listen with you?" Jen asked.

Ethan's voice was soft. "I don't know if the headphones will reach you."

Jen stared back at him. The look on his face made her flush. He inched closer to her, until they were only half a foot apart.

"I'm contagious," she whispered.

"I don't care." Ethan lowered himself so he was lying down facing her. He reached over and brushed her hair aside, slipping one of the earbuds into her ear.

The narrator's voice was gentle. Jen had no idea what the story was about, but she could have listened for hours.

When she woke up several hours later, the space on the bed next to her was empty. She felt around, desperate for some sign she hadn't imagined the whole thing.

On the pillow next to her, something crinkled. She came away with an orange Post-it note stuck to her hand.

You fell asleep around chapter three.

Maybe we can find out what happens together.

Chapter Sixteen

I spend the walk to class trying to rationalize Carly's reason for blocking me. Maybe I've been a little aggressive, trying to get her to talk to me. Any reasonable person would be creeped out.

But there's little evidence to indicate that Carly Amato is, in fact, a reasonable person. She lied about being friends with Juliana. She said she *barely knew her*, which just isn't the truth.

I force Carly out of my mind when I get to first period. I can't afford to bomb another AP chem quiz; there's time in the quarter to pull my average up, but Mr. Franken will call my mother if I get lower than a 70 today.

Coefficients. Add the coefficients first.

Why would Carly lie?

I shake my head and add an O_2 to the equation. Next to me, I catch Dave Camarco stealing glances at my paper. If I wasn't so sure Mr. Franken would accuse *me* of cheating, I'd lean over and hiss *Good luck with that* at Dave.

I'm the second-to-last person to finish the quiz. After I turn it in and get back to my desk, I sneak my phone out of my backpack's side pocket while Mr. Franken is distracted stapling the test Scantrons to the long answer sheets.

"Monica."

I wince at my name, closing my eyes. When I open them, Mr. Franken is staring at me. He beckons me to come up to the front of the room.

"I'm sorry," I whisper when I reach his desk. "I just had to look something up real quick."

He silently picks up the wire basket where he puts confiscated phones. I drop my phone in and Mr. Franken tells me I can pick it up at the end of the day. I want to cry as I do a walk of shame back to my desk.

I'm so eager to talk to Ginny about Carly blocking me that I'm about to explode. Without my phone, the minutes to lunch creep by more slowly than they usually do. When the bell rings after fifth period, I bolt for the stairwell.

When I get downstairs to Mrs. Goldberg's room, the lights are off and the door is locked. I knock three times, but no one comes. I have to fight off tears as the bell rings.

I turn to stalk off to the cafeteria, nearly colliding with Ginny.

"Sorry," she says breathlessly. "I texted you that I'd be a little late."

"Mr. Franken took my phone away."

A man's voice booms down the hall—a security guard, doing his post-bell sweep to make sure no one is lingering. Ginny slips a key into Mrs. Goldberg's door and herds me inside the room, locking it behind her.

I follow her into the back office, where she sets her lunch bag on the round table in the corner. Below is a mini-fridge. Ginny grabs a yogurt from inside; she offers me one, but I shake my head.

She plops into one of the chairs at the table. "What's going on?" she asks.

"Saturday night, I went through the files again. I found one from a woman on Norwood Drive who said Jack Canning broke into her backyard—she said the Berrys put up a privacy fence because of him. I didn't remember at the time, but it's true. They had a really high fence around their backyard."

Ginny cocks her head a bit, as if she's not sure where I'm going with this.

"Ethan couldn't have seen anything in the Berrys' backyard from the woods," I say. "I met him at Osprey Lake this morning to ask why he lied."

Ginny freezes, her fingers on the foil seal of her yogurt. "Wait. You met up with him alone?"

"A ton of people were around." I try to ignore how unsettled Ginny looks. "Anyway, he told me the real story. He was in Jen's room that night and saw the argument from the garage roof when he snuck out."

"You believe him?"

"He described Jen's room," I say. "And there's more. Jen told Ethan she felt like she was losing her friends, and he thinks it's because Juliana was spending all her time with Carly Amato."

"But Carly said she barely knew Juliana." Ginny drums her fingers against the side of her yogurt. She stands, abandoning her lunch on the table. "I need to show you something."

I follow her to Mrs. Goldberg's computer and stand behind her, watching as she enters the URL for the proxy we all use to get around the school's blocked websites.

Ginny opens up Facebook and enters login information. The page loads, displaying the news feed of someone named Elizabeth Lewis. She's a round-faced blond woman. Late twenties, maybe.

"Who is she?" I ask. I've never seen her before.

"A member of the International Honor Society of Nursing." Ginny flushes. "I don't know who the woman in the photo is. I found it on Google."

Ginny moves so I can check out Elizabeth Lewis's news feed. Elizabeth likes to post humorous photos about nursing school, various slow cooker recipes, and photos of her chocolate Lab, Luke.

I look up at Ginny. "Wait. You made all of this up?"

Her face is sheepish. "I had to make it convincing so Carly would accept my friend request."

"No, it's impressive. How did you do all this today?"

"I didn't. After we went to the library, I checked Carly's page again. She made it private. I wanted to look through her pictures and see what else I could find out about her."

Ginny gets up so I can check out the profile. I scroll up to Elizabeth's friend list; she has forty-nine friends, one of whom is Carly Amato.

I stare at Ginny. "You're a genius. How'd you get all these people to add you?"

"I just added a ton of random people who have nursing listed as their major. I made sure to get a bunch from

OCCC. Most people just click accept."

Ginny drags a free chair over to Mrs. Goldberg's computer. She rotates the monitor so we both have a full view of the screen. "Anyway, I didn't find anything in her pictures that seemed important and I forgot about Elizabeth's profile until this morning when you told me Carly blocked you."

Ginny pulls up Carly Amato's page. She loads Carly's album of profile pictures. "I had study hall last period, so I went to the library to look through these again."

The buzzing in my ears has reached a crescendo. "What did you find?"

Ginny silently enlarges a photo of Carly in ripped denim cutoffs and a white tank top. She's holding a Corona bottle, a slice of lime stuffed down the neck. The sky behind her is black, starless.

She's standing in the bed of a black pickup truck.

Ginny's voice is in my ear, pulling me back. "I looked through all her other pictures. This is the only one with the truck in it."

I deflate. "So no license plate or anything."

"I also looked for any pictures from the same night to see who she may have been with, but there aren't any."

I rub my eyes. "God*damn* it. We can't even message her and ask her whose truck that is, because she'll get suspicious and block Elizabeth."

"I thought of that," Ginny says. "But she has a lot of other pictures. If we can figure out who else she was friends with at Sunnybrook . . . There's got to be someone who knows who drove that truck."

267

I cycle through Carly's profile pictures again, starting with her oldest ones. Carly at prom, in a black satin dress, a slit up to her thigh. I pause and point at the black girl standing next to Carly in the prom photo. She's wearing a white gown with a beaded sweetheart neckline, her silky hair loose and wavy over her shoulders. "I recognize her—I'm pretty sure she was a cheerleader."

Ginny leans in to get a look at the girl's face.

A rap on the door makes us both jump in our seats. Then, a woman's voice: "Who's in here?"

Ginny winces. "I left the classroom light on."

My stomach plummets as Mrs. Goldberg's office door opens. Mrs. Coughlin looks around the room, her gaze finally resting on Ginny. "What are you doing in here?"

Ginny looks like she's going to throw up. "Yearbook stuff."

"Oh really." Mrs. Coughlin clutches the lanyard around her neck. She peeks around Ginny, her beady eyes lasering in on me. "*You're* not on yearbook."

"I'm helping," I say stupidly.

"Mrs. Goldberg is out today," Mrs. Coughlin says. "I'm covering her class next period. There is absolutely no reason for you to be in here unsupervised."

"We have permission," I say, when Ginny doesn't speak up.

"Monica, do not pee on my leg and tell me it's raining." Mrs. Coughlin tears out a referral sheet from her attendance ledger and nods to Ginny. "What's your name?"

Ginny stares at Mrs. Coughlin like she's just undergone a lobotomy.

"This isn't fair." My voice is quaking; Mrs. Coughlin is just being spiteful because I didn't help with the memorial.

Mrs. Coughlin tears out another referral sheet, violently. The ripping sound shuts me up. "Would you like detention for *two* afternoons, Monica?"

Something in Ginny seems to have come unglued. Her eyes are blazing as she stares at Mrs. Coughlin. "I told Monica it was okay for us to be in here. I deserve detention. Not her."

"By all means, be a martyr." Mrs. Coughlin scrawls something on the referral and hands it to Ginny. "You can keep each other company in detention tomorrow."

A parent has to sign your detention slip, just so they know that they raised a fuckup. I could forge my mother's or Tom's signature, but I wouldn't put it past Mrs. Coughlin to call her.

Mom's sitting at the kitchen island when I get home from practice, bent over a booster form. I watch her for a moment, absorbing her idiosyncrasies—she taps her pen to her chin when she's thinking, sighs through her nose when the thought is unpleasant. She shakes her head and crosses something out on the paper, not noticing me standing across the island from her.

"I got this." I set my detention slip on the counter and push it toward her.

She looks up at me. Sticks her fingers beneath her reading glasses and rubs her eyelids before peering at me. "What is it?"

"I have detention tomorrow."

Her expression is flat. "What did you do?"

"Nothing. I was in the yearbook office during lunch and Mrs. Coughlin wrote me up for not having a pass. It's stupid."

My mother ignores the detention slip and turns back to her booster form. "I'll call her after dinner and get you out of it."

"No."

"Excuse me?" She takes off her glasses and sets them on the counter. "You're going to miss practice if you're in detention."

And so will Ginny. "I don't care. Coach is ready to cut me from the competition team anyway."

I wait for her to yell. But she just sighs. "Fine. No computer or cell phone until the weekend."

Now I feel a flutter of panic. "You can't take my computer. I have to write a paper for English tonight."

She pushes her stool away from the counter, jolting me. She storms down the hall off the kitchen, making a right into Tom's office. A beat later, Petey shouts from the living room: "HEY! Who turned the Wi-Fi off?"

My mother steps out of Tom's office and zeroes in on me. "There. You don't need the Internet for an English paper."

"This is such bullshit."

"Do you need to see Dr. Feit?"

My stomach starts pumping acid. Dr. Feit is her

therapist; my sister saw him once after Juliana and Susan were killed. I don't know how my mother can stand the sight of him.

"Are you seriously threatening to send me to a shrink?"

"I don't know what else to do, Monica. I'm tired of watching you turn into someone else." Her cheeks flush. "If you keep acting like this, you're eventually going to do something Tom and I can't fix for you."

"I didn't ask you to fix anything," I say.

She turns away from me and I scream inside my head, *Don't fucking cry.*

"Do you realize that you didn't even hug me?" I ask. "After Dr. Bob's. You wouldn't even touch me."

My mother flinches at "Dr. Bob's." Cranes her neck to the living room, obviously worried that Petey heard, like my little brother has any idea what she's talking about.

"I took care of you. Everything I do is for you and your brother."

"You hug him," I say. "You won't come near me. Do I really remind you of her that much?"

"Go upstairs, Monica. I'm tired of talking about this."

"Talking about what? Jen? You won't talk about her. That's the point." I'm about to erupt. I'm tired of keeping this shit to myself and I'm sick of my mother acting like my sister's name is a forbidden word in this house.

"No, I do not want to talk about her." My mother looks as livid as I am. "I don't want to think about the worst day of my life and every way I could have stopped it. I couldn't protect her, and I can't protect you."

271

I don't know what to say. I spin on my heels, because I don't even want to look at her anymore.

"Monica. Wait."

I turn around. My mother's hand is outstretched. "Give me your phone."

I pat my pocket and flinch. I totally forgot to stop by Mr. Franken's office and get my phone back from him.

"My chem teacher took it away," I say. "I don't even have it."

"Wonderful. Upstairs. We're eating in an hour." She shakes her head and all it does is infuriate me, because it's like at this point she's expecting me to screw up every day.

I stomp out of the kitchen and up the stairs. It's not until I'm shut in my room that I silently thank God Mr. Franken has my phone and that my mother can't go through four weeks' worth of texts between Ginny and me.

The sky is cornflower blue and cloudless in the morning. Rachel and Alexa don't say much on the ride to school, casting furtive glances toward me whenever there's a beat of silence. I don't have the energy to ask why they're treating me with kid gloves.

When we get to school and see the white lilies resting against the flagpole outside the gym, I understand their awkwardness. Tomorrow is the anniversary of Bethany's and Colleen's deaths, and today is the memorial.

After homeroom, Mrs. Barnes's voice comes over the loudspeaker, instructing all students to report to the courtyard for a special ceremony. A freshman science class pours out into the hall after the announcement, some of the kids whooping and hollering. *No first period! Sweet, I have gym!*

I can't do this. Even with Rachel beside me, I can't go out there and deal with the stares from my classmates. I don't want to be the suicide girl's sister today.

The tightness in my chest gets worse when we reach the crowd funneling through the double doors leading out to the courtyard. Mrs. Coughlin swoops by, holding a bouquet of pink balloons.

I feel my free hand curl into a fist. "What the hell are those for?"

Rach fiddles with one of her pearl earrings. "I heard someone say they're doing a balloon release."

"A balloon release? Seriously?"

Rach looks over her shoulder. "Jesus, Mon, calm down."

"Do they know how bad that is for the environment? Balloons kill birds. They eat the balloons and they die."

"Mrs. Coughlin wanted to do it," Rach says. "Cut her some slack. Her daughter died."

I picture Mrs. Coughlin's face yesterday when she gave me detention, how gleeful she looked. As if nothing pleased her more in that moment than to screw me over.

Heat crawls up my back as bodies press against mine, angling for the door. "I can't do this," I say. Before Rachel can call out to me, I pivot and head for the exit at the end of the hall, away from the courtyard.

No one notices me slip out of the building, toward the parking lot. I make a break for the fence lining the soccer field, hoping to duck behind it before I get caught. I don't know where I'm going, but I can't be in that goddamn building a second longer. I'll walk all the way home if I have to.

"Monica."

I halt in my tracks, ready to break out into a run, but when I turn I spot Brandon. He's heading in the opposite direction, toward the school.

He hikes his backpack up his shoulder. He looks like he could be a student, with his Sunnybrook High Cross-Country warm-up jacket. His face is shaved, a small nick blooming on his neck. "Where are you going?"

"I don't know," I say. "Are you going to tell on me?"

Brandon's mouth forms half a smile. "I don't think that would be very wise of me." He jerks a hand toward the school. "Are you sure you want to miss the ceremony?"

"I can't—" I start, and suck in a breath. "I just can't handle it."

Brandon's at my side, putting a hand on the small of my back, so lightly he's barely touching me. "Security is going to see you if you just stand here. Come on."

I let him guide me past the staff section of the lot. His Jeep is parked at the very end of the row, by the tennis courts.

Brandon unlocks the car and opens the passenger side for me. I duck in and shut the door, even though we're far away from the school and no one can see me.

As I'm wiping my eyes, his voice sounds next to me. He's climbed into the driver's seat, shutting us both in. "You can stay in here as long as you need. But you shouldn't cut the rest of the day."

I hate that I'm crying in front of him. Brandon takes my hand. "Hey. You're going to be okay."

He laces his fingers through mine. Or maybe I started it, I don't know. But my lips wind up on his and then he's kissing me back. Even though we're so far back in the lot and no one can see us, it's so stupid—

Brandon rests a hand on my shoulder. Pushes me away gently. "This is a really bad idea."

"I know." I swipe a finger under my eye; a smear of mascara comes away on my skin. "I know. I'm sorry."

"There are so many reasons this can't happen anymore, especially—"

"Now that you have a girlfriend. I get it."

"I don't want to be that guy," he says.

I nod. "You don't have to explain."

Brandon sighs. Tilts his back against his headrest. "Can I ask you something?"

"Do people ever say no to that question?"

"What made you do it?" he asks. "What you did. With me."

I don't know what he expects me to say. I'm sure he doesn't want to hear the truth: that having sex with him was like being someone else. But I can't make myself say the words. *You're hot and my boyfriend broke up with me and you were just there.*

"Because I was sad."

Brandon puts his head in his hands.

"I'm sorry," I say. "Why did you do it?"

"Because I liked you." Brandon laughs. "And I told

myself that you looked older, and you acted older, so it wasn't as wrong."

"But now you do think it was wrong."

"I don't know. It just feels like you used me to avoid your problems."

My throat tightens. He's right—I knew what we were doing was wrong, and I didn't care because I was ready to set my perfect life on fire and walk away while it burned.

"Go back to the memorial," I say. "I'll wait until everyone starts clearing out after and head inside."

For a moment it looks like he wants to stay. I'm not even entirely sure I want him to, but my heart sinks when he reaches for the door handle.

Brandon climbs out of the Jeep and looks at me. "What just happened—I'm not gonna pretend it was all you or that I didn't like it. But it can't happen again."

I don't want to stay, thinking about what happened in this car over the summer, but I can't go back just yet. So I tilt the passenger seat back and stare at the sky over the school until I see the pink balloons floating upward—five of them, one for each girl.

Chapter Seventeen

Detention on Friday is held in the basement, next to the weight room. I had to ask a random teacher how to find the classroom, because as many times as teachers have threatened me with it for being *chatty*, I've never actually gotten detention before.

A chorus of hollers greets me when I step into the classroom. In the row of desks by the window sit the usual suspects—the class-cutters, the big mouths, and the guys who will fight anyone who looks at them. One of them is in my grade: Chris Tavares, a wiry kid with pants that sag low on his hips. Boxers printed with red peppers stick out over his waistline.

He cups his hands over his mouth to mime a megaphone. "RayBURN! Oh, shit!"

The teacher at the desk in the front of the room—a sub, no doubt—sets down his copy of the *New York Post*. "Tavares. You want to sit next to me for the next two hours?"

"No, sir." Chris slumps back in his seat. But it's too late; every pair of eyes in the room is now focused on me. I keep my head down as I check in with the teacher at his desk. He crosses my name off a list and tells me to sit anywhere.

I spot Ginny toward the back of the room, face buried in *The Grapes of Wrath*. I slide into the seat next to her and whisper her name.

She sets her book down. "Hey."

The teacher snaps his fingers twice to get our attention. "No talking. You may do homework, read, sleep, or silently stare into the void."

I glance over at the guys by the window. Most of them have nailed the last two options. One of them has his hands stuffed in the front pocket of his sweatshirt. I hope he's secretly texting and not doing something else.

When the teacher turns back to his newspaper, Ginny reaches into her messenger bag. She produces two pieces of paper, stapled together, and sets them on my desk.

It's a printed page from the Internet. The header says *The Pioneer;* it's the online edition of Newton High School East's newspaper.

Back when our football team still won, NHSE was our biggest rival. The year after all the girls were killed, before the first game of the season, some kids from NHSE snuck into our parking lot and hung a bloody cheerleading uniform from the flagpole.

I shoot Ginny a confused look. She points to the bottom of the page.

PIONEER CHEER NABS GOLD AT ULSTER COUNTY REGIONALS

There's a brief paragraph about the cheerleading squad's path to victory, complete with a quote from Coach

Patrice Johnson. Ginny moves her finger to the team photo accompanying the article, resting on a gorgeous black woman in a coach's warm-up jacket. Patrice looks familiar.

"She was in Carly's prom photo," Ginny whispers.

The sub locks eyes with Ginny and me. "I said *silently*."

As if on cue, someone shouts in the hallway. There's an explosion of laughter. When it doesn't die down, the teacher sighs and gets up. "I'll be back in *one minute*," he says as he steps out of the classroom.

As soon as he's gone, Ginny leans over and whispers, "Newton East has a football game tomorrow. Patrice should be there."

Before I can answer, Chris Tavares shouts in our direction. "Yo, Rayburn, what are you doing here?"

"Yeah, what're you in for?" One of the guys by the window, an enormous senior, stares at Ginny and me. His friend—a guy with a patchy beard—pipes up: "Why don't you come sit by me? This is where the party's at."

"Thanks for the tip," I say.

Chris and the other guy howl with laughter as the huge kid tells me he'll give me a tip any time I want. Ginny stares at her fingers, her face scarlet.

"Yo, you're making the other one blush," the guy with the beard says.

"I'd take her, too. She's got no tits. But that ass, though."

"I seen her on the school website," Beard says. "In one of those gymnastics leotards. Gimme your phone, I'll show you."

The big kid hands over an iPhone, and Chris Tavares turns in his seat. Lemmings gathering to leer at Ginny's body.

279

I stand, the sound of my chair legs squealing against the floor startling the guys. They're taken so off guard that Beard doesn't even fight when I snatch the phone from his hand.

"Put this away, or I will shove it so far up your ass a doctor won't be able to find it." I slam the phone on the desk and walk back to my seat, Beard's friends howling with laughter.

"Man, she is *savage*." Chris Tavares lets out a whistle of admiration, while the substitute teacher wanders back into the room, shouting for us to settle down unless we want to join him again for detention on Monday.

"Thanks," Ginny whispers as I sit down. The guys by the window don't say another word, or even look at us, until the teacher tells us we can leave.

Detention and dance team practice both end at five, so I can still grab a ride home with Rachel and Alexa. I wait for them outside instead of meeting them by the gym, because I am a coward and can't face Coach right now.

Regionals are in two weeks, and I missed practice. I'm well aware that, when she gets here, Rachel might have to relay the message that Coach has thrown me off the team. And I can't even blame her for it.

"Was she mad?" I ask. We're at Rach's car; she's digging at the bottom of her bag for her keys.

"I don't know," Alexa says, glancing at Rachel nervously.

But Rach is watching me over the roof of the car. "Why did you get detention?"

"Mrs. Coughlin," I mutter. "I don't want to talk about it."

Alexa opens her mouth, but Rach freezes her with a look. She must have told Alexa about my meltdown before the memorial this morning. They both must assume I had it out with Mrs. Coughlin at some point today, because neither of them asks me why Coughlin wrote me up.

Rach lets us into the car. Neither she nor Alexa questions why Ginny missed practice either, and I don't offer that information. Ginny already left to catch the late bus on the other side of the school.

"Well, at least it's Spirit Night," Alexa says.

I wince. I completely forgot to tell them that I'm not allowed to go tonight.

"About that," I say. "I can't go."

"What the hell, Monica?" Rachel is studying me, silent.

I can't look at her. "My mom flipped out because of the detention."

Alexa leans forward and puts her arms around my headrest. "Let's go to your house. Rach and I will convince her you have to go."

"Lex. Seriously. You do not want to do that."

My voice must be scary, because Alexa promptly shuts her mouth. She buries herself in her phone for the rest of the ride to her house; Rach has to turn the radio up, the silence is so awkward.

When we drop Alexa off at her house, Rachel looks at me head-on. "I'm worried about you."

"Don't be," I say. "Things are just messed up with my

family right now. They always are at this time of year."

Rachel puts the car in reverse and inches out of Alexa's driveway. When we're on the main road again, she eyes me. "Why can't you talk to me about it? Bethany was my cousin. I understand."

I look away from her so she can't see my face flush with annoyance. She can't possibly understand. Jen was my sister, and her death will never compare with Rachel losing a cousin she didn't even like.

"I don't talk to anyone about it," I say. "It's nothing personal."

After a beat, Rach speaks, her voice frosty. "Do you talk to Ginny Cordero about it?"

I close my eyes and tilt my head back. "Rach, don't do this."

She doesn't have much else to say to me until she pulls into my driveway and I get out of the car. "I got the triple today," she says. "In case you were wondering."

I don't want my mother to figure out that barring me from going to Spirit Night is the best gift she could have given me this week, so I make sure to be quiet and sulky during dinner.

As I'm clearing the table of pizza grease–stained paper plates, I force myself to look at my mom. "Can I go to the Newton versus Shrewsbury football game tomorrow?"

She blinks, as if she can't grasp how I could possibly have the balls to ask her that. "You're still grounded."

Tom's head snaps up from the garlic knot he'd

been polishing off. "Grounded? Why?"

Mom doesn't look at him as she collects balled-up dirty napkins from the table. "She got detention."

"Seriously?" Tom looks at me.

"For the stupidest reason," I say. "I'm really sorry. I'll come straight home after the game."

My mother inhales sharply as Tom sits back in his chair. "Why do you want to see Newton versus Shrewsbury anyway?"

"My friend Ginny's cousin is playing," I say. "He's Newton's running back."

Tom is incapable of saying no to football. He raises his eyebrows at Mom. Her lips form a line, and I can tell she's feeling guilty about making me miss Spirit Night when she can't stand Mrs. Coughlin either.

"Fine," she says. "Straight home, though."

When her back is turned, Tom gives me a triumphant smile. For some reason, it makes my stomach turn over.

I wake up early in the morning. I went to bed at ten, for lack of anything better to do, and the sunrise leaking in through my blinds has me flopping between positions, unable to fall back asleep.

Mrs. Cordero doesn't have to work until tonight, so Ginny can borrow her car to drive us to the game. I shower and blow-dry my hair, and when Petey wakes up at eight, I even sit at the kitchen island with him as he eats breakfast, listening to his plans for the model Vietnam Veterans Memorial he's designing for his social studies class.

The game doesn't start until two, and the school is

only twenty minutes away, but Ginny picks me up at one. Newton High School East's team is ranked first in the county. Their games sell out quickly, and we want to make sure we find a parking spot.

Newton East's campus is a lot bigger than Sunnybrook's, and even though the game doesn't start for another half hour, Ginny has to fight for a parking spot several hundred yards from the field.

The spot is a tight squeeze; I climb out of the car to help direct Ginny into it. When she gets out of the car, she's put on a knit cap with earflaps. "Ready?"

I nod, and we fall into step with a crowd of people heading for the field. A group of tailgaters gathered around a charcoal grill starts to boo. I tense up, worried they've somehow recognized Ginny and me. Then I see the real object of their scorn—a pack of high school kids behind me, wearing green and white. Shrewsbury's colors.

Ginny protests when I pay the fourteen-dollar admission fee for the two of us.

"Stop," I say. "It's the least I can do."

"I'm seriously not mad about detention." She thrusts her hands into the front pocket of her hoodie as we pick our way up the bleachers in search of a free spot. We settle into a row three-quarters of the way up the first level. As soon as we sit down, Ginny produces a steel thermos from her bag and hands it to me. "Hot chocolate."

The thought of hot chocolate, and Ginny pouring two packets into the thermos, warms me before I even take a sip. I peel off my gloves so I can unscrew the top of the thermos. The last time I was here was for a NHSE vs. Sunnybrook game freshman year, with Rachel and Alexa and Matt. One of Matt's friends had smuggled in a flask of rum, which we mixed with hot apple cider from the concession stand. It was only the first weekend of November, but the forecast said there was a chance of snow flurries. Under the blanket we brought, Matt traced a finger up the inside of my thigh and I shivered, thinking, *If I weren't me, I would kill to be me.*

"Are you okay?" Ginny asks.

"I'm good," I say, and in spite of everything, I mean it.

"Look." Ginny points across the field, where a bunch of girls in navy-and-white skirts are huddled. Someone shouts, and they break apart, staggering into groups of three. Ginny and I watch them bend, pop the fliers up into formation. The fliers pull their legs up into scorpion positions. They hold them while someone shouts a count to three before the bases drop them back down. The girls march into a pyramid formation.

The counter—a slender and tall black woman—is off to the side, admiring the pyramid as if it were a piece of art. Her hair is in a high bun, and she's wearing a navy-and-white warm-up jacket to match the girls' uniforms.

"That's Patrice," I say.

I keep my eyes on her through the anthem, the home team's ceremonial entrance set to an AC/DC song, and through kickoff.

"Have you figured out what you're going to say to her?" Ginny asks.

Shrewsbury picks up a first down, and the crowd boos. Below us, at the bottom of the bleachers, a line of cheerleaders in green and white attempts to lead our side of the stadium in a cheer, waving their pom-poms.

"Not exactly," I say. "But Patrice isn't Facebook friends with Carly. I'm not that worried about it getting back to her."

At halftime, the score is 21 to 14, Shrewsbury. The field clears so the NHSE cheerleaders can perform their routine; a techno remix of this summer's most played-out pop song blares from the speakers. The girls are out of sync in a way that would make Coach claw her eyes out, but the crowd goes wild for their tumbling passes.

Shrewsbury winds up winning 34 to 27. Ginny and I stay seated while the bleachers around us clear out. I say a silent prayer that no one from Shrewsbury gets the shit kicked out of them on the way back to the parking lot.

Down on the field, Patrice is giving the cheerleaders a pep talk. They raise their pom-poms in a cheer of solidarity before breaking apart and heading through the locker room entrance below the box. Patrice hangs behind, collecting pom-poms.

"Let's go," I say.

Ginny is at my heels as we hurry down the bleachers. Patrice looks up. Looks through us and goes back to packing up the pom-poms.

"Patrice?" I say.

Her back tenses as she takes Ginny and me in. "Yeah?"

"Do you have a minute?"

Patrice studies my face. "Where do I know you from?"

"I'm Jennifer Rayburn's sister."

Patrice's onyx eyes soften. "Monica, right?"

I nod. "This is Ginny. We're both on the dance team."

Patrice's mouth tightens in a polite smile. "I'm glad

you came and said hi." No doubt wondering what the hell this is all about.

I swallow to clear the nerves from my throat. "I wanted to ask you—were you friends with Carly Amato in high school?"

Patrice blinks. "Carly? I knew her. I wouldn't call her a friend."

"I was just wondering, because I saw a picture of you guys together at prom."

Patrice's forehead wrinkles. "Yeah, I know what you're talking about. I mean, we were friendly, kind of, but I only took that picture at prom because she asked."

"But you were on cheerleading together," I press.

"For a little while." Patrice closes the top of the pom-pom box and pauses. "Why do you guys care about Carly? That girl was bad news."

I glance over at Ginny; I can tell she picked up the ominous note in Patrice's voice too. Somehow, I don't think Patrice said Carly was bad news because she snuck cigarettes in the school parking lot.

"Bad news how?" I ask.

Patrice straightens and brushes a stray pom-pom string from her palm. "I mean, I didn't know her that well. She only went to Sunnybrook her senior year. She got kicked out of Catholic school for fighting. She ripped out a chunk of this girl's hair and bit her so hard she needed stitches," Patrice says. "At least, that's what people said."

"That's horrible," I say. When I met Carly, I'd gotten the vibe that she was scrappy. But Patrice is describing someone who is downright vicious.

Patrice shrugs. "She got into a couple fights at Sunny-brook, but she was mostly talk. She was kind of desper-ate, like always hanging around me and my friends as if it would give her street cred or whatever. I don't know, everyone called her a skank or wannabe ghetto but I just felt bad for her. She didn't have any friends."

"What about Juliana Ruiz? Everyone says they were friends." Everyone except Carly herself.

"Yeah. Sweet little Jules." Patrice sighs. "It was hon-estly kind of sad."

"What do you mean?" I ask.

"At practice, Carly would make it a point to talk really loudly about the parties she and Juliana went to over the weekend with these older guys Carly knew. I think Carly wanted to show off, like she was too cool for high school shit. But that, like, wasn't Juliana at all. None of us really understood the power Carly had over her."

"When you said Carly was only on the squad for a little while," I say, "do you mean she stopped cheering before Juliana died?"

Patrice shakes her head. "She got kicked off the squad before."

I glance at Ginny. Her eyebrows are raised, eyes on Pa-trice. "What did Carly do to get kicked off?" Ginny asks.

"There were rumors. But no one knows what really happened except Carly and Allie."

"Allie?"

"Our coach," Patrice says. "You never met Allie?"

A flash of my sister's coach, in the bleachers at one of Jen's regional competitions that my mother dragged

Petey and me to. Cheerleader Barbie.

I shake my head. "What was the rumor?"

A gust of wind flies past us. Patrice zips her warm-up jacket to her chin. "That Carly slept with Allie's boyfriend."

"That's nuts," I say.

Patrice shrugs. "If it's true, it's the least scandalous thing that would have happened when I was in school. A girl in my grade had a threesome. When we were *freshmen*. God, I do not miss that place."

Patrice picks up the box of pom-poms. "I've got to head out. Why do you guys care about Carly anyway? Can't you talk to her yourselves?"

"I think she can tell me something that happened between my sister and her friends," I say. "She wasn't exactly cooperative when I tried to talk to her."

Patrice balances the pom-pom box on her hip, looking thoughtful. "Maybe you should ask Allie."

"She knew everything that was going on with us. She was always comforting some crying girl in her office." Patrice's voice suggests that she was definitely not one of those crying girls.

Some shrieking draws our attention to the other end of the football field; a handful of football players in navy-and-white uniforms are almost forehead to forehead with two guys on Shrewsbury's team. I recognize the hulking kid in the center as the linebacker who got a nasty penalty off of Shrewsbury during the game.

There's some cursing and scuffling, a crowd gathering around the guys, voices swelling like a melee is about to break out. Patrice drops the box of pom-poms and starts jogging toward them, shouting, "Are you *for real right now*?"

Something occurs to me. I call out: "Patrice, wait! One second!"

Patrice stops short. "What is it?"

"Did Carly have a pickup truck?"

Patrice blinks at me. "No. She couldn't drive."

Parents are hurrying down the bleachers, toward the fight. Patrice disappears into the chaos; Ginny and I hurry off the field and duck out of the stadium, wending our way through a crowd thick with tension. Jubilant people in green avoiding the somber throngs of people in navy and white.

When we get back to the car, the sky is a pearly gray with threatening-looking clouds rolling in. Ginny unlocks the car and I pour myself into the passenger seat, suddenly in a very foul mood. "So that was a huge waste of time. I dragged us out here to hear about locker room drama, and we were almost part of a football field brawl."

"It wasn't a waste of time," Ginny says. "She did say that Allie was always listening to the girls' problems."

Would my sister open up to her coach about what was going on between her and Juliana and Susan? When Jen was happy—which seemed like almost all the time before that year—she spread her joy around like it was sunshine. Every other emotion, though—fear, sadness, and loneliness—she'd kept them locked up. After Jen died, one of the only times I heard my mother lose it was when she was on the phone with Grandma Carlino: *She never told me anything. I tried so hard, but she would never tell me anything.*

"I don't know," I say. "Jen was pretty private."

Ginny turns the heat on. Wiggles her fingers in front of the vents. I glance at the side mirror; there's still chaos in the parking lot. Too many people trying to leave at once, boxing us into our spot.

"Juliana, though." I turn to Ginny. "If she was in some sort of trouble and couldn't tell her mom or Jen, I could see her going to someone older that she trusted. Someone like Allie, maybe."

Ginny turns down the heat so I can hear her over the air rattling in the vents. "Maybe Juliana found out something that she felt like she had to tell Allie."

I look at Ginny. "You think Juliana told Allie her boyfriend was cheating on her?"

Ginny shrugs. "Juliana might have been more loyal to her coach than to a girl she only knew for a few months. Especially if she wanted to rid herself of Carly."

I turn this theory over in my head. "If you were Allie, and Juliana told you that your boyfriend was cheating on you, and then Juliana was murdered a little while later . . . would you be suspicious of Carly?"

"No," Ginny finally says. "I wouldn't think it had anything to do with the murders. Especially if the police said they knew who did it."

A thumping noise rattles Ginny's car. We jerk in our seats; in the side mirror, I see a pack of guys whooping, weaving between cars, giving each one a hearty slap on the back. I wonder if the brawl on the field has died down.

"You're right," I tell Ginny. "Carly sounds scary, but her *killing* two girls because Juliana ratted her out to their coach . . . it doesn't fit. Also, Patrice confirmed the pickup truck wasn't Carly's."

"It doesn't mean Carly wasn't there that night or that she wasn't involved somehow."

Ginny looks lost in her thoughts. I keep quiet, letting her piece them together.

"I just keep thinking about something Patrice said. How no one understood the power Carly had over Juliana." Ginny lifts her thumb to her mouth, ready to gnaw at her cuticle. When she catches me eyeing her, she drops her hand to her lap. "What if Carly got Juliana mixed up in something really bad? Maybe Juliana was in over her head and confided in Allie. We should talk to her," she says. "If we can find a way to contact her."

"We can." I look out my window, my stomach suddenly feeling very tight. "The first person in my sister's contacts is named Allie."

I head straight for my closet when I get home and open my jewelry box. Jen's phone rests on top, where I left it.

I sit back on my heels and open her contacts. At the very top of the list is the name *Allie Lewandowski*.

Mango wanders into my closet, nose in the air, trying to sniff out food. He sees me on the floor, empty-handed except for Jen's phone, and turns to leave, bored.

Stealing Allie Lewandowski's phone number from my dead sister is wrong. Obviously I know that. But Ginny and I got this far, and I'm not going to stop because of some false sense of decency. Decency went out the window long ago.

I copy Allie's number into my phone and tap out a text message.

> Hey, Allie—this is Monica Rayburn. I hope you don't mind that Mrs. Barnes at the high school gave me your number. You were my sister Jen's cheerleading coach. I'm thinking about applying to Oneonta, and I was wondering if you had time to chat with me with any tips or advice you might have? I'll buy you coffee! Thanks so much 😊

I stay up until past midnight, watching my phone, waiting for her to reply. But my text inbox stays empty until I fall asleep, and it's empty when I wake up.

It's Monday evening, after practice, and I'm unlacing my shoes in the locker room. Alexa and Rach are refilling their water bottles at the fountain outside Coach's office, voices echoing through the locker room. Their conversation bounces from the male kickline routine they're planning for Spirit Night to regionals in two weeks, and hearing it makes me feel so lonely I could puke.

Ginny pokes her head around the corner. She sits on

the bench next to me. "Anything from Allie?"

I shake my head. I swing my feet off the bench and wiggle my toes, finally free of the restrictive dance shoes. "Texting her was probably a bad idea. I probably freaked her out like I freaked Carly out."

I wait for Ginny to disagree, but she shrugs. "That number is five years old. She may have gotten a new one."

We walk into the hall together. The cross-country guys are spilling out of their locker room, bringing the cocktail of body odor and Axe spray with them. My body tenses up. Cross-country practice letting out means Brandon is nearby.

Next to me, Ginny's voice is quiet. "Are you okay?"

I nod. "Yeah. Just exhausted."

She studies me, wearing that curious look that says she doesn't believe me but she won't push it. "I've got to catch the bus. Let me know if you hear from her."

"I will."

As I'm watching Ginny head down the hall, toward the parking lot, a guy says, "Hey, Monica."

Jimmy Varney is walking toward me, hair clinging to his sweaty forehead. Over his shoulder, I spot Brandon emerging from the locker room, talking with a boy half his height. He looks up; his eyes connect with mine as he gives the kid a pat on the shoulder. Brandon is still watching me as the kid takes off down the hall. I swallow and turn to face Jimmy.

"Hey."

"How are you?" Jimmy asks.

"Sweaty and disgusting." It sounds a lot like *Go away*,

so I slide my voice up to a friendlier octave. "How was your practice?"

I uncap my water bottle and start chugging. Jimmy grabs one of his biceps and rolls his shoulder back until it gives a small *pop*. "State qualifiers are next week. Coach is riding us pretty hard."

I think of Brandon, mere feet away from us, and I choke on the water sliding down my throat. Cough until my eyes water and concern knits up Jimmy's forehead. "You okay?"

"I'm good. Sorry." I force out another cough and wipe my lips. Steal a look at Brandon; he's in the doorway to the athletic office, using a sneakered foot to scratch the back of his opposite calf.

Jimmy's voice draws me back. "What are you doing after the dance Saturday? Kelsey G's house?"

I remember what Alexa said the other day. *Varney wants to ask you to homecoming.* The parade, the dance, the party—they're the furthest things from my mind this year. "I don't know. Are you going to Kelsey's?"

"I am," Jimmy says. "I think Kelsey hopes you'll come."

I'm pretty sure that Kelsey Gabriel doesn't think about me much at all, but the nervous blush in Jimmy's cheeks makes a smile tug the corner of my mouth. The urge to flirt with him takes me by surprise. "Is that your way of indirectly saying you hope I'll come to Kelsey's?"

"Yes." Jimmy grins. "Yes, it is."

More cross-country guys pour out of the locker room, and Jimmy is swept up into a group of them asking him for a ride home. He meets my eyes over their heads—he towers over most of them—and smiles again.

My giddiness evaporates when I spot Brandon watching us. He looks away, palming the door frame to the men's athletic office, talking to someone inside. He's trying hard to angle away from me, suggesting he heard everything Jimmy and I said to each other.

My stomach does that suction-cup thing it does whenever Brandon is around. I think about last Tuesday in his Jeep, the tug of his fingers through my hair. Tamp down the image, because the thought of Jimmy knowing what we did makes me feel ill.

I don't feel like setting my life on fire anymore. I want to fast-forward to the part where I look at Brandon and don't feel anything at all.

Alexa's voice echoes from the locker room into the hall; she and Rachel wander out, fanning their armpits. Like a hawk, Alexa zeroes in on me. "Why are you blushing?"

"Because we just finished a ridiculous practice," I say.

"No, that's a flirting blush." Alexa looks down the hallway, past Brandon, whose back is turned to me. When she spots Jimmy Varney and his friends, she pokes me in the shoulder.

"Stop," I say, "seriously."

Rachel slides the elastic from her ponytail, letting her hair spill over her shoulders. "Monica, he's been in love with you for, like, ever."

I'm about to tell them both to shut the hell up when my tote bag buzzes at my hip. I dig out my phone. There's a text from a number that's not in my contacts.

Allie Lewandowski replied to my message.

> Hi, Monica! Sorry for taking so long to get back to you. I'd love to chat about Oneonta. You still live in Sunnybrook, right? I teach an 8 PM class in town, so I can meet up any night before then.

It's a little after five now; I fire off a response to Allie.

> I'm actually just getting out of practice now. Are you free tonight by any chance?

I chew a fingernail absently, keeping my eyes on my phone as Rach, Alexa, and I head outside the gym doors.

> That should work. How does Earth Lily Café sound? Does 6:15 work?

I look up at Rachel. "Hey, do you think you could drop me off in town on the way home?"

Earth Lily Café is two blocks away. I step into the library vestibule for show, keeping an eye on the window overlooking the street. When Rach's car disappears from view, I zip my North Face up to my chin and head for the café.

Earth Lily opened a year ago, but I've never been. Tom once called the food *hippie shit* during one of his rants about how Sunnybrook will eventually be taken over by young, crunchy types like in Millerton.

I don't want to take up a table without buying anything, so I order the only thing on the menu I recognize—a cappuccino. I order it decaf and when it's ready I grab an open seat in the corner of the room, in a velvet armchair. It's twenty after six, and Allie isn't here.

"Monica?"

Allie Lewandowski is wearing a black off-the-shoulder sweatshirt. Her hair is twisted in an elegant bun at the top of her head. "I'm so sorry. Parking is awful around here."

"It's okay." I wedge my hands between my knees, realizing they're trembling. "Thanks for coming. I know you probably have better things to do."

"No, don't be silly. I'm going to grab a drink and then we can chat?"

I nod. I keep my fingers wrapped around my mug to warm them, trying not to stare at Allie as she orders at the counter. She's the most beautiful person I've ever seen. When she returns, she plops in the armchair across from me. Shoots me a warm smile.

"What do you teach?" I ask.

"Pilates at Barre-ing It All." Allie gives a small smile. "It's not a dream job, but I'm getting my master's degree full-time. What do you want to major in?"

My mind goes blank. My sister was the one who was always so sure about what she wanted to be, while I gave a different answer every year. A ballerina. A teacher. A magazine editor. "I don't know," I say. "Maybe psychology."

Allie's eyes brighten. "That's what I majored in! I'm in school to be a social worker."

"That's awesome," I say. "Really awesome."

Allie pulls her straw up to her lips and sneaks a glance at her phone. I'm making this totally awkward, and she's looking for an excuse to bail.

"Sorry I'm being weird," I blurt. "It's just that my sister also wanted to be a social worker. Or a veterinarian."

"Oh." Allie's eyes soften as she twirls her straw through her iced latte. "Jen was such a good kid. She would have been really good at both of those things."

"She talked about you a lot," I say. It's a lie, and it's a shitty one. All Allie has to do is ask what Jen said about her and I'm done. Once my sister started high school she never talked to me about Allie or about cheerleading or anything, really.

"You must really miss her." Allie tilts her head, giving me an encouraging look. There's sympathy in her expression, but no pity. She's going to make a good social worker.

The backs of my eyes prick. "I wish I could talk to her. I just want to ask her what happened."

Allie's fingers go still around her straw. "What do you mean?"

"I don't know. Even before her friends were killed, I noticed something was going on with Jen." I collect my cappuccino off the coffee table, keeping my eyes on the cup. "There was this other cheerleader my sister couldn't stand—Carly Amato. She was kicked off the team."

There's a brief flash of something ugly in Allie's expression. "I never kicked Carly off. She quit."

My thoughts swirl. Patrice had sounded so sure that Allie had kicked Carly off the team. "Oh. It's just that I heard this rumor. . . ."

"I know the rumor." Allie's bubbly voice has gone flat. "Is that why you asked me here? To find out if my boyfriend cheated on me with Carly?"

My throat has sealed up. I can't find the words to defend myself, if there even are any.

Allie stares at me, her expression frosty. "I don't know why you care, but no, it's not true. The whole thing got blown out of proportion. I found Carly's earring in my boyfriend's car," Allie says. "Obviously I asked him how it got there. He said that his best friend had met Carly over the summer, and they'd been hanging out. One night Carly called them up asking to buy her beer. They picked her up, and her earring must have fallen out in my boyfriend's backseat."

"And you believed him?"

"His friend backed the story up. And this might sound mean, but my boyfriend never would have gone for a girl like Carly." Allie's eyes flash. "It was still really stupid of them. I mean, hanging out with a high school girl and buying her alcohol? They could have gotten in a ton of trouble.

"Anyway, I didn't kick Carly off the team. Before I knew what really happened I said some horrible things to her. I just kind of lost my mind. She quit and the rumors started." Allie stares back at me. "What does any of this have to do with your sister?"

It's exactly what I came here hoping she could tell me. Allie is one of the only links left between Carly and my sister and her dead friends, and all I've done is piss her off.

Connect the dots. Maybe Carly and Allie and her boyfriend were never dots to begin with.

"I don't know," I say. "I didn't mean to waste your time."

"It's fine. I have to go teach now." Allie stands up, looking at me as if she's not quite sure how she got here. "Good luck with Oneonta. If you even really want to go there."

Chapter Eighteen

My mom can't pick me up until the rehearsal she's supervising at the playhouse is over at 7:30, so I have to kill time in the library. I grab a chair in the magazine section and text Ginny.

> Talked to Allie. It was a disaster

> Uh-oh

> Yep. She says she caught her boyfriend buying Carly beer. Allie fought with her about it and Carly quit.

> You think that's what really happened?

I pause, thinking it over.

> I don't know. I feel like there was something Allie wasn't telling me. She didn't mention Juliana being under Carly's spell.

> Maybe Allie just didn't know that Juliana was hanging out with Carly?

> I don't know. Either way, Carly's obv not going to tell us

An ellipsis appears and disappears. Appears again. As if Ginny keeps typing out a response and deleting it. Then finally:

> I might know someone who can get Carly to talk to us

> ??? Who??

> Elizabeth Lewis ☺

It's almost ten o'clock, and Ginny hasn't texted me an update. She messaged Carly as Elizabeth Lewis hours ago, inviting her to coffee to talk about the International Honor Society of Nursing.

The society doesn't exist, which Carly could figure out very quickly from Google. Our plan to lure her to the college student activity center relies on Carly not being the brightest bulb in the box.

There's also the chance that her guard is still up after my visit; Carly may not have thought twice about adding Elizabeth Lewis as a friend, but the invitation to meet up in person might be suspicious to someone with something to hide. And ever since I talked to Ethan at Osprey Lake, I've been convinced that everything Carly told me is a lie—and that she holds the key to figuring out what really happened the night Juliana was killed.

If Ginny and I can't pry anything out of Carly, I don't know where that leaves us. We can try to track down the guy she was seeing—Allie's boyfriend's friend—but after Allie's abrupt exit after I brought him up, it's clear she's not interested in indulging my poking around into the events of five years ago.

When Ginny calls me, I pick up on the first ring.

"She's free Friday at six-thirty," Ginny says. "She has practical exams this week, so that's the only night she can do."

"That's fine."

Ginny hesitates. "You'll have to miss a good part of float building."

"I don't give a crap about float building if you don't."

"Monica, I've never once gone to float building," she says. "I could not give less of a crap about it."

There is still the issue of faking enthusiasm for Friday's pep rally, and Saturday's parade, game, and dance. I don't know how long Alexa and Rachel will tolerate my moodiness.

If anyone else has noticed how unpleasant I've been, apparently it doesn't bother them. On Thursday morning, the student council president announces that I'm on the junior class homecoming court.

I sit up a little straighter, cheeks burning from a dozen sets of hands in my homeroom clapping for me. I strain my ears to hear the rest of the girls' names.

"Alexa Santiago and Sharaya Tompkins! And for the boys . . ."

I tune out, my stomach sinking. Rachel looks absolutely crushed.

During our pep rally routine, she turns the wrong way when we're changing formations and collides with Kelsey G.

After practice, when Alexa asks what time we're getting to float building later, Rach mumbles an excuse about cramps and says she's not going. I wait until I get home to text Alexa that I'm not going either, so the worst thing she can do is send me a picture of herself giving me the middle finger.

Alexa will get over it; she always does. But I can't stop thinking about Rachel, and how every day it feels like I'm letting her slip away from me. When Ginny picks me up at six, she asks me what's wrong.

"Just bullshit with my friends," I say.

Ginny doesn't reply; as if sensing I don't want to talk

about it, she turns the radio on. My parents think I'm going to float building, so I have Ginny make a right out of my driveway as if we're going to school, just in case anyone is watching from my house.

We—or Elizabeth Lewis, rather—are meeting Carly at the Orange County Community College student activity center, where there's a coffee shop.

"Are you sure we should confront her?" I say to Ginny as we pull into the parking lot. "This has the potential to get ugly."

"I know." She chews on a hangnail. "I brought this."

She dips a hand into the V-neck of her shirt and emerges holding a small purple whistle. "My mom gives these out at the sexual assault prevention class she holds at the hospital every month."

I don't tell her that the whistle is a small comfort. The cars in the parking lot are sparse, and I wish that Carly could have met us earlier, when more people would be around.

At 6:30 on the dot, a Volkswagen pulls into the parking lot. Carly gets out of the car. Holds her keys over her shoulder and locks it.

"There." I point to the Volkswagen. "That's her. Let's go."

Ginny and I climb out of her mom's car and follow her, darting between cars. I signal for Ginny to go around the SUV blocking our view of Carly. I run around the other side, cutting Carly off.

"Hi," I say.

Carly Amato jumps back. "What the *fuck*?"

"We just want to talk to you," I say. "Ten minutes. Please. And you'll never see us again."

Carly shoves a hand into her bag, and I shrink back into the car behind me. Squeeze my eyes shut, bracing against a shot of pepper spray to the face. But she pulls out her vape stick and puts it to her lips.

"I've got nothing to say." Carly blows smoke through her nostrils.

"You were friends with Juliana," I say. "So why did you say you barely knew her?"

"You don't get it," Carly says. "I did a lot of stuff I regret in high school. I have my life on track now, so excuse me if I have a problem with you two digging up old shit."

"We know you hung out with Allie's boyfriend and his best friend," I say. "You introduced them to Juliana, didn't you?"

"So what if I did?" Carly's eyes dart between Ginny and me, like a hamster's. "What does it even matter?"

"It matters if Allie's boyfriend or his friend drove a pickup truck."

Carly's lips part. "Why?"

"Because someone saw Juliana get out of a pickup truck the night she was killed. Someone else heard her yelling, 'Don't tell me to calm down.'"

Something flashes in Carly's eyes. She swallows. I glance at Ginny.

"Carly," she says. "We don't care if you did drugs. We just want to know who really killed Juliana."

Carly folds her arms across her chest, burying her hands in her cardigan. "That big creep next door killed Juliana."

"You don't believe that," I say. "We just want the name of the guy who drove the pickup truck."

"Fuck no. I bought from one of those guys. I saw him beat the shit out of a kid who told his parents he bought Oxy from him."

I balk, even though I'm not sure why anything surprises me anymore. "You bought pills from your cheer coach's boyfriend?"

"Not him. His friend." The small of Carly's throat twitches. "She attacked me, you know. Allie. She thought I was screwing her boyfriend. I would have loved to throw it in her face that his best friend was pulling in thousands selling pills."

"This guy. Did Juliana buy from him?" I ask.

"Juliana didn't do drugs." Carly takes another pull from her vape. "She didn't want to hang out with him anymore once she found out he was selling. We were hanging out one night, just drinking, the four of us. He had to stop to do a deal, and Juliana kind of freaked."

"And you didn't think to tell anyone this when she was murdered?"

Carly snorts. "Who the hell would believe me? These were Hamilton guys."

"Hamilton?"

"The college. Preppy and rich and shit. And I didn't have any proof that they even *knew* Juliana. Aside from the party where I met them, we never hung out with them in public or anything."

A blood vessel under my right eye pulses. "What are their names, Carly?"

She blows a stream of smoke into my face. "The neighbor killed Juliana and Susan. That's all I got to say."

"And what if Jack didn't kill them?" Ginny blurts.

I look over at Ginny; her face is scarlet, and she's breathing heavily. "How can you live with yourself if those guys are guilty and you helped them get away with it?"

For the first time, Carly Amato actually looks sad. "Guys like that always get away with it. Sorry to be the one to tell you that."

We did it—we found out who else would have wanted Juliana and Susan dead. Allie's boyfriend and his friend must have gone to the Berrys' house that night to confront Juliana. Maybe they wanted to reason with her, or intimidate her into being quiet about the drug deal.

Instead, she fought back.

Ginny and I are in her room, sitting on her bed.

"It makes sense," I say. "They got into a fight with Juliana downstairs, and they killed her—and when Susan heard the commotion, she got out of the shower. So one or both of them chased her back upstairs."

Ginny sits butterfly style, pressing the bottoms of her feet together. "It definitely makes more sense than Jack Canning sneaking into the house and killing Juliana just to get to Susan."

I press my fingers to my eyelids. "This is infuriating. We have two guys with a motive and no idea what their names are because Carly Amato is a coward."

Ginny's eyes blaze. "*No.* We're going to find them."

The forcefulness of her voice takes me aback. I stare at Ginny, unsure of when this happened to her. Maybe she was always like this and no one bothered to pay attention.

"And then what?" I say. "Who would believe us if we accused two random guys of a five-year-old crime?"

"Ethan could testify." The pink in Ginny's cheeks deepens. "If they can tie the pickup truck to the guys—"

"No one is going to believe Ethan."

Ginny goes quiet. "I hate this."

"Me too," I say.

I don't just hate this—I feel completely wrecked. The idea that Juliana and Susan's killer is alive and walking free and there's nothing we can do about it is worse than not getting answers at all.

Is this where Jen found herself? Did she figure it out? She was closer to Juliana than anyone.

Did Jen find out something she wasn't supposed to? Did they get to her?

I need to know what happened to my sister.

Jennifer

"I can't do this."

Jen lay balled up on her side, the pillow beneath her stained with tears and drool. Her mother was sitting on the bed next to her, stroking her hair.

"You have to, baby. For her."

Jen's throat felt like it was closing. Her mother never called her *baby*, not once in her life. Jen cringed under the bony feel of her mother's fingers. She had lost so much weight in the past week. They both had.

Her mother had to help her into her dress. Jen didn't even care that her mom was seeing her in her bra and underwear. When her mother left to change into her own dress, Jen sat on the edge of her bed. She stared into her full-length mirror, unable to pick up the hairbrush lying next to her.

In the mirror, Jen caught a flash of brown hair in her doorway. She craned her neck in time to see Monica dart back down the hall.

Jen called her sister's name and Monica slunk back to Jen's doorway, silent in her black velvet dress. When Jen opened her mouth to ask Monica why she'd been spying, all that came out was a strangled cry.

Monica stepped inside Jen's room. She silently picked up the brush and began working at Jen's tangled ends. Jen sat, staring into the mirror, tears rolling down her cheeks as her sister—her little pain-in-the-ass sister—braided her hair with all the care and tenderness she used on one of her dolls.

The line for Juliana's wake wrapped all the way around the side of Maroney's and spilled into the parking lot. When Jen got out of the car, she felt her knees go wobbly. *I should wait out here for Susan.*

She was aware of her mother's eyes on her, and when Jen looked up, the realization crushed her. Susan was dead too. Her wake was in two days.

Her mother took her hand, but Jen stayed planted to the ground. People were looking over, their eyes lingering on the Rayburn/Carlino family a beat too long.

"They're looking at me," she whispered.

Tom put a hand on her mother's shoulder. "We can go in the back. No one will mind."

Jen kept her eyes down as Tom ushered them around the side of the building, to the emergency exit door. It was propped open, a man just outside in a suit—Mr. Maroney sneaking a cigarette. Even he looked beaten down.

Mr. Maroney nodded to Tom and let everyone inside without question. Jen let herself exhale as the door shut behind them. The hall was empty, save for a man dressed like Mr. Maroney. He seemed to be standing guard over the smallest room in the parlor. The door was cracked open; Jen caught a glimpse of the photo on the end table, surrounded by white lilies. Her stomach bottomed out.

"They had his wake here?"

Tom placed a hand on Jen's shoulder. "His mother deserves to bury him too."

Jen shrugged herself away from Tom. "He's a *monster*."

The man stationed outside the door to Jack Canning's viewing was looking over at them now; Mr. Maroney had stepped back inside at the commotion. Even Monica and Petey were looking up at Jen like they'd never seen her before.

Jen covered her mouth, running outside. She gagged over the railing, but nothing came out. Probably for the best. She would have ruined the pansies below her. The pansies hadn't done anything wrong.

"The trick is to stick your finger down your throat."

Jen looked up. Carly Amato, eyes red and eyelashes clumping together, was watching her. A cigarette burned between her index and middle finger.

"Don't talk to me," Jen said.

"That's right. Take it out on the skank." Carly stamped out her cigarette with the heel of her lace-up boot.

Jen felt a surge of anger. She thought of the blood staining Carly's lips, the manic look in her eyes when Allie had gone after her. The fight had felt like it was weeks ago. But it had only been six days.

"You had something to do with this, didn't you?"

Carly smirked. "Yeah. I told that creep to go over and kill them. You got me."

Jen had to stop herself from charging at Carly, transferring her rage to her like Allie had. She thought about saying something cruel. *You do a line of coke in the bathroom, Carly? Because you sure look like it.*

But Jen couldn't be cruel, no matter how much she wanted to be. The cruelest people were the ones who seemed to coast through life, as if all that nastiness was a shield.

"I wish she'd never met you," Jen said. "Maybe she'd still be here."

Carly blinked. Jen thought maybe she saw tears in her eyes before she turned and left her standing there.

When they got home from the wake, Jen said she was going to bed early. She climbed out the window and cut across the backyard, the glow of the TV in the den behind her.

He let her in. "Are you okay?"

Jen bit her lip. Shook her head. "Can we go to your room?"

Ethan slipped a hand in Jen's and led her down the hall. With his free hand, he opened his bedroom door. Jen looked from him to his bed. She lay down, and Ethan followed, keeping about a foot of space between them. His comforter was cool against her cheek.

Jen took Ethan's face in her hands. He held her back, winding his fingers through her hair. He didn't move to kiss her; this time, she kissed him first. He kissed her back until their faces were flushed and they had to break apart to catch their breath.

Jen stared at Ethan's face. Ran a finger down his lips. He kissed the pad of her finger and she reached behind her, unzipping her dress. Ethan put his lips on her shoulder.

Jen moved her hand lower, lower, until she felt the hot flesh of his belly. When she reached for the zipper on his pants, he laced his fingers through hers. Pulled her hand up his chest.

She sat up. "You don't want to?"

Ethan's face was flushed, his lips plump from the kissing. "I really, really want to." He scooted closer to her. Pulled her so she was tucked in the space between his legs. "I just don't want to do it when you're sad."

Jen's eyes stung as he moved her hair off her bare shoulder, brushing his lips against her collarbone. "I'm always sad."

She didn't realize she'd said it out loud until he paused. She turned to face him, her face wet now. "I'm always so goddamn sad."

Ethan reached and wiped away a tear with his thumb. "When was the last time you were happy?"

She didn't know. Even when she dug up her happiest memories, it was as if she were viewing them on a film reel. Things that had happened to another girl.

"I don't know if I ever was happy." Jen wiped a tear with the back of her hand. "It doesn't even matter. They're gone and I was supposed to be with them and every day since I've woken up wishing I could die too."

Ethan's finger, the one stroking her cheek, went still. "I tried to do it in eighth grade. Die."

It felt like the air was sucked from her body. "How?"

"I'm not telling you that. It's not the point. I changed my mind and I'm still here." Ethan cupped his hands around her face, inches from his own. "You have so many people here who love you."

That was the problem. Jen knew she was loved and that she'd always been loved. She knew that even if she did the unforgivable and destroyed them, they'd still love her. And that made it so much worse.

"I was supposed to be there," Jen whispered. "It was supposed to be the three of us."

Ethan said nothing. He moved his fingers from her cheek to her forehead. He brushed aside a lock of hair that had become wet with her tears, sending a shiver across her skin. Ethan didn't say *You can't think like that* or *you can't beat yourself up* like everyone else did. For that, Jen was grateful.

When he spoke again, his voice was a whisper in her ear. "You're still here. That's all that matters now."

Jen shut her eyes. A tear trailed down her cheek, over her lips, pooling in the crook of her collarbone.

Ethan wiped it away. "Say it. *I'm still here.*"

Jen obeyed, her voice straining against the invisible grip on her throat. "I'm still here."

She repeated the words in her head. But the longer they played on their loop, the less the words felt like an affirmation.

I'm still here.

It was starting to feel like a curse.

Chapter Nineteen

Mango scratches at my door around midnight. I shoo him back to my mother and Tom's room. He gives me a look that makes me feel like the most evil person who has ever lived.

I wait another half hour to make sure he doesn't come back before tiptoeing out of my room. Tom's snores carry out into the hall; I take the stairs, pausing on every step to listen for the sounds of the snores behind me.

Tom's computer is password protected. I try my mother's name, Petey's name, even mine with every permutation of our birthdays. None work, even when I substitute our names with *NYGiants*.

I open the top drawer of his desk, searching for a stray Post-it with passwords scribbled on it. I move my hand down to the third drawer, but it doesn't budge when I tug the handle.

Dread pools in my stomach. I left this drawer unlocked—Tom must have found it that way and known someone had been inside. I think of him searching through the contents. Realizing Jen's phone was gone. Figuring out there's only one person in this house with a reason to steal it.

I stand so forcefully the desk chair rolls backward. I need to get the hell out of here. When I turn and face the office doorway, I yelp.

Tom's arms are folded across his chest. He looks at me as if there are a million things he wants to say, but he settles on one word: "Sit."

Tom points to the love seat by the window. I comply while he flips the light on and sits at his desk. He steeples his fingers in front of his mouth. Shuts his eyes and spins small semicircles in his desk chair.

I don't know if he's waiting for me to defend myself or not.

"What are you doing?" I finally ask.

After a beat, he says, "I am trying to decide if there's a way to ream you out that doesn't involve your mother."

"Didn't you tell me that Mom doesn't need to know everything that goes on around here?"

Tom's eyes fly open. "You think this is funny? I keep my gun in the safe in here."

His voice cracks on the word *gun*, sending my guts into a knot.

"How did she kill herself?" I've asked him before, of course. The answer never changes. But now Tom's refusal to tell me the truth feels like another notch in Ethan's column.

Tom stares back at me, unmoved. "I swore to your mother that I would never tell you that."

"That's bullshit. I can handle it."

Tom slams a hand on his desktop. "It's not up to you."

For a second, I really think he's going to lose it on me.

But his expression softens. He runs his hands down his face. Takes an audible breath and stares at me as if for a moment he'd forgotten that I'm sitting here.

"You've got to be up early for the parade tomorrow," he says. "We'll talk about this some other time."

"I want to talk about it now," I snap, hating how I sound like a petulant child.

Tom sighs and reaches for the second drawer of his desk. He roots around and emerges with a bottle of bourbon and a glass. I blink at him as he pours himself two inches and tosses it back.

"Why do you have that in your desk?"

Tom swirls his glass, his eyes on the dregs clinging to the bottom. "Your mother doesn't like me drinking."

"Because you did it too much after Jen died?"

Tom pours himself another generous helping of bourbon. "Right you are."

As he knocks back the second glass, the pit in my stomach widens. "Do you need to do that?"

"Monica, if you want me to talk about something I really don't want to talk about, then yes. I need to."

Tom closes his eyes. Tilts his head back. When he opens his eyes again, they focus on me. "What do you want to know?"

Everything. "Why didn't you confront me when you realized I took Jen's phone?"

"I wasn't entirely convinced it wasn't your mother who took it. She doesn't know I kept it when I canceled Jen's phone number."

"But why did you keep it?"

"Monica. If your child took her own life, you would want to examine every single thing she did leading up to that moment to figure out why."

"So you knew she'd been talking to Ethan McCready. He was the last person who called her."

"Yes. When I learned it was his number, I lost my head and said some things to him that I shouldn't have. Accused him of things."

"You thought he had something to do with it?"

"The kid had a suicide attempt in his past." Tom swirls the dregs of liquid in his glass. "So yes. I thought he had something to do with it."

"But he knew something was wrong, and he tried to tell you. And you didn't listen. You didn't listen when he tried to tell you about what he saw at the Berrys' the night of the murders."

"He didn't *see anything*, Monica."

I swallow the bulb of anger tightening in my throat. "Have you *ever* stopped to consider that maybe he did? That maybe Jack Canning didn't do it?"

"A number of times, yes."

It's not what I expected him to say. The steely resolve he had when I confronted him weeks ago is gone.

"Then why didn't you try harder?" I demand.

"We talked to Juliana and Susan's friends," Tom says. "We didn't leave any stones unturned. No one wanted to hurt those girls."

"Did you talk to Carly Amato?"

Tom blinks with droopy eyelids. "Who?"

"She was friends with Juliana."

"The name doesn't sound familiar. But if they were friends, someone must have talked to her."

"Well, she could have lied to protect whoever did it. You *just* said you've considered that Jack Canning didn't do it."

"Sweetheart." Tom's eyes are red and glassy. "Just because I'm not one hundred percent certain doesn't mean that I don't believe in my heart of hearts that he did it. I believe the man who killed those girls is dead."

Hearing him say it feels like a fist coming down on my heart.

"I believe the man who killed Jen is dead," he says, and my eyes water with hot tears. "I blame Jack Canning for killing her. I know you wish there was someone still here who we can blame. I wish it sometimes too."

I wipe my face with my pajama sleeve. Tom grabs the box of tissues on his desk and hands them to me before sitting back down.

Once I've wiped my nose, I look up at Tom. "Did you know it was Ethan McCready sending you the letters in your desk?"

Tom shuts his eyes. "I suspected it, yes."

When Tom opens his eyes, he pours himself another shot of bourbon. When he meets my gaze, he sets the glass down on his desk instead of knocking it back.

"Why?" I whisper. "Why did you keep her phone?"

Tom watches me through bleary eyes. "Every now and then, I look at those calls. I've memorized the numbers, but I just keep going back to them like they're a code I can't crack." He pauses, his gaze flitting to the

322

bourbon on his desk. "I listen to her voice mail, hoping I'll hear something new. I assume it's the same reason the McCready kid sends me those letters. We think if we ask enough times, the answer will change."

My throat is tight. "I can't stop hearing the sound of Mom's scream," I say. "In the car, after she picked me up that morning. Are there things you can't stop seeing or hearing?"

Tom nods. He closes his eyes and tilts his head all the way back until I can barely see his face. When he sits upright again, he says, "The dog was curled up next to Susan's body, shaking. The damn thing had Jules's blood all over his paws."

Tom has never told me anything about what he saw in the Berrys' house. He must be drunk to be telling me something as intimate as Beethoven, Susan's beloved dog, lying next to her lifeless body.

Something occurs to me. "The dog. Wouldn't he have tried to attack the killer?"

"Someone Jack's size would have been able to throw a dog off of him."

"But was the dog hurt? Limping or something?"

Tom's face falls, and I know that he hadn't thought of that. Or he did, because he's a good cop, and he wrote it off, because even good cops make mistakes.

A perfect storm for a shoddy investigation. The police were blinded by emotion, more prone to overlook small details.

Like how strange it was that Jack Canning walked out of the Berrys' house without a very large dog bite.

Preparing for the homecoming parade in the morning feels like sleepwalking through Monica 1.0's life. I don't recognize myself in the bathroom mirror as I go through my game makeup routine, applying false eyelashes and lining my lips in red. Everything is the same, but it's different.

We're marching in the parade and performing to the marching band's music; it's a watered-down, simple routine centered on a kickline. Still, Coach ordered us to be in full competition dress: slicked-back buns, rhinestones adhered to the corners of our eyes.

The parade starts in the high school parking lot; once we're all here, Coach lines us up for inspection. The parking lot is filling rapidly with sports team members in uniform, band members carrying unwieldy instruments. A girl is blowing into a clarinet, tuning it shrilly.

A whistle pierces through the din. Around the parking lot, people are dropping what they're doing to find the source of the noise. Mrs. Lin, the student council advisor, climbs onto the back of the pickup truck hitched to the senior class float. She sticks two fingers in her mouth and whistles again.

"Find your groups, please. Class court members should report to their floats. If you're marching *and* on homecoming court, find your class float at the end of the parade route for the crowning ceremony."

The band launches into a practice run of Sunnybrook's fight song, and we run through the routine. They kick off the parade, us dancing behind them, and the other sports teams and the class floats bringing up the rear.

When we reach the corner of Main Street, someone shouts my name from the crowd. My brother is jumping up and down, waving at me. He's camped outside of Alden's grocery with TJ Blake and his mother. The sidewalks are packed, and the police have the side streets blocked off. The crowd goes wild at our high kicks. While they're clapping, I sneak a wave at my brother.

A flash of blond hair, and our eyes connect. Me and Allie Lewandowski. She stares back at me, coldly, and I stumble, sashaying forward with the wrong foot.

What is she doing here?

She didn't go to Sunnybrook High School; she hasn't coached here for years. Paranoia wallops me as I entertain the idea that Allie being here has something to do with our meeting.

I screw up the routine and add in an extra step, colliding with the dancer in front of me. We're at the end of the route, in the CVS parking lot. I can't think over the buzzing in my ears.

Ginny. I have to find Ginny and tell her Allie is here. I wade through the crowd at the end of the route, looking for her strawberry-blond bun. We all look the same in our uniforms, our identical hairstyles.

Someone grabs me by the shoulder, pulling me back.

"Monica," Alexa says. "We have to go to the float for homecoming court."

I open my mouth to give her an excuse, but the crowd starts going wild. The class floats are approaching the end of the route, a police officer directing the trucks pulling them into the parking lot.

Alexa tugs on my hand, and we follow the junior class float. It's a giant papier-mâché of a shark head. Hanging between two palm trees is a banner reading GRAB SHREWSBURY BY THE JAWS.

The other court members are already on the float, plastic leis around their necks. The driver—one of the juniors' parents—slows to a stop in front of CVS.

"Come on, come on." Mrs. Lin hurries over to Alexa and me, passing us each plastic leis. This part always annoys her, how all the girls on the team who make homecoming court choose dancing in the parade over riding on the float. Or at least, she thinks we have the choice.

One of the guys on the float holds a hand out to Alexa, helping hoist her up. Once she's settled, he reaches for me. I balk.

"Monica," Mrs. Lin snaps. "I need you on that float so we can start the ceremony. The police have to reopen the road in fifteen minutes."

"I decline the nomination," I say. "Give it to someone else."

Alexa stares from me to Mrs. Lin. "Can she even do that?"

Before I can open my mouth, two guys on the float reach down and grab me by the forearms, pulling me up.

Mrs. Lin hurries off to make sure the Kelseys, both on the homecoming court, have made it onto the senior class float behind us without incident. I rub my forearms, the skin smarting from where the guys grabbed me.

The sight of the crowd gathering in the parking lot waiting for the coronation sends a shot of panic through me. I drape my lei over my head, heart hammering, scanning the throng of people for Allie Lewandowski.

I finally spot her in front of the post office adjoining the CVS. She's standing next to a tall guy wearing a beanie and a Sunnybrook cross-country sweatshirt. He's almost a foot taller than she is; his head is turned to the soccer coach standing next to him, but his arm is around Allie's waist.

Brandon. Brandon and Allie.

Somewhere, someone is shouting into a bullhorn.

"And now, your junior class homecoming court!"

More cheers, nearly drowning out our names. When they get to mine, I try to duck behind Alexa, but it's too late; they've both seen me. Brandon is clapping, slowly, a deer caught in the headlights. Allie's arms are folded across her chest. They both seem oblivious to the fact that the other is staring straight at me.

Chapter Twenty

Kelsey Butler and Joe Gabriel win homecoming queen and king. While they're being crowned, I hop off the float and wend my way through the dispersing crowd. The cop manning the end of the route is having little luck shooing people out of the street.

I pass through the CVS parking lot and out onto the sidewalk. Keep walking until I spot them in front of the playhouse. Ginny and my brother. Petey is talking a mile a minute, and she's smiling down at him, nodding along. Always a good sport.

"Where's Mom?" I ask Petey when I catch up with them.

"At home doing work. TJ's mom brought me."

Ginny's eyes meet mine—she can tell I'm upset. I shake my head. *Not here.*

I put a hand on Petey's shoulder. "Can you go find TJ? Ginny and I have to be somewhere for dance team."

"But she downloaded *Clan Wars*. I was telling her about the update," he whines.

"Petey. Please."

He gives me a frosty look and trudges off to where

TJ and Mrs. Blake are chatting with a woman outside of Alden's. Ginny's voice is in my ear: "What's the matter?"

I nod to the alley walkway between the playhouse and the library. Ginny and I slip down it and emerge in the rear parking lot.

"Allie Lewandowski's here," I say. "With Brandon, the cross-country coach."

I can't tell if she's putting two and two together— seeing me inside Brandon's office and my reaction to seeing him here with Allie today. My calling him Brandon and not Mr. Michaelson, like everyone else does.

If Ginny knows, she doesn't say anything. But her face is grim. "Last night . . . I poked around online a little. I tried to find the names of guys from the Sunnybrook area who also graduated from Hamilton the year before the murders."

My mouth goes dry.

"There were only three guys who met the criteria. One of them is Brandon Michaelson." Ginny eyes me. "I looked into him more and found him on Newton High West's athletic records website. Allie was on it too. She graduated the year before. She got a scholarship to Oneonta for cheerleading."

I lower myself to the curb, sit, and lean forward, resting my elbows on my knees. If Brandon was dating Allie at the time of the murders, it doesn't mean he's involved. Carly had said Allie's boyfriend's friend was the one who was selling pills. He was the one Juliana was afraid of.

But Brandon knew. If Carly was telling the truth,

Brandon was in the car when the other guy stopped to make a deal. Brandon helped his friend beat the shit out of the guy who ratted him out.

It was five years ago. People change.

A dueling voice in my head jumps in. *He was still older than you are now. He knew better.*

"It doesn't matter," I whisper it, as if saying it out loud will make it true. It doesn't matter who Brandon was back then, because nothing is going on between Brandon and me anymore.

You made out with him in his car during the memorial.

I bury my face in my hands. Breathe deeply for a minute before I look up at Ginny. "Brandon was Allie's boyfriend, and his best friend was the drug dealer. Carly didn't say which one the pickup truck belonged to."

"So what do we do?" Ginny says.

"I don't know. We have no proof of anything. We have a rumor from Carly that Brandon was friends with a drug dealer who may have possibly killed Juliana and Susan. We have a dead man's statement that he saw a pickup truck that night. And then a story about someone fighting with Juliana on the deck that the cops already think is a lie." I rub my eyes. "Who's going to believe us?"

Ginny's mouth forms a line. Shouts of excitement echo in the alley behind us. People are filtering through it, heading for their cars parked in the lot.

"Congratulations!" A man accompanied by a trio of kids gives me a thumbs-up. It takes me a moment to remember the lei around my neck. When he and the kids are loaded into their car, I tear the lei off.

"I can't do this," I tell Ginny. "I can't go to the game or the dance and act like everything is normal."

"You have to," she says. "There's nothing we can do right now. You're just going to make your mom and step-dad more worried about you."

She's right. My eyes prick with tears. "Can you come? I know you didn't get a ticket to the dance, but you can come to Kelsey's party."

The faintest trace of a smile passes over Ginny's lips. "Monica. That would be the exact opposite of acting like everything is normal."

To everyone's surprise, Sunnybrook defeats Shrewsbury 50 to 44. It's the first homecoming game we've won in four years; as a result, the mood at the dance is even more raucous than normal. Three seniors are thrown out for showing up drunk, and all night teachers have to pry people off each other for violating the no-grinding rule.

Alexa is breathless on the ride back to her house, un-daunted by the fact that Mrs. Coughlin reamed her out for dancing inappropriately with Joe Gabriel, even going so far as to threaten to tell Coach.

"I love him," Alexa says, lowering the window and tilting her face to the cool night air. "I'm going to lick his face tonight."

"You're demented. He's a douchebag." Rach isn't look-ing at either of us, her eyes on the road. She's been quiet all day. It worries me; her being this moody means she's more likely to get obliterated at Kelsey's party.

They bicker all the way to Alexa's about whether or not Joe Gabriel is a douchebag. I can't keep up; Brandon won't stop invading my thoughts. The look on his face when he saw me at the parade.

Was he just nervous, having me in proximity of his girlfriend? Or does he know I talked to Allie last week, and he's panicking because I asked her about Carly Amato?

Rach, Alexa, and I head straight upstairs when we get to the Santiagos'. I park myself on the edge of Alexa's bed, peeling off the glittery flats I wore to the dance. We're staying here tonight; Alexa's mom is always saying that she knows we drink, and if we're going to do it anyway, she'd rather we have a safe ride home. Rachel and I don't have chill moms; they think we're sleeping at the Santiagos' tonight and braiding each other's hair or whatever.

Tom gave me a look and a sigh when I told him and my mom I was staying here.

While Rachel strips off her homecoming dress, replacing it with skinny jeans, I get my phone out of my purse. I have a missed text. I recognize the number as Brandon's.

Need to talk to you.

I try to control my breathing as I type out a response.

About what?

"I can't wear this." Rachel is studying herself in Alexa's full-length mirror, running her hands over her glittery black tank top. "My boobs are falling out."

"It's that stupid juice cleanse." Alexa is winding a lock of hair around her wave iron. My phone vibrates.

I think you know what.

I pocket my phone, feeling sick. He knows I talked to Allie. If she told him everything, he may have put the pieces together. He might know I've been looking into the murders.

"Here. Wear this. It's going to be freezing by the lake anyway." Alexa tosses Rach a boatneck sweatshirt. She tugs it over her tank top. Examines herself in the mirror.

"Just don't let anything happen to that one," Alexa says, turning back to freshening up her waves. "I like it."

Rach's face darkens, no doubt thinking of the dance team sweatshirt she borrowed from Alexa and lost.

I shrug out of my dress, almost positive Rach and Alexa can hear my heart racing. I want to talk to Ginny, but I'll have to tell her why Brandon Michaelson has my phone number.

I just won't respond to him. He can't push it, can't try to corner me at school on Monday. Not without having to answer uncomfortable questions about our relationship. The thought soothes me enough to laugh as Mrs. Santiago and Rachel taunt Alexa about Joe on the car ride to the Gabriels' house.

Kelsey lives on a secluded estate on the north side of

Osprey Lake. It's one of those houses that have a driveway with a gate. Her back deck overlooks the lake and has a hot tub.

Almost everyone is inside, because it's forty degrees out—probably the coldest night of the season so far. A few brave morons are in the hot tub.

The party is a shitshow. Rachel is drunk within fifteen minutes of our arrival, and Alexa is stuck to the beer pong table like a barnacle. I leave her and make myself a vodka cranberry in the kitchen. Drain it in two gulps, hoping it will loosen me a bit, before I'm dragged into a group of dance team girls.

"We're doing a shot together," one of them crows. I don't fight it; when we're done I do a lap around the house for Rachel. Unable to find her, I pour another drink and head back to the garage.

Alexa is still at the beer pong table. I watch her play against Joe Gabriel and another senior guy.

"Hey." Jimmy Varney sidles up next to me, a can of Diet Coke in hand.

"Is there rum in there, at least?" I'm surprised at the effort it takes to get the words out. I look down at the dregs of my vodka cranberry. My head is fuzzy, and I can't remember if it was my second or third. No, definitely second. I always stop after two. The shot I did, though—that was a mistake.

Jimmy smiles. "Driving," he says. "Rachel Steiger is looking for you."

Disappointment needles me. Is that the only reason he sought me out? I'm immediately disgusted with myself.

My pathological need for attention from guys is why I'm in this mess with Brandon.

"Thanks," I say. "I'll go find her I guess."

Jimmy nods to the beer pong table. "Partners next game?"

Before I can respond, my back pocket vibrates. I set my drink down and scramble to get my phone out, my fingertips numb from the cold garage.

I turn away from Jimmy so he can't see the message from Brandon.

> I'm parked down the block. Can you come out?
> We need to talk. Now.

My heart comes to a full stop. The noise in the garage dulls; I lean against the wall for support.

Jimmy rests a hand on my upper back. "Mon, are you okay?"

"Yeah. Fine. I need to get something from inside."

I head up the stairs into the house at the same moment Rachel is stepping down into the garage, wobbling on her heels like a newborn giraffe. Her eyes, mascara already smudged, lock on me. "Babe! Whatcha doing?"

"I have to go somewhere for a minute," I say, sidestepping her. "I'll be right back."

Rachel pouts. "But *where* are you going?"

"Outside for a minute. I'll be right back."

"Can I come?"

"No." It comes out more forceful than I intended.

"Jesus, Rach, I'll be *right back*."

Rach takes a step back at the forcefulness of my voice. Her cup sways with her, splashing cranberry juice down Alexa's sweatshirt.

"Nooooo." She screws up her face like a toddler who dropped her ice cream in the dirt. "No no no!"

"It's okay," I say. "Ask Kelsey if she has seltzer."

"Alexa is going to kill me! I'm always borrowing her shit and losing it or ruining it."

That's when something in me snaps. "Rachel. You need to get a grip."

She bursts into tears. Alexa, who has been watching us from the pong table, looks at me like I'm a monster. I'll have to apologize later, but right now, I need to get the hell out of here before anyone sees Brandon's Jeep.

How the hell could he come here? Does he realize how stupid that is? If he's caught near a high school party—

My gut clenches at the sight of Brandon's Jeep parked at the end of the cul-de-sac, his lights off. I rap on the window. He lowers it. "Door's unlocked."

"I think I'll stay out here." I wrap my arms around my midsection.

Brandon sighs. Turns his engine off. "Fine."

I take a step back as he gets out of the Jeep. He rakes his hair off his forehead and looks at me. "You talked to Allie. What the fuck, Monica?"

"It wasn't even about you. I didn't know you two were together."

"Still," he says. "Do you realize what could happen if she finds out?"

"I'm not going to tell her anything. Are we done here? Good. Bye." I suddenly realize that I am drunk and need to remove myself from this situation. When I turn to leave, Brandon grabs my wrist.

"Wait. Why were you asking Allie about Carly Amato?"

My knees are quaking beneath me. I press my legs together to still them. "You and Allie were together when she was the cheerleading coach, weren't you?"

Brandon is quiet. "I don't know where you're going with this."

"Just answer the question, Brandon."

"You're obviously wasted," he says. "Why don't you let me take you home?"

It occurs to me that he's still holding me by the wrist.

"Get the hell away from me." I yank my arm away from him so forcefully that I pull a muscle in my shoulder. Brandon takes a step back. Holds his hands up. "Jesus, Monica."

"Don't ever come near me again," I say.

He gets back into the car, and I start crying. I collapse on the lawn of the house Brandon parked outside. And I call my mom.

My mother looks deeply unamused as she pulls up outside Kelsey's house. I yank open the passenger door and stumble in.

Mom sniffs. "How much did you drink?"

"Two vodka cranberries and a shot."

She sighs and pulls away from the house. I lean

back in the seat, eyes closed, tears pooling under my lids.

Once we're home, she turns off the engine, but she doesn't move to get out of the car. Finally, she speaks. "Just tell me what to do. I'm out of ideas."

My throat is dry and scratchy. I swallow, but I can't find any words. The sobs come out of me like violent dry heaves. "I hate myself."

I don't know what she was expecting me to say, but that wasn't it. She flinches like I've cursed at her. I can't stand looking at her, so I cover my face in my hands and cry. It's an ugly, awful sound—any louder and Tom and Petey could probably hear from inside the house.

"Monica. Listen to me."

I hiccup. Gulp for air. My mother says my name again; she grabs me and holds my head to her shoulder. She rocks me like a child and lets me cry.

"I hate who I am. I hate myself so much."

"Monica," she says, still cradling me. "Even at your worst, I love you more than life itself."

Mom makes me drink a full bottle of water before I go up to bed. I eye my bathroom, but I'm not ready to throw up yet. I stumble to my bed and text Ginny.

> he came to kelset gs brandon

My phone starts vibrating moments later. She's calling me. I hit accept.

Ginny's voice is soft in my ear.

"Monica? I couldn't understand your texts. Are you drunk?"

"Yes," I say. "Brandon came to Kelsey's party. We argued and I told him to stay away from me."

"Monica, hold on. Brandon Michaelson?"

"Yes. Allie's boyfriend."

"How did he— What was he doing showing up at Kelsey's party to talk to you?"

"He . . . We . . . I fucked up *so bad*," I whimper, and hiccup, and Ginny cuts me off by saying my name.

"Monica, look, it's not your fault. He's so much older . . . Monica, you understand what happened to you, right?"

"I know. I think I have to tell Tom everything."

"Is he awake now?"

"No. I think I should wait until the morning. He . . . he's not going to believe me when I'm like this.

"Ginny," I say. "I don't deserve a friend like you."

I don't know what she says in response, because the room around me spins into darkness.

I wake up ready to throw up and stumble into my bathroom. Not much comes out. I flush the toilet and lie back against the vanity, not ambitious enough to stand just yet.

Finally I'm ready to drag myself back to bed. Before

I get comfortable, I check my phone. It's only two in the morning; I must have passed out briefly after ending my call with Ginny.

I have a text from Rachel, time stamped almost an hour ago.

> Babe you okay??? Someone said
> your mom picked u up
> I'm sorry I was such an asshole.
> I got the juice off lex's shirt with
> seltzer

I text her back, my eyes tight, cheeks stiff with tears:

> I'm the asshole. I love you.

I wish I were piled onto Alexa's bed with my friends. On a normal night, we would be laughing by now at Rach's lack of ability to give us back anything she borrows. Earrings, sweatshirts, books. We don't know where it all goes, but we keep lending her shit anyway because that's what friends do.

I jolt, sitting up straight and banging my head on my headboard. A single thought crystallizes. Something is wrong. Why can't I figure out what's wrong?

Brandon and Carly. Brandon was not cheating on Allie with Carly. Allie said the guys shouldn't have been hanging out with a *high school girl*. Not *girls*.

Allie didn't know about Juliana. Brandon didn't *want* her to know about Juliana.

I cover my mouth. Whimper, tasting bile coming back up my throat.

I made myself delete the picture a few weeks ago. I took it at work this summer. Brandon on the lifeguard stand, sticking his tongue out at me playfully.

I fumble for my phone. My trash bin stores deleted pictures for thirty days.

I zoom in on Brandon's tan and muscular legs. It feels like my bed is bottoming out.

Just above his right ankle, on his calf, is a crescent-shaped white scar, the size of a bite from a large dog.

Chapter Twenty-One

I wake up facedown on my bed, still in the outfit I wore to Kelsey's party. My phone tells me it's almost noon. I head downstairs, every step rattling my brain. I want to die.

My brother is on the living room couch, watching an Avengers movie. An explosion on-screen makes the throbbing in my head quicken.

"Where is everyone?" I ask.

"Dad is at the range, and Mom is at her play, duh."

A fresh wave of panic hits me. My parents left Petey and me alone—of course they did. It's broad daylight on Sunday, and we're not infants. They don't know what happened last night. Maybe Ginny was right, and I should have woken Tom up to tell him everything.

"They said you have a hangover and I shouldn't wake you up but if you do, I'm supposed to tell you not to set one foot outside this house," Petey says.

"Got it." I massage my temples.

I plod into the kitchen, wincing at the light coming in through the window over the sink. Water. I need to rehydrate, maybe force some food down so I can take a Tylenol.

The sound of a car door shutting makes me freeze.

Maybe Tom, back from the range already. I look out the window, but the driveway is empty.

There's a knock at the door leading from the kitchen into the garage. Tom must have left the garage door open when he left.

I swallow back the urge to vomit. I creep over to the door, opening it the slightest crack.

Brandon stares back at me. My stomach plummets.

"I just want to talk," he says.

I have a flash of him at Susan Berry's back door. "You need to leave before I call my stepdad," I say. "Did I mention he's a cop?"

"And tell him what?" There's panic in Brandon's voice. "You have the wrong idea about everything."

I think about my brother, lounging on the couch. Mango curled at his feet, unable to hear the knock at the door because of the volume of his movie.

I angle myself so Brandon can't see me and fumble until I find the sound recording app on my phone and hit START. I slip my phone into my pajama pants pocket and step into the garage, pulling the door shut behind me.

"What do you want, Brandon?" His name tastes foul in my mouth, but I need some way to prove it's him on the recording.

"I'm sorry about last night. I was out of line." His eyes are pink around his pupils, the skin underneath them gray and shiny. "But we need to talk about why you care so much about Carly Amato and Allie."

"You know why I care about them." I think of the security cameras Tom never got. Did anyone see Brandon

343

come here? Will it even matter if he drags me out of here and gets me into his car? My brother won't hear my scream over the movie, and if he does, I have no idea what Brandon will do to him.

"Monica, whatever you're thinking, it's wrong."

"So you didn't cheat on Allie with Juliana Ruiz?"

His reaction to her name is all the confirmation I need. He flinches, and his expression hardens. The lightest twitch in his jaw. I almost buckle over. I'm right—the earring, Carly's earring—

"I met her through Carly," Brandon says. "It was stupid of me. I ended it quickly."

"The night she was killed, right? Someone saw you outside Susan's house."

Brandon's lips part. I'm shaking so hard. His eyes drop to my pocket, from which I've forgotten to remove my hand. Realization dawns on his face. "Are you recording this?"

He takes a step toward me at the same moment the kitchen door opens.

I whip around; Petey is standing in the doorway. He looks from Brandon to me. "Who is that?"

"No one. Go back inside, Petey."

I pull Brandon aside by the arm, my pulse ticking in my ears. "He knows you were here. What you look like. You're not a kid killer, Brandon. Please just leave and I'll pretend you were never here."

Brandon's eyes flick from me to my brother, who hasn't moved.

"Please," I say quietly. "You didn't think this through.

He's just a kid. And if you take me, he'll be able to lead the cops straight to you. You won't get away with it."

A bead of sweat crops up on Brandon's lip. I've gotten through to him. He's not a kid killer.

When I feel the tension leave his body, I knee him in the balls and scream for Petey to run. "Go straight to Ginny's house. Number eighty-four. Call the police there."

Brandon doubles over and yelps with pain. He stands up straight as I'm stumbling toward Tom's workbench and grabs me by the shoulder.

He's hurting; I can hear it in his labored breathing. I could probably fight him off, but I need to give my brother a head start. I struggle against Brandon, keeping my eye on the open garage door; as soon I spot Petey running down the street, I twist and elbow Brandon in the face.

When I start to scramble away from him, pain sears the back of my head. He has me by the ponytail; I scream as he yanks me to a stop. He covers my mouth with one hand. I bite him, hard. While he recoils, I grab Petey's baseball bat off the rack next to the workbench. I use one hand to keep the bat pointed at Brandon.

"You move, I bash your head in. Hands up."

Brandon complies. The hand where I bit him is pink, blood drops forming where my teeth met his flesh. I think of Susan Berry's dog, trying to stop Brandon from smothering her. I tighten my grip around the bat.

"Sit there." I nod to the rack where we keep our dirty shoes. Brandon obeys.

"Okay," I say. "You said you wanted to talk. Talk."

He winces, from the pain in his groin, his hand, or

both. "I don't know what I'm supposed to say."

"Why'd you kill them?" I ask. "Did Juliana threaten to tell Allie?"

Brandon shuts his eyes, muttering, "Oh my God oh my God oh my God." He probably thought this moment would never come.

I hit him in the kneecap with the bat, yelling over his moaning and cries of *Oh my God*. "Why did you kill them, Brandon?"

"It wasn't just about Allie finding out. I was twenty-two, and Juliana was fifteen," he says. "If she told anyone, I could have gone to *jail*. You should know that."

The snideness that's crept into his voice makes me want to hit him in the knee again, harder. "What happened that night?"

"I told Juliana we had to stop, the morning after Allie found the earring in my truck. Juliana was really, really mad. She'd thought I would break up with Allie for her—she didn't *get* it, that I couldn't be with a fifteen-year-old." Brandon swallows. "She asked me to come to Susan's house to talk. We sat in my truck. It was fine, at first, but when I told her again I wasn't leaving Allie, she started crying and yelling about how she was going to tell her. She got out and slammed the door."

"You followed her inside."

Brandon closes his eyes. Tears drip down his face, over his lips. "She wouldn't answer the front door. When she said she was going to call the cops, I freaked. I climbed the fence, and I saw the back door—she saw me and opened it and started yelling at me. When I followed her into the house she went nuts. I was afraid Susan would hear, so I covered Juliana's mouth. She bit me, and when she jerked away, she fell back into the mirror. Her head was bleeding, and she came at me with a shard—I just panicked."

"So instead of calling to get Juliana help, you killed her and Susan."

"Susan heard. She came downstairs at the noise. She started running back upstairs when she saw everything, so I ran after her and grabbed her." Brandon chokes out a sob. "I didn't go there planning to hurt anyone. It just got out of control."

"You're disgusting!" I scream. "It was all an act with me, wasn't it? You pretended sleeping with me was a bad idea because of my age, while you were really a fucking *pedo*—"

He lunges at me, mashing his fist into my mouth before I can lift the baseball bat. I stumble back, but he presses his forearm into my throat, pinning me to the wall. When he reaches for the bat, I throw it as far as my short reach will allow. It clatters when it hits the ground, but Brandon doesn't go after it; his eyes are locked on me. I'm staring back at a cornered animal.

"Is this what you did to her?" I gasp.

Black spots are swimming before my eyes. Then, screaming. His screaming. He releases me, stumbling backward; I'm bent over, clutching my throat, trying to process the scene in front of me.

Ginny is standing over Brandon, the bat in her hands.

She's calm, her hands steady around its neck; Brandon is on his back, not moving.

"Where's my brother?" It comes out garbled; my lips are swollen and my mouth tastes like blood. "Where's Petey?"

"He's at my house. We called nine-one-one, and Tom."

I look from Ginny to Brandon. It's just the three of us now. I don't hear sirens yet. Brandon is watching me from the floor, his temple leaking blood. I realize that Ginny hit him in the head with the bat.

Brandon's eyelids flutter. He needs an ambulance; he has a concussion, or worse. I look at Ginny again.

"Give me the bat."

"Monica," she says.

"Please."

Ginny hands it over. Brandon's eyes roll back. He's finally passed out, either from the pain or from the sight of me standing over him with the bat. He must see it in my face—how badly I want to kill him. I've never wanted anything more in my life. It would just take a few swings.

My fingers tremble around the handle of the bat. I look at Ginny. Her face is calm. "If you do it, I'll say whatever you want."

She'll tell everyone it was self-defense. That I had no choice but to kill Brandon.

"I want to." A tear slips out of my eye. "I want it so bad."

"I know," Ginny says.

The thoughts swirl through my head, landing on what my mother said to me last night in her car. *Even at your worst, I love you more than life itself.* She will still love me if I execute Brandon right here. I know Tom would, too, and maybe even Petey as well.

But the Ruizes, the Berrys—all the people whose lives he destroyed—they deserve the chance to look Brandon in the face as well. If I take that from them, I won't be able to live with myself.

Brandon's eyes open again. I hold his gaze as I kick him in the stomach. I keep kicking and kicking until I'm out of breath, until a siren blares from down the street, until my foot's gone numb and Ginny has to drag me away from his limp body.

Chapter Twenty-Two

"We can go home now."

Tom's voice snaps me out of my trance. He sets his phone down on his desk and rubs his eyes. My mother has pulled her seat so close to mine she is practically on top of me.

When Tom speaks, her grip on my shoulder tightens. "What about *him*?"

"Being treated. Won't be able to talk to him until tomorrow, most likely."

"Why is he getting medical care?" Mom demands. "He should be in a cell."

Tom shuts his eyes. Holds up a hand. "Phoebe, please."

I touch the tender skin on my neck where Brandon tried to choke me. The first responders said to expect nasty bruises there. They checked me for any serious injuries at the house and cleared me, which is the only reason my mother let me skip going to the hospital.

I saw them carting Brandon off to the hospital. I can't be in the same building as him. I don't even want to breathe the same air as Brandon Michaelson.

A flutter of panic. "They can't let him go, right?"

"They have enough to keep him for assault." Tom doesn't look at me as he says it, but my mother moves her hand to mine. "They'll move to charge him for that and the statutory rape as soon as possible."

My mother flinches at the last part.

"What about the murders?" I ask. "I have him recorded practically confessing."

"Once they finish up interviewing Ginny about what happened today, someone is going to talk to you again. After that, the DA will want to hear from you." Tom massages his beard. "I've been asked to step aside while they investigate."

My eyes go prickly. If Brandon is charged with Juliana's and Susan's murders, the department will reopen the inquiry into Jack Canning's death. Tom could lose his job.

"I'm sorry," I say. "All of this is my fault."

My mother moves her hand to my knee and squeezes. "Stop it."

She's crying and I'm crying, and soon Tom is crying and wrapping his arms around both of us and we're all crying.

"What if Jen knew it was him?" I manage to choke out. "What if she knew and he found out and he made it look like she did it herself—"

"Monica." My mom tightens her grip on me. "She left a note. Jen left a note. She mentioned you. She wanted you to see California for her—"

"Stop," I say. "Please stop."

"Honey, no. You have to understand."

I'm sobbing too hard to get out what I want to tell her: I'll never understand.

I wake in my bed to my mother's hand on my forehead and sunlight assaulting my eyelids. "Ginny's here, if you want to see her."

I sit up. "What time is it?"

"Almost ten. I wanted to let you sleep. Do you want me to send her up?"

My head is throbbing. "No. I'll come downstairs."

Ginny is on my living room couch. She cranes her neck. Stands when she sees me.

I wave a hand. "Sit, sit."

Ginny lowers herself onto the couch and I plop down next to her. "God, this hurts so bad."

"Your neck?"

That, and everything else. "Yeah."

"I just wanted you to know—I didn't tell the police anything," she says. "Well, obviously I told them stuff. But not the last part of yesterday."

"Thanks. But you don't have to lie for me anymore." I pinch the bridge of my nose until I see white. "Everyone's going to find out about Brandon and me. My life is pretty much over anyway."

"You didn't do anything wrong." Ginny's voice is soft. "He used you, like he used Juliana."

"I used him. I was tired of being numb and I wanted to prove to myself I could feel something."

Ginny is quiet for a moment. Then: "Did you?"

"I do now."

I don't realize I'm crying until Ginny throws her arms around me.

Tom said to expect the murder case to move slowly. When the news breaks Brandon is being charged with statutory rape and assault, there's no mention in the news of Juliana's and Susan's murders.

There's no mention of Brandon Michaelson's unnamed victim, but everyone at school knows it's me.

I'm not sure who figured it out, but it doesn't take a detective to put everything together. My two-day absence starting the morning that Brandon was fired from Sunnybrook High, rumors already swirling that he'd been arrested.

Rachel and Alexa are the only ones I've told outside of Ginny and my family. They shield me on the way inside the school building; when the news broke last night, my mother said I could stay home today, but there's something I've been meaning to do.

Instead of nasty looks and a scarlet letter painted on my locker, I arrive to sympathetic smiles. I suspect Rach and Alexa did damage control.

I am a victim, whether or not I feel like one. Maybe one day I will wake up crushed under the weight of what Brandon did to me. For now all I feel is the memory of that baseball bat hitting his body and my foot in his ribs.

At the end of the day, before dance team practice starts, I find Coach in the athletic office, filling out registration forms for the upcoming competition. She looks up at me; she doesn't seem surprised to see that I'm not dressed in my dance clothes.

"I quit," I say. "I should have done it sooner. But you have a week before regionals to rework the spots."

Coach works the top of her pen with her thumb, giving it a click. "Are you sure this is what you want?"

I couldn't eat the morning after dance team tryouts freshman year. I tried to strike a deal with God: *If I make the team, I promise I'll be nicer to Mom and Petey and give all my Christmas money to the animal shelter.* I'd never wanted anything so badly.

Freshman-year Monica would want to punch me in the face.

"Yes," I tell Coach.

She blinks at me, the ghost of a smile on her lips, before going back to her paperwork. "You're all right, Rayburn."

I don't know which way she means it. But when I leave her office, I feel lighter than I did when I stepped inside.

I catch the three-thirty bus home from school. The days are getting shorter. It feels strange, being home before dark. As I climb the driveway, I see my mother's silhouette in the window, hanging a strand of orange holiday lights. The outside of the house looks different too; she's stretched cotton cobwebs over the bushes, and a skeleton in a top hat hangs off the hook on the front door.

When the door clicks shut behind me, Mango starts

barking. My mom pops her head into the foyer, the tangle of Halloween lights in hand. "You're home."

"I quit dance team."

She comes to my side, draping an arm around my shoulder and pulling me in for a hug. I'm almost as tall as she is now. I let her squeeze me for a solid minute before putting my hands on her shoulders and gently pushing her away. "Do you need help with the lights?"

After the lights are strung, I head up to my room and shrug out of my jeans, replacing them with pajama pants. I plop into my desk chair and open up my email, bracing for anonymous hate messages about what a life-ruining slut I am.

I only have one message, and it's from Daphne Furman. My heartbeat skips; there's no way she knows that I'm the Sunnybrook High victim. There was no mention of Brandon's connection to the cheerleader murders in the media—

The gears in my head grind to a halt when I see the subject line.

Phil Cordero.

I pull my feet onto my desk chair and tuck them under me.

Hi Monica—
   My contact had a tough time with this one. He couldn't find any record of employment, taxes, or

incarceration for Phil Cordero in the last five years.

Four years ago, his wife filed a request to have him declared dead, but it looks like the judge denied it. The record shows that Phil's wife posted a five-thousand-dollar bail for a previous DUI charge he was set to appear for before he disappeared (unrelated to the domestic violence charge—this guy seems like a real winner). If a defendant dies before a case goes to trial and bail is paid in cash, whoever posted the bail can get the money back. It's pretty difficult to provide proof of death without a body or evidence that a person met foul play.

Anyway, the motion to have Phil declared dead states that the last time his wife saw him was the morning of October 27. Several other people saw him at a bar that evening. I'm sure you've realized that this means Phil Cordero was last seen a full week before the murders.

I'm sorry—I know you were hoping this would turn into a viable lead. I'll admit that I was too. My guess? Phil Cordero was facing upward of fifteen years in prison for the domestic violence charges and the DUI and fled. Wherever he's hiding, he's doing a good job of it. Probably shacked up with some poor woman who has no idea what he did.

Let me know if there's anything else I can do to help.

Best,

Daphne

I read it again to make sure I have it right. Ginny said her father left on October 18, a full three days before this report says he was last seen.

Either Ginny has the date her dad went missing wrong, or she lied about it.

Ginny's father was last seen the night of Bethany and Colleen's accident.

I wake up on the morning of the anniversary of Jen's death feeling different than I did last year. The numbness that I always feel is still there, but I can feel too.

I can cry, so I do, in the shower. Rachel texts me that she's outside while I'm still dabbing concealer over my dark circles. I stick the wand back in the tube. Stare at myself in the mirror, watching the rise and fall of my chest as I exhale.

No one at school, aside from Rach and Alexa, is delicate with me today. They don't know what today is, and that's fine by me. I don't want to be treated as if I'm breakable.

When I stop by my locker at the end of the day and find Jimmy Varney waiting for me, my breath gets caught in my throat. His older brother was in Jen's grade; he must remember. He must be here to say how sorry he is, how he's been thinking about my family and me today.

The last thing I'm expecting him to say is, "Do you want to go to Big Hero's?"

"Now?"

"Well. Rumor has it you quit dance team, and seeing how I don't have a cross-country coach anymore, I figured we're both free this afternoon."

He must sense how I stiffen at the mention of Brandon. "Monica," he says softly. "I don't care about that."

I meet his eyes. "This is just a sandwich among friends?"

"A sandwich among friends. That's it. As long as it's a Louisiana Lightning."

I smile. "Obviously."

Jimmy doesn't needle me at all for details about the events of the last few weeks. In fact, he seems to be going out of his way to prove that he doesn't care about anything that happened between Brandon and me.

Once our sandwich is ready, he must be able to tell that I don't want to eat in the busy deli, because he asks if I want to go somewhere quieter.

"What about Osprey's Bluff?" I say.

He agrees, and we spend the ride talking about his college options. He's being scouted by SUNY Binghamton, where Matt goes, but Jimmy doesn't want to go there because Matt says it smells like cows.

Jimmy turns onto Osprey Road; on the other side of the street, I spot several wilted bouquets of flowers, including a hot-pink bunch of tiger lilies. Bethany's favorite.

"Can you pull over here?"

Jimmy parks on the shoulder, a safe distance from the road and the sign reading IN MEMORY OF BETHANY STEIGER AND COLLEEN COUGHLIN. Jimmy stands, his back against the car, feet crossed at the ankles. Arms folded. He doesn't ask what I'm doing as I cross the street to the side overlooking the lake.

The guardrail is weathered, but there's the faintest trace of red paint on it. The steep embankment slopes all the way to the edge of Osprey Lake. It would be so easy for a speeding car to fly over that guardrail and roll down into the lake.

I think of Ginny's visceral reaction to Mrs. Coughlin in the yearbook office that day. The way Ginny went out of her way to avoid Rachel that fall. I swallow, shoot one last look at the lake before rejoining Jimmy at his car.

"What's the matter?" Jimmy says, seeing my face.

"Absolutely nothing at all."

When I get home and search the mail, there's no letter from Ethan McCready. There is no reason for him to write to Tom, asking if he cares about the truth. The truth is out there now.

But I text him anyway.

> No letter today.

He responds right away, as if he was waiting to hear from me.

You sound surprised.

> No. Grateful, maybe.

After a minute goes by without a response, I text him again.

> Why did she call you that morning?

> We listened to part of a book together. She wanted to know how it ended.

> Did you tell her?

> I said I'd tell her when I saw her next.

I cover my mouth. Hold in a sob while a tear trickles down my face, over my hand. She knew she was going to die that day. Knowing it for sure doesn't make it hurt less. I blink away my tears and read the message that's just come through from Ethan.

> Thank you.

> For what?

He doesn't reply for several minutes.

> Because maybe now I can let her go.

It sends a fresh wave of hope through me. Maybe Ethan is right, and now we can all move on. We can forget about the heinous act and what it did to us, and in the process, the burden of missing the girls might just become a little lighter.

I make a promise to myself to try to move on. To think about them a little less every day. I'll never forget Bethany and Colleen and Juliana and Susan and Jen.

I can't, because my story is tied up in theirs forever.

Ginny

She always loved the way the rain looked when it hit the windshield of her father's truck. It was only a gentle mist, but the forecast called for a thunderstorm later.

"Where are we going?" Ginny asked, even though she knew the answer.

It was a Friday night and her mother was working at the hospital. The last time she came home at two in the morning and found Ginny on the couch, watching infomercials on Nickelodeon, Daddy nowhere to be found, Mom called and said she'd kill him if he ever left her daughter alone again.

He came home from the bar, stinking of cigarette smoke and cheap whiskey. Mom told Ginny to go to her room, to her closet that locked from the inside. In the morning, Mom's eye was purple and swollen and when she got up from the kitchen table, her spine went stiff and her face pinched like she was trying not to cry.

This time, she went to the emergency room for a

broken wrist, taking Ginny with her. This time, when the hospital social worker asked if she should call the police, Ginny's mother nodded through the tears, her body limp as if all the fight had left her.

Mom tried to shield Ginny from everything that came after—talk of bail, a court date, the seriousness of the charges her dad was facing, and murmurings about him staying at a motel in Beaverton. Earlier that night, Mom had had no choice but to drop her off at Grandma Cordero's, since no one else could watch Ginny.

When her father showed up to his mother's house, he screamed at Grandma Cordero until she let him take Ginny with him. *She's my daughter. I'm allowed to see my goddamn daughter.*

"We're going to get ice cream," Daddy grunted, his yellowed, calloused fingers tapping against the steering wheel of the truck. "I just have to make a quick stop first."

Ginny wondered what kind of ice cream place was open at ten-thirty at night, but she knew better than to question it. Her father had never touched her, but she wasn't sure if someday that would change.

Daddy pulled up outside the 7-Eleven and thrust the truck into park. "Don't go anywhere."

Ginny knew better than to ask him how long he'd be inside. Was it enough time to make it to the pay phone? She wasn't sure her dad was allowed to pick her up and bring her anywhere and he'd obviously already had a lot to drink. "Okay."

He left the engine running and swung himself out the driver's side, wincing. As he walked up to the store, past the boys with skateboards who were always smoking in the parking lot, Ginny noticed that his lopsided gait was getting worse. That fact, coupled with how foul her father's mood had been, made her suspect that his orthopedist wasn't prescribing him as many pain pills as he needed.

Ginny looked in the side mirror, craning her neck to see behind her, at Jessie's Gym across the street. When she was four, her mother signed her up for "toddler tumbling," and she'd liked it so much she wound up going to class three nights a week, once she was old enough. She would have signed Ginny up for every class Jessie had to offer, if they could've afforded it. Ginny knew she wanted to get her out of the house, away from her father.

Ginny closed her eyes and smelled sweat and rosin. Heard her father squealing up to the curb outside Jessie's Gym in his truck, nearly taking down the sign listing a sandwich special for the deli next door.

When Jennifer Rayburn saw and marched off to tell Jessie what she'd seen, hair flying out behind her, all Ginny could think was that Jen was an angel. A blond-haired, green-eyed angel.

But then Ginny would get embarrassed, worrying about everyone else at the gym thinking she was a loser whose parents never picked her up on time or who showed up drunk.

Her father had managed to ruin gymnastics too.

Outside the truck, someone was yelling. Her *father* was yelling. She'd recognize that sound anywhere. Ginny peered out the window.

Her father was standing in front of a beat-up pickup

truck. A man was leaning against the side, and one was seated in the driver's seat, his arm dangling from the window. Ginny swallowed back fear and lowered the window just enough to hear what they were saying. She caught her father midsentence.

"S'matter with you?" he was shouting. "Those girls are less'n half your age."

The guy leaning against the side of the truck laughed, clearly unthreatened by her father. "Whatever, old man."

Ginny's blood ran cold as her father stood up straight. "The fuck did you just call me?"

The driver of the truck stopped smirking. He opened his door, sending a flood of panic over Ginny. She lowered the window and called out to her father.

"Daddy, please. Don't."

The man standing outside the truck swung his head toward her. He gaped, then turned back to her father. "You're standing there blitzed out of your mind, and you got a fucking kid in the truck?"

Ginny flitted back and forth between hoping the men would call the police and praying that her father wouldn't put his beer down and go after the driver. He may have been stronger than her mother, but this was a fight he couldn't win.

"Daddy," she pleaded. "Let's go. Come on."

To her surprise, he didn't take another step toward the men in the truck. He hoisted his twelve-pack of beer up and headed around to the driver's side of his own truck, while the other man got into his truck. They peeled off, leaving Ginny trembling in her seat.

"I told you to stay out of shit like that."

Her father's voice jolted her. He tossed the beer into the backseat and slammed the door shut. Ginny's heart thumped as he climbed into the driver's seat.

"I didn't want you to get hurt," she whispered.

Her father grunted. Ginny picked up the stench of beer on him that wasn't there when he entered the store, and she strongly suspected that one can was missing from the twelve-pack in the backseat.

"Those men were harassing some girls," he said. "I don't like when animals like them look at girls like that. One of them could be you someday."

Ginny breathed through her mouth as he fumbled to put the truck in reverse. She didn't say it, but she didn't think there was a man out there who was more dangerous to her than her own father was.

The rain was falling sideways in sheets now; one of those fall storms that shifts gears with little warning.

"It's really rainy," Ginny said. "It's too dangerous to drive." *It's too dangerous for* you *to drive.*

Daddy grabbed her by the chin. "Hey. Look at me. Have I ever put you in danger before?"

His words slurred together. Ginny shook her head. Her father released her, and Ginny felt a red spot bloom on her face where his fingers had dug in. "I don't put my family in danger. You're safer with me than 'nyone else, you got that?"

Ginny nodded. She thought of the cell phone in the pocket of her father's jacket. If she could sneak it without him seeing—

He leaned over and began to cycle through the radio stations. The moment his eyes left the road, the truck swerved onto the shoulder. "What d'you think? The Stones or the Moody Blues?"

Ginny squeezed her eyes shut.

"What, now you're not talking to me?" Daddy whipped around in his seat to face her, jerking the car into the oncoming lane. Ginny grabbed the dashboard, seeing the headlights of the other car through the rain—

She felt like she was leaving her body, like it was someone else screaming *Daddy Daddy Daddy*—

He yanked the wheel back. The sickening sound of the other car's horn, then the screech of metal on metal; Daddy slammed on the brakes and the truck spun a complete three-sixty. Ginny felt the tires leave the pavement—they were falling, both of them screaming. Her skull cracked against the ceiling and then everything went still.

Upside down. They were upside down. With trembling hands, Ginny unbuckled her seat belt. Next to her, her father was motionless, blood trickling down his face.

Ginny lowered the window and climbed out, the scene swirling around her. The truck had flown over the guardrail; the ground sloped below her, her feet sucking into the mud. The water from the lake below was rising with the rain.

She stumbled up the hill back toward the road, her sneakers sounding like suction cups in the mud. She walked through the pain in her shoulder, or maybe her collarbone. She had never broken a bone before, but she imagined this was what it felt like.

Help, I have to help them—

Ginny came to a halt when the other car came into focus. It was split in *half*, the front end wrapped around a tree.

When she saw a limb, completely detached from its body, lying on the grass, she stumbled forward and vomited.

Both of the girls—Ginny thought they were girls, at least—in the car were dead. That much was clear. They were dead because of her father—or maybe it was *her* fault; she hadn't answered him when he asked what music she wanted to listen to, and he'd gotten angry and taken his eyes off the road.

In both directions, there was only blackness and rain. Why wasn't anyone coming? Where were other drivers? Ginny ran back across the road, sliding down the embankment, grabbing on to branches as she went so she wouldn't fall. If she could get to her father's cell phone, she could call the police.

That's when she heard him moaning her name. The film of vomit still sour on her tongue, Ginny climbed over the embankment. Her father had managed to lower his window. His face was purple from the blood rushing to his head.

"Ginny baby," he said. "I need you to unbuckle me so I can climb out."

Ginny looked from his arm, twisted at an unnatural angle, to the blood dripping from his forehead. She thought of Mom's eye, purple and swollen.

Daddy's voice cracked through the pain in Ginny's

skull. "*Now,* Ginny. I'm fuckin' bleeding over here."

Ginny touched her eyebrow and examined her fingers, stained with blood.

Her father's eyes were pleading. "Come on, baby. You gotta help me out of here. I can't unbuckle myself."

All she had to do was reach through the window, undo his seat belt so he could wiggle out the driver's window. The embankment was flooding, the truck teetering, threatening to topple into the lake—

Daddy was screaming her name now. Thunder sounded over the lake, and she knew no one in the houses, if they were even listening, could hear his screams. She watched, one arm around the tree, as the truck rolled into the lake.

Then she turned and headed back up toward the road, away from the sounds of the sirens approaching, disappearing into the rain.

Hours later, when her mother got home and wanted to know why Ginny was lying in bed with a bag of frozen carrots pressed to her fractured collarbone, Ginny said her father had done it before he left.

It was the truth, after all.

She knew the image of that wrecked car would haunt her for the rest of her life, but what was there to gain from admitting what had really happened? Hadn't her father gotten what he deserved for killing those two girls, for hurting her mother, for destroying almost everything he touched?

No, Ginny decided. She wouldn't tell anyone.

There are some things not everyone has to know.

Acknowledgments

This book was a team effort with my editor, Krista Marino. Thank you for responding to my brainstorming emails in the middle of the night. Thank you for your patience, guidance, and enthusiasm (as well as our shared love of dark and creepy things).

Thank you to my agent, Suzie Townsend, who has been by my side for seven years and counting. I'm also so lucky to have the team at New Leaf Literary in my corner: Sara Stricker, Joanna Volpe, Mia Roman, Kathleen Ortiz, Pouya Shahbazian, Chris McEwen, and Hilary Pecheone.

Thank you to the team at Random House Children's Books: Monica Jean, Barbara Marcus, Beverly Horowitz, Cayla Rasi, Elizabeth Ward, Kate Keating, John Adamo, and rock star publicist Aisha Cloud.

Thank you to the Sleuthers, the best fans a gal could ask for: Mithila, Brittany, Gabriella, Ashley, Maren, Eileen, Natasha, Ryley, Olivia, Emily, Chelly, Anna, Angel, Jess, Joe, Lisa, Jordan, Inah, Rachel, Bianca, Kristen, Nicole, Alice, Bailey, Danielle, Diana, Emma, Sarah, Veronica, Whitney, Jeddidiah, Stephanie, Jessica, Hazel, Kaitlin,

Tawney, April, Amber, Hallie, Krysti, Kat, Jessica, Troix, Desirai, Regina, Meigan, and Kester.

To my patient husband and family and my friends, especially my hags.

About the Author

Kara Thomas is the author of *The Darkest Corners*, *Little Monsters*, and *The Cheerleaders*. She is a true-crime addict who lives on Long Island with her husband and rescue cat. To learn more about Kara and her books, visit her at kara-thomas.com and follow @karatwrites on Twitter.

MYKINDABOOK.COM

LOVE BOOKS?
JOIN MYKINDABOOK.COM
YOUR KINDA BOOK CLUB

READ BOOK EXTRACTS

RECOMMENDED READS

BE A PART OF THE MKB CREW

WIN STUFF

BUILD A PROFILE

GET CREATIVE

CHAT TO AUTHORS

CHAT TO OTHER READERS